MICHAEL ARDITTI

Good Clean Fun

MICHAEL ARDITTI

Good Clean Fun

For Hilary Sage

Published in 2004 by
The Maia Press Limited
82 Forest Road
London E8 3BH
www.maiapress.com

ISBN 1 9045590 8 5

A CIP catalogue record for this book is available
from the British Library

Printed and bound in Great Britain by Thanet Press

Contents

———

Uncle Brian   7

Haverstock Hill   27

Bedtime Story   45

Good Clean Fun   65

The Night Out   81

The Pillar of Strength   99

Contentment   117

The Fig-Leaf   141

The Marriage of Convenience   163

Virtual Love   189

The Isolation Ward   209

Visiting Hour   233

Uncle Brian

UNCLE BRIAN isn't my proper uncle but I call him it because he's married to Mum. Dad is married to Jayne but I don't call her Aunt. Jayne spells her name with a 'y'. Mum used to laugh at her, but she can't now she's married to Uncle Brian because his dad's got a tattoo. My name's Joseph but most people call me Joe. Mum calls me Joey, which Dad hates because he thinks I'll never grow into a man. Uncle Brian calls me Jay, which is the capital letter of Joseph but, when he writes it down, he adds 'ay' to make it a word. 'A jay is my favourite bird,' he says, 'just like you're my favourite boy.'

Here, I'm only called Joe in letters. The Warden and staff call me Pargeter like they're talking to Dad. The other boys call me Yid, which is a bad word for being Jewish. I'm not Jewish – I'm not anything though Granny taught me the Lord's Prayer – but, on the first day I was sent here, three of the Intermediates followed me into the toilet and pulled down my pants. 'Look, he's a Yid,' one of them said, 'he's had the top chopped off.'

'It's more hygienic,' I said, 'my dad's a dentist.'

'You'll be all right then,' another one said and punched me in the mouth.

The only people here who ask what I want to be called are the doctors. 'Jay,' I tell them. But, when they ask me why, I don't say.

They're always asking something. I used to want to be eighteen so I could stay up all night, but now I want to so I won't have to answer any more questions. When you're eighteen, you can say 'I'd like to speak to my solicitor.' When you're eighteen, you can say 'I reserve the right to stay silent,' like they do on TV. When you're nine, you don't have any choice. My grandpa Pargeter used to give me 50p every time I got ten out of ten in one of his tests. If I got 50p every time I answered all the questions in here, I'd be rich as the Queen. 'Did your dad ever hit your mum?' they ask in voices that sound like smiles. 'No,' I say, and I know they think I'm lying. But it's true. They just used to shout – sometimes until it was midnight. 'You bitch,' he'd say. 'You bastard,' she'd say. But I'm not going to tell tales.

Mum stopped loving Dad when I was four. She told Aunty Janet she sent him packing, but that was a lie because he just piled his clothes straight on the back seat of the car – which is another thing that's allowed when you're eighteen. Mum said she did it for us – that's me and Rose. Rose is my sister: she's four years older, but she says, since girls grow up quicker than boys, it's more like eight. Mum said she did it to protect us because, if you live next to waste, you end up becoming contaminated. Rose said that was a lie too and she did it for herself so that she wouldn't have to share Dad with 'that woman'. Mum never calls Jayne 'Jayne'. Sometimes she calls her 'the slag', although I was the only one brave enough to call her it to her face. Dad gave me three smacks and drove us home early. At first Mum was cross but, when she found out what happened, she kissed me and called me her 'knight in shining armour'. I wish I'd been wearing armour on my legs. She said, if Dad smacked me again, I must tell her straightaway so she could report him to the police. I think she was sad when he never did.

Ever since Dad went to live with Jayne, he's only allowed into our hall – even though half the house belongs to him – and Jayne isn't allowed on to the doorstep. Mum won't speak to Jayne. The one time when she saw her in a shop, she turned away like she was a witch and marched us straight out. Rose cried and said that it was embarrassing. But there's not much chance it'll happen again because Mum can't afford to take us to the sort of places where Dad takes Jayne. 'They're living it up on our money,' she says when her friends come round and tell her where they've seen them. The thing that upsets Mum most is that Jayne gave up her job as Dad's hygienist so she could spend the day painting her toenails, when Mum has to go out to work in Aunty Janet's wine bar. Which is strange because Dad tells us over and over that Mum is bleeding him dry. He gives her money every week. 'Like pocket money?' I asked her. And she screamed like she'd stood on a nail. 'I can see you're your father's son all right!' But you'd think she would have seen that before.

Rose and me weren't allowed to go to Dad and Jayne's wedding. I didn't care because it only happened in an office but Rose cried for weeks because she wanted to wear a special dress. When the day came, Mum stayed in bed with a migraine (which is grown-up for headache), so Rose made us toast for lunch. Mum kept moaning that she was thirty-two and time was running out. It seemed to me like time was going extra slow – especially since she wouldn't let us watch TV because of her head. But I know about time going quicker for grown-ups. At first when Miss Bevan told us how time was different depending on where you were, I thought she meant like the way you had to put your watch forward when you go to Spain. Then she said it was much more complicated and when we went to big school we'd understand. But I understand already. It's like when Granny says it seems only last week that it was Christmas when, for me, it's felt like a whole year. Time starts slowly when you're young and then gets faster and faster when you're eighteen until, when you're really old like Granny, it whizzes by in a flash. But what I don't understand is why, when I'm older than I've ever been before, it's never gone so slowly as it does in here.

Granny came to stay. I looked forward to it, but Mum said that was because I've never had to live with her. She told Mum to pull herself together. She's allowed to say that because, although Mum's more than thirty, she's still her 'little girl'. Mum shouted at her but she still took notice of what she said. She put on lipstick again – more even than Jayne (though she'd have been furious if I'd said so) – and started going out in the evenings. Rose said it was with her boyfriends, but I said that was stupid because they were far too old. Sometimes, when they came back late from a party, the men had to stay overnight. Rose didn't like it but I said they were safer. I'd seen on TV how grown-ups shouldn't drink wine and drive. I felt safer too because I knew that, if burglars came, there'd be a man there to beat them up. Ever since Dad left, I'd lined up all my animals around me on the bed, with Rory at the front because, although he's the softest material, he's a lion. It helped, but it wasn't the same.

Mum met Uncle Brian when he went into the wine bar for some soup. He couldn't eat anything more because he's a student. When Dad heard that, he called him 'one of the great unwashed', which isn't fair because Uncle Brian's always washing. Sometimes he has three showers a day. Mum teases him and asks him what's so dirty. Granny says it's because he grew up in the working class. Granny doesn't like Uncle Brian. When Mum told her she wanted to get married to him, Granny said he was only after her money. Mum said she was a frustrating old bitch. So Granny called a taxi and said she would never set foot in our house again. But she did. Mrs Stevens – who's Uncle Brian's mother – was even crosser. She shouted at Mum that she was snatching a cradle. Which didn't make any sense at all. Then they both shouted at me when they heard me giggling at the door.

The only people who were pleased that Mum and Uncle Brian were getting married were Rose and me – especially me.

When Mum's other friends played with us, it felt like Helen Clarke handing round her crisps because Miss Bevan was watching. When Uncle Brian played with us, it felt like he wanted to. Mum said most men ran a mile from a woman with kids. Uncle Brian said he would run a hundred miles the other way. He said no one would believe somebody his age could have such a grown-up family. So I said we should call him Uncle to make it clear. Mum didn't agree, but it was three against one. When we were on our own, I asked Uncle Brian who he liked best: Rose or me. He said that he liked us both equal – the way grown-ups always do – but I knew that wasn't true, or else why didn't he lift her up on his shoulders and ruffle her hair? He said he understood boys better on account of his five older brothers. I said how I'd always wanted an older brother and he said I was welcome to all of his (although Geoff was ruled out because he was in prison). When he was young, they'd used to pick on him and call him names. Then, when he grew up, they hated him because he went to college. He was the only one who'd bettered himself. 'Like Joseph in the Bible?' I said 'In a way,' he said, 'although at least he was his father's favourite. My dad used to pick on me too.'

Rose and me went to Mum and Uncle Brian's wedding, but Mum said it was far too small for Rose to be a bridesmaid: just Rose and me, Granny, Aunty Janet and Mr and Mrs Stevens. After the wedding, we went out to lunch and Mr Stevens, who smells of petrol, rolled up his sleeves and we saw his tattoo. Mum smiled all afternoon, even after Aunty Janet had stopped taking pictures. She was allowed to smile now she was married again. She still lost her temper with Rose and me, but it was a crackly little temper not a big thundery one. Sometimes she lost her temper with Uncle Brian. He used to play jokes on her, like when he switched her toothpaste with a tube of sauce. She said it felt less like having a husband than adopting a kid. Then she dropped her voice to stop me listening and said he should remember how he had married her not Joey. He said he didn't want me to feel left out. Then she said I wasn't the one feeling left out. She must have been feeling sorry for Rose.

Uncle Brian said that because I was eight and he was twenty and Mum was thirty-two, he was exactly the same distance from both of us, but we shouldn't talk about it to her. I said I expected she'd already worked it out because she was wicked at sums. He said he was sure she had but she didn't like to be reminded of it. I said I didn't see why, since Dad was even more years older than Jayne. He said it was different when the younger one was a girl. I said everything always was and it wasn't fair. He asked me what I meant. I said how girls are allowed to wear trousers and skirts but boys can only wear trousers – except for Scottishmen and kilts. Girls are allowed to kiss men and ladies but boys can only kiss ladies.

'Do you want to kiss me?' he said, which made me shiver.

'I just don't think it's fair,' I said.

'I'll kiss you if you like,' he said and, instead of waiting for me to say 'yes', he gave me a kiss on my cheek that smacked like in a cartoon. I laughed. 'Right,' he said, 'now who's for a tickle?'

'No,' I screamed and curled up into a ball. 'It's not fair. Your fingers are longer, so you always win.' But he didn't take any notice and tickled me until I had a stitch and it stopped being funny.

'Do you want me to give you another kiss?' he said, like he was offering me a piggyback.

'All right,' I said, even though I knew this time I ought to say 'no'. It wasn't like he was saying goodnight or thank you or leaving for the airport. It was a grown-up kiss like he did with Mum. It was weird and tasted of tongues.

'Promise you won't tell anyone,' he said. 'It'll be our secret.'

'I promise,' I said. I'd never had a secret before – at least not one I'd shared with someone else. It was the secret I wanted to share with him, much more than the kiss.

In the summer, Mum took us all on holiday (it was abroad, even though it was called Brittany). At first, she was just going to take Uncle Brian to celebrate because he was twenty-one and had finished his exams, but he said he would rather take us and she had to say 'yes', because it showed we were a family. He made all the bookings through a man on his hotel course but, when we arrived, we found that there'd been a mess-up. We'd been given one single room and one double and all the others were full. Rose sat down on her suitcase in the middle of the hall and said there was no way she was going to sleep in the same bed as me. I thought it would be fun, but she said that in any civilised country it would be against the law and, if they tried to force her, she would sleep on the beach. I thought that would be fun too. But no one was interested what I thought. Uncle Brian suggested that, for the sake of peace, Rose and Mum should have the double room and he would sleep in the single one with me. 'Some holiday!' Mum said and she made a lot of rude remarks about the hotel. I'm sure the manager understood them even though he was French.

Uncle Brian and me were supposed to sleep top to toe like he used to with one of his brothers but, when he came into bed, he flopped his head on the pillow next to mine. 'You don't want to snuggle up to my pongy feet, do you?' he said. I didn't think it was fair of him to wake me just for that, so I turned away. 'That's all right then,' he said. 'Budge up!'

We were so squashed that he had to put his arm on top of me, but I didn't mind. I turned to face him. 'You smell of wine,' I said.

'I do, do I?' he said. 'It's time you were taught to respect your elders, young man.' Then he began to tickle me, which wasn't fair as I was too tired even to curl up.

'I give in,' I said, but he didn't take any notice. 'I want to go to sleep.'

'So give me a goodnight kiss,' he said. Then he gave me one, but it didn't feel like goodnight at all. It was hot and breathy and it felt more like something waking up than going to sleep. 'How much do you love me?' he said.

'I'm tired,' I said.

'Tell me or I'll tickle,' he said.

'Lots and lots,' I said. 'More than anyone in the whole world.'

'Really?' He sounded surprised. 'More than Mum and Dad?'

'Yes,' I said, which I know was bad but it was true.

'And I love you more than anyone too,' he said, which was even worse because he was a grown-up.

'What about Mum?' I said.

'More than anyone,' he said, like he hadn't heard. 'Are you pleased?'

'Yes,' I said. But really I was only half-pleased because I knew Mum would be sad.

'So how are you going to prove it to me?' he said.

'I haven't got any money,' I said, and he laughed.

'You don't need any.' He took my hand and pulled it along his chest to his tummy-button, which is lumpier than mine. I rubbed it, which is one of my favourite things in the whole world, but it can't have been one of his because he pulled my hand down on to his leg to where I knew it shouldn't go. At first I thought that it couldn't be his willy because it was so thick and hard. 'Put your hand on my prick,' he said, in a voice that was thick and hard too. I said 'no': Jonathan Hurt and David Simmonds were sent home from school for measuring each other's willies in the cloakroom. Miss Bevan said that, just like you should never pick a mushroom in case it was a toadstool, so there were parts of people's bodies it was dangerous to touch.

Uncle Brian said that was rubbish – which is rude to say about a teacher – and you could touch anything you wanted if you loved someone. He said Mum touched him there all the time. That's when I knew he was lying, because she never even dried me there after a bath. I pulled my hand free. 'So that's how you much you love me,' he said and turned on to his side. 'All talk, you!'

'No,' I said. I didn't want to make him cross so I put my hand back.

'That's more like it,' he said and he jigged my hand up and down, which hurt. He turned back towards me and kissed me and stroked my face. Suddenly, he began to make noises like he was choking. He pushed up and down and fell back like he'd done a giant sneeze. That's when I found out grown-ups could still wet the bed. I felt it through my pyjamas – not a lot but a little. I was scared Mum would think it was me. He laughed and said not to worry: she would never know. His voice and his body went all soft again. He ruffled my hair and said how much he loved me. Then he hugged me till I was as hot as him. I felt safe.

The next day the manager found an empty room and we all moved, except for Mum, who stayed in the double room with Uncle Brian. I tried not to think about what had happened but I couldn't help it because, any time no one else was looking, Uncle Brian would wink at me. After we went back home, he got a job in a hotel too. He'd done exams to be a manager, but he was only a receptionist. I felt sad for him, but Mum said it was a good step. Sometimes he worked in the night, so he would pick me up after school to give Mum extra hours at the wine-bar. 'You know what we're going to do when we get home?' he said. I always wished he wouldn't ask because, if I said 'yes', it sounded like I was looking forward to it and, if I said 'no', he said I was playing games. 'You like being dirty,' he said. But it wasn't true. What I liked was lying on the bed – on Uncle Brian

– and feeling warm. I didn't like any of the rest of it, especially when he pushed my head down and made me kiss his willy – or his lollipop, as he started to call it, so as to make me feel better about the taste. He said it was the nicest thing anyone could do for you but he didn't seem grateful. He pulled my hair and banged against my mouth till the moment when he peed stuff and got kind again. And I couldn't help crying, though I knew it upset him. Then he kissed me and stroked me and called me his own boy and hugged my head against his chest. And I felt safe.

The thing I hated more than anything was when Mum and Uncle Brian had a row. It wasn't like the rows she used to have with Dad, where their voices went up and down like singing. It was more like the row Dad had with the man who stole his parking space and they both stood in the road with their fists clenched like they were going to hit each other, until the man told Dad that he had his number (though he didn't write it down) and drove away. Once, when they didn't know I was listening, they had a row about me. It started when Uncle Brian said he was taking me fishing. 'You spend more time with the boy than you do with me,' she said. She'd started calling me the boy to make it sound like I wasn't a proper person. 'Don't you want me to take an interest in him?' he said. 'Yes, of course,' she said. 'But your job is to give me satisfaction.' That wasn't true – only he was too polite to tell her. She was speaking like she was a guest at his hotel.

Whenever we went fishing, he found a time for us to be dirty. I didn't mind because I knew how happy it made him. I just wished he would find a time to hug me afterwards. But he said there were too many risks. So I said that I wasn't going to play with him any more. Then he got really cross and said I was clinging, just like Mum, and he didn't know why he bothered with either of us. He should get on his bike and ride off. He said he'd given everything to our family and all he'd got to show for it was grief. He said, if he did leave, Mum would make life into a misery for Rose and me. He asked if I knew who she'd blame for driving him away. But, when I tried to tell him, he said it was one of those questions you weren't supposed to answer (I wish they asked more of them in here). So, for the first time, I put my hand on to his trousers without him asking, and I put my head inside them. I didn't pull away even when I felt like I would choke. Then he started peeing stuff so I knew he was pleased. 'I can see you love me,' he said. 'I promise I won't leave you now.'

Uncle Brian changed everything for me at school, even though he never came inside. He said it made him feel like he was a kid again, then he winked. I wasn't scared of the teachers any more. When Mr Batty told me to clean the blackboard, I called him Mr Botty and acted like it was a mistake. When Miss Bevan made us sing 'I'm a shrimp, I'm a shrimp and I live in the sea,' I sang 'I'm a shrimp, I'm a shrimp and I live in the pee.' That made everyone laugh – except for Miss Bevan who sent me to see the Headmistress. I thought I'd be in big trouble, but she must have read the note wrong because she just asked me if I was happy at home. Then she said that her door was always open (which was a lie) and I should speak to her if I had any problems. But I wasn't going to fall for that, since we all know she's an alien who uses everything we say to take over our brains.

The next time I was sent to see her was when I stabbed Pete Simpson with my compass. He'd snotted on me in the playground, but she said that was no excuse. Half an inch higher and it would have gone straight in his eye. She phoned Mum to take me home. She came with Dad – not Uncle Brian – so I knew it must be serious. They put on voices like at the doctor's and said it was their fault – which was much better than I'd expected. They said their getting divorced had disturbed me more than they realised. From now on they promised to put me first.

Dad decided we should spend quality time with each other, which is the same length as ordinary time but more special – like travelling first-class on a train. One of his patients played football and he gave us tickets for a game. The teams were neighbours so they called it a derby, like they were horses. The seats hurt and, as soon as anything happened, the people in front jumped up so you couldn't see. I enjoyed it, but I was glad when the man refused to pay for his canal treatment, which meant we didn't have to go again. Instead, we played crazy golf and went skating. After a few weeks we went back to ordinary time, where Dad made things in his shed and I watched videos and played on the computer. Rose was busy helping Jayne look after her babies. She had two, one exactly a year after the other. Mum said it was obscene, but I said it should be printed in the *Guinness Book of Records*. The babies cried a lot and Jayne was always tired. They couldn't talk properly, so you could pinch them and no one would know.

Dad plays golf but he's got fat around his tummy. Jayne calls it love handles, which is soppy, but Mum calls it a spare tyre. Uncle Brian doesn't play anything but he's thin. He said if I wasn't careful, I'd end up like my dad. 'So we'd better build you up.' Then he wrestled me to the ground. He got cross because I wouldn't fight back. 'You can't just let blokes walk all over you.'

'I don't,' I said, 'only you.'

His voice changed like it always does when he's starting to be dirty. 'I could do anything I want to you,' he said. 'You're completely in my power.' I giggled because it was safe and scary at the same time. 'What would you do if you were me?'

'Hold me,' I said. Though I knew it would only make him crosser.

'You're just a big girl, you are,' he said.

'Don't say that,' I said. 'You can do anything. And I promise I won't shout.'

'Anything?' he said. And I nodded. Which I wish I hadn't, because he did that thing with his fingers that hurts. But I didn't cry. I didn't even moan. He told me how pleased he was with me. He could see I was a boy who kept his word. Then he pulled down his trousers and pressed up against me and I found out why he didn't call it a willy but a prick.

Rose has got a boyfriend. At least she says he's a boyfriend; Mum says he's just a crush. They hold hands and stare at each other's eyes like they were watching cartoons. I found them kissing in the kitchen. 'You're in my power,' I said to her after he went home. 'Swear you'll be my slave or I'll tell Mum you're a slag like Jayne.'

'Who's in whose power?' she said. 'Don't you realise you're on probation? The next thing you do wrong, Mum and Dad are going to send you to boarding school for ever.'

'No way,' I said. 'Uncle Brian'll never let them. We'll escape into hiding, far away from everyone else.'

'You're such a baby,' she said. 'Uncle Brian doesn't give a toss about you. He's just using you to score points with Mum.'

She made me so angry that I told her lots of things I shouldn't have. Like how it was me he loved best, not Mum. And how he came into my room at midnight when she was asleep. Rose twisted my arm and began to ask me a whole load of questions. I knew straightaway I'd been stupid, so I tried to laugh. 'You believed me,' I said. 'What a sucker!' But it didn't stop her crying. 'Sucker!' I said. But she didn't see the joke.

Mum slapped me across my legs like nettles. 'You're nine years old,' she said. 'How can so much filth come into your head?' I supposed it must be from the stuff I'd sucked out of Uncle Brian but I knew if I said that, things would get even worse. 'Why do you always have to ruin everything?' she said. 'It was you that drove your father away. It's your fault he stayed late every night at the surgery, making himself easy game for that woman!' Rose was right about them plotting to send me away. 'If you breathe one more word of these disgusting lies,' Mum said, 'I'll put you straight into care. Let somebody else try to cope with you. Lord knows, I'm at my wits' end.' Then she did the worst thing anyone's ever done to me: she made me say 'sorry' to Uncle Brian. He was waiting in the lounge. He looked me right in the eye. He didn't wink (in fact, he never winked at me again). He just gave a big sigh and offered to forgive me, but he said he could never forget the abuse of his trust.

The next day was when I tore up all the pictures at school. I don't know why everyone made it into such a big deal. They were just a load of crappy paintings that we'd done of our holidays. Mr Batty only pretended they were good because we were kids. He gave them stars and stuck them up on the wall. He might as well have stuck up scraps of Christmas wrapping. They were rubbish: they belonged in the bin. So that's where I put them. Even then no one punished me. They took me to see a special doctor, who had an office not a surgery, which was full of dolls – but they weren't girl dolls like Rose's, they were boys with pricks like Uncle Brian's. He told me to play with them, so I did. Then he asked me questions, but my head got all in a tangle. Usually, when grown-ups ask you questions you know what they want you to answer, but he was no help at all. Then they took me to a different doctor, who had a nurse. He asked me to describe what Uncle Brian had done and I said it was a secret. But he must have found out, because he did the exact same thing with his fingers. And I howled, a bit because it hurt but most because it had stopped being a secret. Then he gave me a lollipop – a proper one – but it had no taste.

When anything had been the matter with me before – if I was sad or sick or had a cut or a splinter – I'd go to Mum and she'd kiss it better. Now she wouldn't even speak to me but only to Rose. She talked about 'your brother' like she was writing a letter. I thought she must be cross with me but Rose said she was cross with herself. It was something to do with being a grown-up that I didn't understand. Rose was being extra nice to me. She was the only one who told me things – like how Uncle Brian had been arrested and wasn't allowed to come within a radius of us. I asked if he'd gone back to live with Mr and Mrs Stevens. She said no. Two of his brothers had promised to kill him, so he was living somewhere secret. I felt sad for him to have a secret he couldn't share with me.

Rose was sad that I hadn't shared my secret with her before. She said she would have stopped Uncle Brian from hurting me. I said I didn't want her to stop him. It had hurt a bit but that wasn't the whole thing. It was like an injection before you went on holiday or going to church at Christmas. When he held me, I felt like I had a hundred bodyguards. She said what he had done to me was evil – it was the most evil crime anyone could commit apart from murder. He had scarred me for life. I know she meant the sort of scars people can't see, but I told her she was wrong. Uncle Brian hadn't done me any harm; he'd made me happy. I loved him. In that case, she said, you must be as evil as him. You must be the most evil boy in the world.

Dad started to cry when he saw me. Which made me cry too. But he didn't lift me up or ruffle my hair. He stood at the far side of the room like I smelt – like he had when I jumped over the log in Ireland and fell into the cowpat. How Mum and Dad and Rose had laughed! I wished somebody would laugh now. But Dad banged his fist against his head and said he blamed himself. Then, when Mum walked in, he changed his mind and blamed her. Rose dragged me out of the room but I could hear them arguing from the stairs. He said Mum had used me as bait (like I was just a worm). He said she was an unfit person to be a mother. That was when they decided I should live with him. Mum said it was time for him to do his share and Dad said it was important for me to have a healthy male model. Jayne was kind. She made a sign that read Welcome. She hugged me to her bosoms, which was nicer now she'd got fat. She said I mustn't feel ashamed about anything since it wasn't my fault. Which was good. Then she mixed me up with one of the babies and said not to worry if I wet the bed.

Dad wants me to forget about what happened. He wouldn't even let me watch *Oliver Twist* when it was a serial on TV. But other people want me to remember. I go to see doctors and policemen and teachers (special ones, not like Miss Bevan) and they all ask me to talk about it in my own words – like they thought I might start cheating. I asked a police lady if I could see Uncle Brian, only for a minute to make sure he was all right. She didn't answer but wrote something down in her book. That's all they ever do. Sometimes I say things just to see if they'll write them down. I play a game with myself where I score a point every time they pick up their pens. I wish I could play it with Uncle Brian. I know now what he did was wrong and his brothers were right to want to kill him (except that two wrongs can never make a right), but I keep trying to explain that he can't have realised. He would never do anything to hurt me. He loved me. He was the only grown-up who made me feel I wasn't a child. 'But you are a child,' one of the doctors said. 'I know that,' I told him, 'but Uncle Brian made it feel safe.'

I went back to school and Miss Bevan gave me a new set of exercise books. All the teachers were extra nice. They wrote 'splendid work' when I got five out of ten and 'good effort' when I only got one. I was even allowed to undress in the janitor's cupboard when we went swimming. None of the other kids knew what had happened. They thought it was like when Alice Jerrold's brother and sister were killed in the crash. Then Louis Preston heard something about Uncle Brian from his parents. He started calling me names – 'Wanker' and 'Cocksucker', like you hear at a football game. Soon everybody joined in. I didn't care. I didn't need to talk to them. I had much better voices inside my head. And one of them – the one that sounded most like Uncle Brian – told me I had power: I didn't need to be frightened of anyone. So when Louis Preston came up to me in the toilets and wiggled his bottom, I didn't run away. Instead, I grabbed hold of his shoulders and shook him. He was so shocked that he didn't fight back. So I shook him more and more, first in the air and then against the pipes. I shook him till there were no screams left in him and the wall was the same colour as his head.

Shaking's not real killing – not like stabbing or shooting or poison. Shaking's more gentle, like when Uncle Brian swung me up till I could touch the sky. But all the policemen cared about was that Louis was dead. I was taken back to the station, but this time they weren't so friendly since it wasn't Uncle Brian who'd done the most evil thing in the world, it was me. I had to go to court. I was glad the judge was a lady until she started to talk. She told me things I didn't need to hear because I knew them already and things I didn't want to hear because they made me sad. Then she made it worse by repeating them to make sure I understood. Mum and Dad were watching, but they felt as far away as at the nativity play when my wings fell off and they weren't allowed to come up on the stage to help. The judge said I must be kept in a secure unit indefinitely (which isn't as long as it sounds), but she sent me here first to find out what's happening inside my mind. There are sixty boys at the Centre, but we're divided into ages, so there are only twenty who count. No one asks you about before (it's not secret, just private). No one cares who's good and who's bad, only who's strong and who's scared, who fights and who cries.

We have activities all day long. They're supposed to keep us out of trouble. We make moulds and draw and go on the assault course. We don't have proper lessons but we're always doing tests. It's important to do well because it's in here they decide where we go next. Sometimes if you're really lucky, then you're allowed home (though not if you've had your name in the papers like me). Otherwise, you're sent to a foster-home or a children's home or a special school or a detention centre. One of the Intermediates told me, when you kill someone – even if it's only by shaking – then you're locked up for life. You're put in a young offenders' institution then, when you're eighteen, you get moved to a grown-up prison. The moment somebody mentions letting you out, the newspapers send petitions to the Queen. I started to laugh. He called me a 'fucking psycho'. But he didn't understand. Now I have a new reason to look forward to being eighteen. I know there are hundreds of prisons all over the country but, as long as I do what I'm told and I don't answer back, then I'm sure they'll find me a cell with Uncle Brian.

Haverstock Hill

SIMON AWOKE with a raging erection, which made him jealous of his dreams. He cast a rueful, recriminatory glance at the empty mattress beside him. No purchase could have been more optimistic than his king-size bed. He had explained to friends that he wanted space to stretch out. Narrow beds brought back memories of school, where they had been known, with characteristic infantilism, as cots. What he really wanted was somebody to stretch out with. It was as if buying the bed would provide the stimulus: part magnet, part charm. On both counts it had failed. He had been celibate for so long that the only way to endure it was to pretend that he had taken vows: that, like some Indian mystic, he had ascended to a higher spiritual plane. He had even enrolled on a course of beginners' yoga, but he had been so intent on sneaking a glimpse of his teacher's midriff during the *cobra* that he had cricked his neck.

He swung out of bed, his erection throbbing before him, and recalled a host of dormitory jokes about elephants' trunks. He refused to risk opening the curtains. He doubted that any of his neighbours would be up so early on a Sunday morning, but it was pointless to court humiliation. There was nothing he enjoyed more than a surreptitious snoop through the windows opposite and he had no wish to present a similar prospect. He pulled on his dressing gown, wishing that he could afford something less sensible and more silky, and made the long descent to fetch his papers. Though all his visitors, of whatever age and shape, felt obliged to complain about the trek to the fourth floor, Simon, who did not play sport and was chary of gyms, welcomed the exercise. He had read that climbing four flights of stairs was the equivalent of playing two sets of tennis or making love for an hour. The thought threatened to revive his erection and he hurried back upstairs, clutching the papers like a shield.

He lingered first over breakfast, then over his shower, and finally over the papers, less for the pleasure they afforded him than to occupy the time. He steeled himself for his weekly phone call to his mother and was doubly resentful of the sound of her voice on the machine. He was full of admiration for those of his friends who managed to integrate their lives – parents and home and lovers and London – but his remained compartmentalised. He used to joke that, if he were to bring the various aspects of his life together, people would discover there was nothing there. He was no longer sure that it was a joke. He dreamt of finding someone who would make him whole, who would unite all the facets of his personality, who would love, excite, protect and forgive. But he was afraid to grant anyone so much power.

On the stroke of one, he headed into the kitchen to prepare his lunch. He could not decide which was the more depressing: that he was eating alone or that he was microwaving a frozen lasagne. He gulped it down without even bothering to remove it from the carton. The telephone rang as if to reprove his indolence. He responded with a curse which he feared for a moment might be audible.

'Hello,' said a pleasing voice: a pleasingly masculine voice. 'Is that Simon?' He confirmed that it was. 'Can you talk?'

Of course I can, he thought. Why ever shouldn't I? But annoyance at the question mingled with satisfaction that someone might think him worthy of a double life. So he simply said yes. The voice identified itself.

'My name's Will. You won't know me. You answered my ad in *Time Out.*'

He felt as sick as when he had collected a prize at school and his joy had been tempered by the fear of his friends' derision. For several months he had been reading the Personals column in *Time Out*. He told himself that it was to keep informed, the way that he read the jazz and poetry sections even though he had no wish to attend any of the events listed in either. At first the announcements had amused him, then intrigued him, and finally enticed him, for one week when he had been feeling – there was no point in denying it – more than usually lonely, he had replied.

He had brooded over his letter for days: whether to be the strong, silent type (at least on paper), leaving much unsaid in the hope that the recipient (about whom he knew nothing but his age, hair colour and certain socially acceptable interests) would be sufficiently fascinated to wish to solve the mystery, or whether to sell himself from the first line, scarcely pausing for commas in the hope that his enthusiasm would prove to be catching. He had hesitated to describe his appearance, being aware of the twin pitfalls of arrogance and false modesty, and was grateful for the injunction to send a photograph (although he had made it quite clear that it barely resembled him and was simply all that he had to hand). When, after two weeks, he had heard nothing, he blamed the silence on the photograph, even though he had not been wearing his glasses and it had made him look young. He deplored the current fashion of judging everything on face value, which he acknowledged might be considered a paradox in view of his work.

Not wishing to dwell on his humiliation, he had put the letter out of his mind. Adverts were no way to meet someone, although he was unable to come up with anything better. His friends could not understand his problem, particularly given all his professional opportunities. What they failed to understand was that the greater the opportunity, the greater the risk. He was almost as afraid of rejection as he was of commitment. He wondered whether, after all, he might not be safer alone.

'Hello? Are you still there?' Will's voice broke into his reflections.

'Yes, of course. I'm sorry. I was just a little taken aback.'

'You did say you could talk?'

'Sure. No problem.'

'You never know. I don't have a phone, so I have to use my landlady's. Well, it's communal really. I grab my chance when everyone else is out.'

'Don't worry, I'm quite alone. Though you were lucky to catch me in,' he added quickly, for fear that he might be sending out the wrong message.

'I thought if I rang at lunchtime . . . Oh hell, I haven't caught you in the middle of eating?'

'Not at all.' He wafted away any abiding trace of lasagne. 'I was just about to go into the kitchen. I fancied something light. *Penne alle vongole.*' The words had slipped out of nowhere. He prayed that he had pronounced them correctly.

'Do you make it yourself?'

'I'll say. None of that frozen rubbish.' He dug his nails into his hand.

'Oh, it's good to talk to you,' Will said, 'it's so hard to make contact like this, don't you think?

'I agree. As I wrote in my letter, this is my very first time.'

'I hope you'll find I'm the right man to take your virginity.'

Simon thought it only polite to echo Will's laugh, but his left leg was trembling and his whole body thrilled.

'You said that you were a photographer,' Will continued.

'Yes.'

'Specialising in theatre.'

'That's right.'

'It must be fascinating. I go as often as I can – for which read: can afford it.'

'I'm afraid I take it pretty much for granted. But then, as a kid, didn't you dream of growing up and working in a sweet factory?'

'I'm diabetic.'

'Oh look. I'm sorry – '

'Don't worry. I had the toyshop equivalent.'

'So you'll know that even the most enviable profession palls over time. What with stars who insist on setting their own lighting, directors who want to call all the shots and editors who choose the most basic close-ups, it's not all roses.'

Simon warmed to his favourite subject and was grateful to Will for drawing him out. He chatted for several minutes until he suddenly realised that he had monopolised the conversation. Afraid that Will might mistake nervousness for egotism, he broke off in mid-sentence and asked him a question.

'Yes,' Will replied, 'one sister.'

'Snap,' he said. 'Both of us come from pigeon pairs.'

'I'm the older.'

'I'm the younger.' His hopes of a ready-made affinity collapsed.

'There are advantages to both,' Will said.

'Absolutely,' he agreed, worried that Will might turn out to be banal. 'So what do you do?' he asked, wary of the question ever since it had been wilfully misread in a gay bar.

'I'm a teacher, for my sins,' Will confessed. Simon wondered why teachers were always so self-deprecating. He supposed that it must derive from a sense of having stayed in the shallow end of life, like people who marry their cousins.

'Any particular subject?' he asked.

'French and music,' Will said.

'What an interesting combination,' he replied. Although, on reflection, it was merely unusual.

'Yes, I enjoy it. It means that I get to take the children to concerts of French music.'

Simon laughed gently at what he presumed was a joke. 'Where?'

'On Haverstock Hill.'

'That's not far from me.'

'I know. Though I'm living in Stockwell. Rents are far too steep north of the river.'

Simon felt his remark like a reproach.

'It must be quite a trek every day.'

'I don't mind. It's straight up the Northern Line and I usually get a seat.'

'It would be good to meet. Maybe you'd like to come round one afternoon after school?'

'I'd like that a lot,' Will said. And Simon felt as if he were taking his clothes off on the phone.

'So shall we fix a date?' he asked. Will then recited a litany of his extramural activities for the forthcoming week, in the middle of which the line went dead.

'Hello!' Simon rattled the receiver, willing it back to life. 'Hello!' There was no reply. 'Damn!' he swore and replaced it on the base. It was typical that they should be cut off in mid-arrangement, but he was sure that Will would grasp what had happened and call back. Never in his life had he struck up such an instant rapport. After ten tense minutes he rang 1471, from which he learnt that 'the caller' – or, more probably, his landlady – had withheld the number. He returned to his phoneside vigil. Every few moments he checked the dialling tone, only to slam down the receiver in case Will should ring and find him engaged. After half an hour he took the remaining lasagne into the kitchen and tossed it into the bin. He made himself a pot of real coffee as compensation for his lie about lunch. The caffeine cleared his head and he realised that Will's failure to phone back must have been caused by his landlady's – or a fellow-lodger's – return. While he was the first to appreciate the value of discretion, he saw no virtue in taking it to extremes.

The telephone rang like a siren and he raced back into the sitting room. He was determined to maintain his reserve, but impatience overcame him and he grabbed the receiver. 'Simon Dune!' He could scarcely conceal his frustration at hearing his mother's voice. 'I'm sorry, Mum,' he said, 'I can't speak now. I'm expecting a very important phone call. From America.' He spoke the name with a reverence that harked back to the days before cheap flights. 'I'll ring you this evening. All right?' He hated himself even more as she hung up. It would have done him no harm to have chatted for a few minutes. Will would have surely understood that he was not – not yet – the most important person in his life. He sunk into a chair and focused his attention on the phone which, contrary to conventional wisdom, rang several times during the course of the afternoon. All the friends in the world, however, could not compensate for a lack of love.

By now he was racked with doubt. Will had been in full flow when they were cut off. It might well seem to him that it was he, Simon, who had put down the phone, hence his not ringing back. As he conjured up Will's sense of rejection, it hurt him even more than his own. There was nothing he could do to make it up to him. He berated himself for not asking for his number, but he had had no reason to expect a fault on the line. He did not know his surname or else he would have worked his way through the entire phone book – even if that name were Smith. All he knew was that he taught in a school on Haverstock Hill and was, at that very moment, most probably locked in despair in his lonely flat – no, not even a flat, lodgings (he

painted the scene in the black-and-white tones of a Fifties film).
The thought that there might be any misunderstanding between
them was unbearable, for the truth was that he had fallen in
love with Will's voice on the phone.

So absurd did it sound that he was embarrassed to articulate
the thought, even to himself. They had talked for all of fifteen
minutes. He had no idea what Will looked like, what he believed
in, how often he smiled. On the other hand, people did fall in
love with voices. The blind did so all the time and he had read
of listeners who were infatuated with radio announcers. Besides,
Will's voice was so enticing: masculine and mellow, soft and yet
self-assured, persuasive but not harsh. He lost himself in trying
to describe it. He felt exhilarated and excited and, above all,
grateful that Will had rung him, that he had thrown out the
possibility of love. There was no need for restraint. Will must
want love even more than he did. After all, he was the one who
had put in the advert. What's more, he had picked out his letter
from the pile. All his schoolboy efforts at writing to pen-pals had
paid off. Now he wanted to step off the page and meet him. He
was approaching thirty. He was beginning to leave hairs in the
bath. Will was an answer to his prayers . . . or, at any rate, he
would be when he rang back.

By the early evening he had turned over so many possibilities
in his mind that he had to test them on someone else. So he
rang Jenny, his closest confidante. He asked for her advice but
what he actually wanted was her endorsement since he had
already come up with a plan to visit all the schools on Haverstock Hill the next day in search of Will. Jenny did not approve.
She suggested that he should contact *Time Out*, explain what
had happened and ask if they would give him Will's number. He
was sure that such information was classified (hence the name).
His voice jumped a pitch and Jenny told him to relax. There was
nothing so unattractive as desperation. Will was sure to call

back soon. But Simon failed to understand why it had taken him so long. It was not as if the whole household would be permanently stationed around the phone like a wartime wireless. Jenny told him that he was gabbling so fast she could barely make out one word in ten, at which he accused her of a lack of sympathy. It was all very well for her. She had Brian. Why could she not understand that he too had found the love of his life?

He dragged himself to bed with no expectation of sleep, only to be confounded eight hours later by the alarm. He was affronted both by the ease with which he had sloughed off despair and the fact that he had not dreamt of Will. He fired himself with a sense of purpose. He was free until four when he was due at the National Theatre for a run-through of a new play set in a crack house. That left him the bulk of the day to carry out his plan.

Step number one was to ring up the local education authority. The official was so helpful that he regretted the intricacy of his cover story. She felt sure that he would find no difficulty in placing his triplets in one of the several schools on Haverstock Hill. He tried to keep the disappointment from his expression of thanks. Armed with the list of schools, he decided to start at Chalk Farm tube and work his way up towards Hampstead. The singularity of his request convinced him of the need to make it in person. Should anyone challenge him, he would say that he had sat next to Will at a concert. They had chatted during the interval when Will had told him of a vacancy for a cellist in his (or a friend's?) quartet. Will had written his name and number on the programme which he had left in the hall. So he had decided to seek him out himself. Such eccentricity would be attributed to his profession. Musicians were allowed to be quirky whereas, to the constant chagrin of one whose heroes were Angus McBean and Cecil Beaton, photographers, since the Sixties, were expected to be, in every sense, straight.

Reeling off a short prayer (which he was afraid might be sacrilegious), he approached the first school. A cacophony of hoots and shrieks warned him that it was breaktime. As one whose contact with boys was confined to the occasional schools matinee, he was quite unprepared for the din. A second shock was the informality. He tried to recall the current orthodoxy on uniforms: whether they were classless and democratic or hidebound and militaristic. Either way, it was clear that, in the absence of an official decree, the boys had imposed one themselves, hence the ubiquitous trainers, sweatshirts and jeans. He entered the yard and asked a solitary boy for directions to the school secretary, whom he had judged to be both the best informed and least threatening member of staff. The boy, seizing his chance to escape indoors with an eagerness that took Simon back twenty years, offered to accompany him. The visit proved to be futile, since the secretary was too new to have mastered first names. With a diffidence that increased Simon's unease, she flagged down a passing teacher, a white-fleeced gargoyle of a man, and put the question to him. He too knew no one by the name of Will (Simon began to wonder whether he would have fared better with a 'William'). 'Besides,' he added as if grossly offended, 'at this school no one teaches both French and Music. There are fully fledged, independent departments for each.' His querulousness was beginning to attract notice so Simon, fearing further interrogation, thanked them for their help and beat a hasty retreat.

Two further enquiries drew a similar response and Simon began to despair. He pictured his visit through tabloid-reading eyes. A scenario unfolded in which a child was abducted and assaulted. The police questioned the pupils at all the neighbouring schools. Several mentioned the presence of a sinister stranger carrying camera equipment (he felt the strap biting into his shoulder). In vain he protested his innocence, his only alibi a dog-eared copy of *Time Out*. He even began to doubt himself – not his motives but his memory. He wondered whether he might have mistaken his hills and, rather than Haverstock, Will had said Primrose or Rosslyn or Highgate (they might as well be in Rome). He had been walking for more than two hours: the strains – and the stains – were beginning to show. Even if he did succeed in tracking Will down, he would be in no fit state to meet him. In the weary, travel-soiled flesh, he would make last summer's photograph look ten years old.

He approached a pair of vast wrought-iron gates that guarded the entrance to the fourth and final school on his list. He gazed through the grille at the children enjoying lunchtime games in the yard. Their youth restored his hope. This was a primary school where the most unlikely subjects would be combined. He searched for an entrance, but the gates were heavily padlocked. In desperation he was considering scaling the wall when a nun sailed past him and through a doorway in the railings. His scripture-soaked brain threw up images of Moses parting the Red Sea on the way to the Promised Land, which were immediately confirmed by the vision in front of him: a young man of such intense beauty that he both longed for it to be Will and prayed that it was not. For, far more than either the rape of a rainforest or genetic engineering, their union would affront the laws of nature. No family romance could breach such a strong taboo. But before he could turn tail, the vision was upon him, asking if he could be of help. Oh yes, Simon thought, in more ways than you can ever know, and he considered blurting out the entire story appealing, if nothing else, to Will's sense of the grotesque. But his courage failed and he heard himself asking for the school secretary. The young man – Simon seized one last hope of anonymity – detailed two small girls to show him to her room while he went back on patrol.

The girls led him down flights of stairs and along labyrinthine corridors, which put him in mind of a mythic quest. They finally reached the secretary's office where he ran through his, by now, depressingly familiar speech. The secretary seemed not at all put out by its anomalies, leaving him to wonder whether she might not have heard something similar before.

'We do indeed have a Will who teaches French and Music: Will Livingstone.' Simon felt even more unnerved by the name's associations and determined that he should on no account meet him in his present condition. He would leave a note, stating that he had happened to be passing and reassuring Will that he had not slammed down the phone.

'What's the time?' the secretary asked, looking at her Dali-esque watch. 'I expect he'll be in the staff room.' The next thing he knew, the girls had led Simon there and knocked on the door. He was ushered in to face a row of disconcertingly jovial nuns. His usual sense of guilt in their presence was inflamed by his particular mission. He had, however, come too far to prevaricate. He stammered his request and was told that Mr Livingstone was on playground duty. So his suspicions had been correct.

He returned outside. Will smiled questioningly at him, leaving him no choice but to respond, even though every instinct told him to slip away.

'Will Livingstone?' he asked, for once at least avoiding the obvious.

'In person,' the young man replied.

'I'm Simon Dune.' He strove to see if any cloud appeared on the man's face but it managed to remain preternaturally calm.

'I'd no idea,' Will said. 'Let's stand over here. I can't go far as I have to keep an eye on the children.'

'Yes, of course,' he replied, with a sudden awareness of the pupils, although none of them was paying him the least attention. It was the role of grown-ups to behave oddly. And he was struck by a wave of melancholy at the prospect of everything that they had to learn.

'You've caught me by surprise,' Will said. 'I wouldn't have recognised you.' Simon wondered whether to take off his glasses, but he was an experienced enough photographer to have identified the disappointment in Will's voice. He remembered the sign that had hung in one of his friends' studios: 'Don't blame the photographer; he's only doing his job.' He knew that his plan had misfired. He was painfully conscious of his heat and the other's cool, of his disarray and the other's elegance, of his grubbiness and the other's freshness. It was so unjust that he should have such overactive sweat glands when he was such an unsweaty person inside. He felt a surge of hope at the sight of Will smiling at him until he realised that he was merely taking his measure, playing him along before disarming him as expertly as he would a madman with a gun.

'I happened to be en route for Hampstead when I saw the school,' he explained, 'so I decided to pop in.' He was aware that he had jumped a stage – what's more, it was a crucial one – and wondered whether Will had noticed. If so, he said nothing. 'I just wanted to make certain that you didn't think I'd hung up on you yesterday.' Will swung round as if the merest mention of that conversation was compromising. Simon wanted to reassure him that he loved him: he would be the last person to cause him any harm. But he realised that he would only make matters worse. So he smiled vacantly, while a drop of saliva formed on his lower lip.

'Oh I know that,' Will said. 'It was my money that ran out. I tried to push in another coin but it jammed. I think the box must have been full.'

'Of course,' he muttered, cursing himself for having ignored Jenny's advice. Fate was so cruel. In books, it was called irony. In life, it was pure spite.

'There was nothing I could do. I was sure you'd understand. I did say that it was a payphone?'

'Yes, you did,' he offered Will a sad reassurance. 'But I didn't hear any pips.'

'No, you wouldn't. It's one of the new models. It drives my mother mad.'

'I can see why.'

'I meant to ring back, but I had to stay in all afternoon and catch up on some marking. Then I went out with friends and I didn't have a chance.'

'No worries,' he said, feeling as small as his playground companions. 'I went out, too.' He pictured himself sitting motionless, staring at the phone as at a sick-bed, and prayed that teachers did not develop a heightened sensitivity to lies.

'Well, at least we've straightened that out. Now I'd better get back to the kids.' Will flashed him a cheerless smile and held out his hand to dismiss him. Simon longed to know his number but, fearing a further rebuff, asked cautiously whether he would give him a ring.

'If you like. Not tonight though. I'm taking the kids out.' Simon wondered if it might be to one of the Fauré or Debussy concerts that he had joked about on the phone. 'But I'll try on Tuesday or Wednesday.'

'Yes, please do. For once you should find me in. I'm enjoying the luxury of a quiet week.'

'Now I really must go,' Will declared, as much the master of the situation as he was of the yard, striding off to arbitrate between two girls, one of whom had stuck chewing gum in the other's hair. Simon, meanwhile, made his tortuous way down the hill.

He had lied about the quiet week. On his return from the National Theatre, he cancelled arrangements for the next two evenings and stayed at home, never further than an arm's length from the phone. Will did not ring. Indeed, as he had predicted, he never rang again. He tried to salvage a modicum of self-respect by commending his own optimism, which came to seem dangerously close to simple-mindedness. His solution was to tell the story (suitably edited) to friends. Moreover, with each telling, the confusions grew more exaggerated and his behaviour more absurd. He was determined to prove the maxim that the ability to laugh at oneself was the key to staying sane. His chief regret was that the story lacked dramatic tension. The fact that his friends could instantly predict Will's response when confronted by a febrile intruder did not reflect well on his own powers of judgement. But, as he said repeatedly, it was all too easy to be wise after the event. And he laughed to the point of hysteria.

For several months he gave up all hope of finding a partner. There was nothing inevitable about falling in love. It was the luck of the draw, not a requirement of being human. He had other outlets for his energies and he plunged himself into his work, his theatre-going and his friendships. But he felt an ache in his groin that was almost unbearable and, as time passed, it spread up his body and into his heart. He was tormented by the paradox that a man who had always prided himself on his sharpness of vision should have been so blind when it came to himself. It was no wonder that he had preferred to remain behind the camera. But, for all his new-found awareness, he could see no way of resolving his predicament until, one evening, Jenny, having run out of gin and refusing to indulge his self-pity, took him to task. She told him that he was a young man who still had a great deal to offer. If he were to realise his dream of leading an integrated life, he had to abandon the pose of being an observer and confront the world head-on.

At first Simon rebelled, charging her with both callousness and betrayal, but her patience was exhausted and required a stronger restorative than straight tonic. She insisted that he had a choice. *I am a camera* was an excellent title for a play but a feeble foundation for a life. The longer Simon reflected on her words, the more apposite he found them. Even falling at the first fence would be preferable to ruling himself out of the running. The prospect made his face relax into a new expression: one that he was determined to capture as both a record and a reminder should his resolution ever start to flag. So he reached for his camera, programmed the self-timer, polished his lenses and smiled.

Bedtime Story

I TALK TO MYSELF. I'm a light sleeper and I welcome the company. It started when I was a child: an only child in a dangerously large bedroom. My parents condemned such soliloquising as roundly as my sucking my thumb or rocking beneath the sheets. They filled my bed with a toy menagerie in an effort to assuage my fears and divert my attention, but my imagination, already far too rational for its own good, was unable to give voice to creatures that bleated, barked or bayed. It needed a human context, albeit one so circumscribed that Thomas the narrator told Thomas the listener stories of which Thomas himself was the hero. Even then, my imagination remained bounded by my experience. Thomas was no Dan Dare or Bobby Charlton, but a young boy clambering for birds' nests or reading in the library or visiting his aunt. The purpose of the stories was not to feed my spirit of adventure, but to give me the illusion of control.

The complicity between narrator and audience removed the need for certain basic information . . . indeed, the fear that, far from honing my communication skills, I was strengthening my solipsism may have inspired my parents' hostility. I am therefore doubly determined to make my position – or, at least, my profession – clear. I am a teacher, here in Cambridge. I say *teacher* rather than fellow or don, because teaching is what I do and what I am proud of. Needless to say, I also write. I am currently working on the first full-scale critical biography of Henry Vaughan to follow up my edition of his poems. Although some of my associates – both colleagues and students – might query my use of the word, Vaughan is my passion. I consider him to be the greatest English religious poet, bar none. For too long he has been relegated to a few pages in an anthology of the Metaphysicals. While lesser poets were hymning their mistresses, coy or otherwise, he was putting the ineffable into words:

> I saw Eternity the other night
> Like a great Ring of pure and endless light,
> All calm, as it was bright.

I have studied enough literature to know about frustrated ambition, yet I still wake up surprised to find myself an academic. Throughout my adolescence, I dreamt of becoming an actor. Lecture theatres notwithstanding, I see no comparison between the professions. Any correspondence is of my own making. In my teens I tried to bury my confusions within the strict contours of a dramatic character, just as now I escape my creative failure in the shadow of a greater man. And yet my dreams foundered not on a lack of talent but on a superfluity of flesh. At school and university, I was always cast in character and comic parts. But I wanted to act with my soul, not my stomach. I had no wish to play Falstaff all my life. Besides, all the best Falstaffs are thin and padded. And I felt so ashamed in the communal dressing room. On the one side were all those lithe young bodies that didn't give themselves a second thought, while on the other was me trying to change behind an empty clothes rack. My analyst – yes, I went through that second adolescence, as long and painful as the first – failed to understand why I did not try to lose weight. But for every Callas with her tapeworms, there is a Thomas with his protein diet, fruit diet, fibre diet – and recalcitrant waistline. So I changed tack. Fortunately, I had not neglected my studies. I got my First, the best of the year, and I could stay in the charmed cloister for the rest of my life.

At the risk of tempting fate, I will say that I found I had a gift for teaching. I loved both my work and the majority of my students, even those who were here primarily for the rowing and the cricket and the champagne. Inspiring others is a vital – if secondary – form of inspiration. I found a natural home in the Senior Common Room, where fellowship became an easy substitute for intimacy. My public persona was mild-mannered and unworldly: donnish, for those who will forgive the tautology. I made no secret of my sexuality, but no spectacle of it either. I let it be known that it was another aspect of my life that was largely academic. Any practical experience had been gained on field trips abroad. These encounters were short, love-less and increasingly pecuniary, but left me with a fertile trove of images which I stored up, camel-like, for the arid periods ahead. I felt no great dissatisfaction. Although I shared a longing for the ideal companion as expressed by everyone from greetings card manufacturers to Platonic scholars, I knew that it was an illusion. I refused to subscribe to an ethos that took sex out of the bedroom and placed it on billboards. And, when all intellectual arguments failed, I took comfort from the ever more grizzled hair on my chest. Then I met Julian.

I search for a word to define our relationship. I usually have little time for his talk of linguistic conspiracies but, in this case, I am forced to agree. *Lover* suggests that we spend our entire life between the sheets and that the experience is perfect, which is false on both counts. *Companion* makes me feel like a dowager. *Friend* is too vague and *boyfriend* too adolescent. *Mate* sounds like an expression – not to say a person – picked up in a London nightclub. *Partner* belongs in a solicitor's office and *significant other* to the obituary pages, where it has made too many appearances in recent years.

Description poses less of a problem, even for one whose natural tendency is to see a person as a whole and not as a set of

49

constituent parts. He is so tall and blond that, hyperbole notwithstanding, he might well be a lifeguard in California. He certainly saved my life, long before he knew that it was at risk. His hair stands on end in the style of the French cartoon character, Tintin. Indeed, in the early weeks of our relationship I adopted Tintin as his pet name, only to drop it when he failed either to respond or to reciprocate. 'You're a natural Thomas,' he said. In what way? Thomas Aquinas? Thomas à Becket? Doubting Thomas? Unlike me, he dresses for display rather than concealment: skin-tight T-shirts and figure- (or, more accurately, crotch-) hugging jeans. No one would ever compliment him on his wardrobe or ask where he bought his sweater. They would be too busy trying to persuade him to take it off. He exudes that particular student smell of cheap after-shave splashed on too quickly: a scent that has never smelt so sweet.

He worships the sun – literally, I presume, given his claim to be a pagan. The merest glimmer in the sky is the cue for him to drag a deckchair from the cellar and soak up the rays. Like the devotee of any religion, he demands genuine commitment, expressing a violent disapproval of solariums and insisting that, if he is to court skin cancer, it should be from the sun itself and not from any artificial aids. He strips stark naked, which I consider somewhat excessive in view of both setting and climate, but he declares an aversion to 'streaks of false modesty'. Gone are the days when I would reply that there was no one to see them but me. Instead, I offer regular warnings that he might be overlooked. Once he picked up an oak leaf and placed it gingerly over his genitals. 'Think of it as a fig leaf,' he said. It blew away in the breeze. 'Fig leaves always do.'

His beauty is not of the passive sort that is draining in its desire for admiration, but rather an invigorating blend of allure and power. I could juggle five carving knives while he stood stock still, yet he would remain the focus of everyone's attention. I am aware that our relationship provokes as much hostile comment as a mixed marriage in the Fifties. Physical incongruity is an affront to a world where the health club is king. I would cite the attraction of opposites – if one of those opposites were not me. Charitable observers suggest that Julian has been deeply scarred by his parents' divorce and longs for a second father. Less charitable ones, aware that I am not dependent on my college stipend, claim that my appeal lies in my wallet. Not that I can blame them. I originally counted myself among their number, assuming that he was looking for a complaisant landlord (although he could surely have found a less costly way of not paying rent). But living with him soon put me right. When I told him that I planned to name him in my will (an attempt, I confess, to guarantee my own security as much as his), he showed a complete lack of interest, declaring that possessions were for dead people, like the luxuries in a pharaoh's tomb.

Our relationship began as that of teacher and student and it never strayed beyond the bounds of propriety. The age of the eccentric don who conducted supervisions in the bath or a loin-cloth has long vanished. There is no place for men such as the Corpus classicist who informed one of my contemporaries that his heavily matted chest came with the word 'Welcome' stamped upon it. Moral turpitude lours over all our heads. I was marking Julian's essays, not his compliance. He came to see me with a fellow student who, I have to admit, sorely taxed my egalitarian principles. He treated literary theory as though it were a branch of topography, picking his way along the routes mapped out by earlier commentators. Individuality was suspect because it threatened critical consensus. Julian, on the other hand, was a maverick whose essays veered from the hare-brained to the profound. I had to check my inclination to indulge his waywardness and force him to engage with scholars of the past. I had no fears, despite his frequent protests, that they would stifle his creativity. He was exhilarated by the wit of the Metaphysicals (and I by his exhilaration) but he preferred the more sensuous images of the Romantics. He declared that his favourite poet of all time was Walt Whitman and, of our own age, Thom Gunn.

It was the invitation to his twenty-first birthday party that changed everything. I was both surprised and touched. Amongst all the crisp white invitations on my chimney-piece there was one bursting with colour. I had initially determined to decline. I told him that coming of age, even symbolically, was a time to rid himself of all the old folk who cluttered up his life. 'You're not old,' he said to me; 'you're the same age as my mother, and she's banned the use of the word. Do come. It will give her someone to talk to.' I must admit that this came low on my list of incentives. On the other hand, it was so long since I had been to a real undergraduates' party, as opposed to cocktails in a college hall or a May Week bash in a meadow, that I resolved to accept. Besides, I was curious. He shared a house with three friends in Thorsby, a village a few miles outside Cambridge. Their domestic arrangements had long intrigued me, as I visualised the hordes of girls who passed through their hands. I clung to the thought that it was girls, although I still cannot decide whether that was for the sake of probability or to place him more securely out of reach.

I experimented with far too many outfits for one who had declared his intention to fade into the background. The choice of gift caused me similar concern. Rarely can the line between ostentation and meanness have seemed so fine. Having dismissed after-shave as self-interested, clothes as overfamiliar and books as dull, I settled on a CD set of Ella Fitzgerald singing Gershwin. Even then, I was faced with the dilemma of whether including the receipt was a courtesy, allowing him the chance to change it, or a vulgar declaration of how much I had spent.

Having negotiated the various pitfalls, I arrived at the house to find the party in full swing. The noise filtered down to the road and would, I felt sure, give rise to a host of complaints. My vision of a police raid in which they discovered vast quantities of dope – or worse – gave way to banner headlines in which I, as the only senior member of the university present, was named. My career would be in ruins. I was on the verge of turning back when I saw Julian standing in the porch, his shadowed features haloed by the hall light. He waved his arm aloft as if directing a plane. I immediately dismissed my fears as the product of self-importance and hurried to greet him. As I drew close, I saw that he was wearing make-up: a scattering of powder on his eyelids and glitter on his cheeks. The effect was less *Cage aux Folles* than Tutankhamun. He was thrilled with the CDs and proposed playing them right away, but my warning that they were no longer dance music convinced him to wait until morning when 'post-party tristesse' had set in. He suggested that I might like to come back and listen to them with him. I felt faint.

He introduced me to his mother, a striking woman with dappled hair pinned high in a bun. She wore a rainbow silk caftan which hit the perfect note, midway between catwalk and thrift shop. I immediately saw from whom Julian had inherited his looks and his charm. I have come to know her well over the past three years but, even on first meeting, I felt an affinity.

'I've been invited to take charge of the catering,' she said. 'What's your excuse?'

'I don't know,' I replied. 'Perhaps to remind them that in the midst of life we are in death?'

'You'd better have a drink,' she said with a generous laugh. She appeared not at all put out either by her son's eccentricities or by his unconventional collection of friends. 'Look at them having such a lovely time,' she said. 'If only we'd had this degree of freedom when we were young . . .' I was on the point of agreeing when I was assailed by the thought that, even had I lived in Liberty Hall, I would have locked myself in my bedroom. I was too great a coward then, as now, which was why I was standing at the side talking to Julian's mother, while I yearned to be sweating on the dance floor with her son. We talked about Julian's prospects. We talked about my research. We talked about her involvement with the National Trust. I was anticipating that the evening would pass in a polite conversational glow when she left me to attend to the food.

I drifted into a discussion with a pair of female students, my interest in whom failed to extend beyond their studies. Their gassy giggles confirmed my indifference. I was planning my escape when it was handed to me in the form of a quiche proffered by Julian's mother. 'I thought you needed rescuing,' she said, offering me a slice. Gratitude for her intervention was tempered by doubts about her meaning. How much had Julian told her about me? We resumed our compensatory conversation until Julian came up and asked why we were not dancing.

'It's not really our kind of music,' I said. 'We're of a different vintage, your mother and I.'

'Oh, Mum likes everything,' he said. 'The original disco queen.'

'I try to keep an open mind,' she said as he hugged her.

'Well, Thomas, that's your cue,' he prompted, leaving me no choice but to take it.

'I'm game if you are,' I said to her.

'You bet,' she replied. 'Let's show these youngsters how it's done.'

I put my arms on her waist and she put hers on my shoulders and we jogged on to the floor. I was surprised at how easy it was to appropriate the beat. We shared an implicit understanding and, without a word, began to twist again as I had not for at least twenty-five summers. When the track ended, we were rewarded with a round of applause, the only ironic element of which was our bows. We retreated to a corner where, despite Julian's mother's entreaty, I determined to remain standing. I was trying discreetly to mop my brow when Julian approached.

'You've been lying to me, Thomas.' My heart pounded. 'I had no idea you were such a good dancer.'

'A dancer is only as good as his partner,' I replied, inclining my head towards his mother.

'In which case let's see how you manage with me.'

He brooked no refusal, citing birthday privileges. So, urged on by his mother and cringing with embarrassment, I followed him into the throng. I determined to take my lead from the self-absorbed heaving all around me.

'Oh no, I want it just like my mum,' he said and placed his arms squarely on my shoulders, removing them only to position my own around his waist. I willed them to resist the heat. As we danced, I pretended that we were in a world of our own, but not for romantic purposes so much as for self-respect. And yet, from the corner of my eye, I could see his mother smiling and tapping her chair to the music, while several others had stopped their writhing and were watching us.

I was dancing with Julian. I did not know what to think. Then his voice cut through my confusion.

'You're very light on your feet.'

'Fat people often are,' I replied, and hated myself more than ever. But, if he heard, he did not respond. We danced on until the music changed. I broke away. He kissed me on the lips, which I convinced myself was mere convention. I bid a hurried goodnight to his mother and drove home. It was late. Sunday or not, I could ill afford an idle morning.

As I suspected, Julian's invitation to listen to the CDs had been rash. I happened to remain within range of the telephone the whole day, and yet it never rang. I was glad to have my judgement confirmed but saddened that he had failed so much as to make the gesture, which I would definitely have refused. With formal teaching over and the students preparing for exams, I knew that our contact would be limited. I might never even have seen him again had not a last-minute phone call from Rosamund Tilner, a fellow Metaphysical, crying off from *The Cherry Orchard*, prompted me to offer him the seat. He responded with unexpected enthusiasm, given his recent pronouncement that the dead weight of the classics was the reason that the theatre could no longer be considered a significant art. I supposed that he must have had a change of heart and, if anything were designed to confirm it, it was the production in question which, to my delight, did not take Chekhov's dictum that he wrote comedies as an excuse for turning the evening into knockabout farce, but brought out the play's full poignancy.

Julian, needless to say, was less enthusiastic. 'Why is it that in Russian plays they always discover their wasted lives too late?' he asked. 'It's so self-indulgent. There's no need to be a victim. Grab hold of the world by the balls and squeeze.' I wondered whether, behind the deliberate provocation, the remark was aimed at me.

I presumed that we had exhausted our quid pro quos and were quits. So I was agreeably surprised when, the following week, I received an invitation to dinner. My only reservation was that it might interfere with his revision, but he assured me that he needed at least one evening's relief. I leave undescribed my agitation over the choice of a suitable bottle of wine or an appropriate interpretation of seven-thirty for eight, except to say that few invitations have ever made me so nervous – a sensation exacerbated when, on my arrival, he informed me that there would be no other guests. His flatmates were busy elsewhere and his friends had no transport. I remonstrated with him for not having told me earlier as I would have been delighted to act as chauffeur. 'I'm cool,' he replied, which was demonstrably true. 'Besides, there'll be all the more for us.' I wondered whether that was a dig at my weight.

The food was palatable rather than inspired. We began with a paté maison, from a maison that was clearly not his, followed by a chicken Kiev, whose provenance was harder to determine. I complimented him on his hidden talents, which he confessed were for unwrapping rather than cooking, adding that his mother had once defined his idea of haute cuisine as a high shelf at Marks and Spencer. We talked with ease, largely about him. It wasn't that he was egotistical, simply young and unversed in conversational niceties. He talked of his hopes for his exams and the importance of gaining a First if he were to return on a research fellowship in the autumn. I assured him that his chances were good, while expressing my incredulity that he had opted to stay and spend his life in libraries. 'You mustn't judge a book by its cover,' he said, which sent a tingle down my spine.

We talked of the forthcoming summer. He intended to go backpacking across America. I found myself offering to put him in touch with various friends, before realising that I would have to provide more of an introduction than just 'one of my students'.

'At least you'll be able to have a bath,' I said.

'Are you trying to tell me something?' he asked, playfully sniffing an armpit.

'Not at all. But I don't want you checking in at the *Psycho* motel.'

'If I do, I promise to steer well clear of the showers. Why not come with me?' He proffered an invitation so improbable that it was almost enticing.

'You're very sweet,' I said, 'or very drunk. I'm tempted to accept if only to teach you discretion.'

'Then do,' he said.

'My backpacking days were over with the age of the ruck-sack,' I replied. 'I can picture you hitchhiking on the highway, nearly causing a smash as cars stop to pick you up only to accel-erate again as I emerge from the undergrowth and you insist on their including me.'

'Why must you always do yourself down?' he asked.

'Saves time?' I said.

'There you go again.'

'In any case, I'm committed to taking my mother on a Baltic cruise.'

'Sounds chilly,' he said.

I agreed.

'So, if I come back in the autumn, I'll be working on my thesis. You'll no longer be my supervisor. No one can impugn either of our motives.'

'You've lost me,' I said, feeling my faint heart quiver.

'Would you like to sleep with me?' he asked: a request that I could only answer with a gulp of wine. 'I'm sorry if I've shocked you. You claim to admire my directness.'

'I was talking about your critical judgement.'

'I'm exercising it now.'

I wondered whether it might be a dare, like a member of the Boat Team dating the ugliest girl in the college. I almost said yes in order to call his bluff. Yet the look on his face was so sincere.

'No hard feelings if you don't. But I'd never have forgiven myself if I'd let the opportunity slip.'

All my instincts . . . all my training was saying no. Years and years of saying no welled up inside me. But something buried even deeper refused to countenance the lie. 'Yes,' I heard myself say. 'Yes, I'd like to very much.'

'Good,' he said, steadying my hand. 'Now I'll serve the dessert.'

I stayed that night and several more besides. I yearned for him with every nerve in my body: a body which, thanks to the miracle of reciprocity, was no longer one that I needed to hide. I held out no hopes of a lasting relationship. I regarded it as a holiday romance in term-time and felt sure that, when term ended and the holidays proper began, reality would intervene. Julian flew off to America to partake of all its fabled opportunities, while I sailed around the Baltic, listening to lectures on Peter the Great and Thomas Mann. He promised to write and I was expecting the odd postcard but not the detailed letters that greeted me from a trail of legendary cities, full of chance discoveries, quirky encounters and expressions of love.

He got his First and returned to Cambridge in the autumn to work on the fiction – or, rather, fictions – of William Burroughs. He looked more burnished than ever. I was sick with desire for him but, true to form, required him to make the first move. He duly made it and, in bed that night, I revealed the proposal that I had been formulating for weeks. I knew that his grant was small and that the pittance he would be paid for teaching would not make up the shortfall. He had given up the Thorsby house so, rather than trying to squeeze into a wretched bedsit, he would be very welcome to move in with me. I had space to spare. I assured him that I was not trying to establish a claim on him, but to resolve his predicament. Moreover, there would be no need to pay rent.

'I'll pay you in kind,' he said, leaning over and giving me an advance. 'You're the most generous man in the world. How could . . . why should I refuse?'

Excitement at the prospect of sharing a house – a life – with Julian mingled with fear that I had acted precipitately. The last time I had lived with anyone had been when I myself was a student. While the house is undoubtedly too big for a bachelor, I enjoy the space. I like to walk into rooms that I never use and

ponder unexplored possibilities. I like to catalogue my possessions: the books and bibelots; the paintings and furniture; some
bought and some inherited, but all invested with powerful
memories. With respect to Proudhon, I believe that property is
personality. Besides, I need the freedom to indulge my fantasies.
I don't mean night-time, behind-closed-curtain fantasies,
but daytime, famous-for-fifteen-minute fantasies. I might be
listening to Mahler – either on the hi-fi or in my head – when I
feel an urge to jump up and play Karajan. And it would be
churlish not to acknowledge the applause. But my bows and
salutation to the orchestra, so natural in my own mind, might
disconcert a stranger.

I have done my best to adjust to his presence, even those
aspects of it that I find less endearing, such as the ring around
the bathtub and the clogged-up sink. He has yet to appreciate
the full function of a wardrobe but, when I try to pick up the
clothes that he leaves scattered on the floor, he informs me that
I am not his maid. 'You're so anal,' he says which, coming from
him, strikes me as a particularly perverse criticism. I have to
admit that I find something satisfying in cleaning up after him,
although it is Mrs Macpherson who bears the brunt of it. She
used to be a bedder at Caius, but she left when they let in
women. Julian charmed her from the first. 'He's such a
gentleman,' she told me as she ironed his T-shirts. 'The sort it's
a privilege to serve.'

In the three years that he has been living here our relationship has inevitably changed. Only an artificial flame burns with
a constant intensity: human passion cannot sustain itself at
such a pitch. Which is why all the great romantic myths end in
death (I must stop comparing our lives to literature). We have
evolved into perfect companions. Each evening at dinner
we discuss our day and the mere fact of his presence gives the
most trivial events significance. We share interests or, more

frequently, swap them, trading a chamber concert at St John's Smith Square (mine) for a conceptual art show at the Serpentine (his). We take holidays together, finding the Mediterranean a suitable compromise between culture and sun. He even came when I took my mother to the Great Wall of China, throughout which she insisted (with what degree of disingenuousness remains unclear) on regarding our association as purely peda-gogic. Of such moments are fifty-year-old scrapbooks made. They offer a far firmer basis for a lifetime of happiness than rumpled sheets.

Lately, he has started to call me Dad. At first, I found it endearing. It gave us an unassailable legitimacy. Then, one day in a restaurant, he asked the waitress to hand the bill to his father. I wondered whether she realised he was playing games (after all, we could hardly be more different physically), but she took my card happily enough. 'Thanks, Dad,' Julian said with a smile. The more I thought about it, the less I liked it. It seemed to define us sexually, or rather asexually. When I asked him not to repeat it, he pretended not to understand my objections I don't want a son: I want a lover. My lover. My love.

I always insisted that he had his own bedroom – even though, at first, I had difficulty in keeping him out of mine. I was eager that he should not feel beholden to me . . . I am paying for my magnanimity now. He told me from the start that he did not believe in monogamy, although, in those early months, his agnosticism appeared purely theoretical. Then, one day, I had a discharge. The doctor told me it was gonorrhoea. There was only one person from whom I could have caught it. So I confronted him. But, whereas I had been wracked with shame in the surgery, he refused to feel any guilt. He called it an occupational hazard, as though it were farmer's lung or house-maid's knee. It was then that he told me that he had been sleeping around. He swore that he still loved me but that sex and love were two quite separate things and it was a grave mistake to confuse them. He threw in a lot of jargon about refusing to abide by heterosexual norms and bourgeois paradigms which, he claimed, were all based on protecting property and securing inheritance. As gay men, we stood apart from all that. If somebody attracted us, we should be free to respond. Where was the harm if it didn't hurt anyone? It hurts me, I wanted to reply. You have no idea how much it hurts me.

I thought about asking him to leave, but that would simply have satisfied my pride – stupid, self-willed pride – when, above all else, I was desperate for him to stay. My acquiescence seemed sure to secure that. If he wants to be free, he can be as free living here as anywhere else. He promises me that I have his heart. The appeal of the other men is wholly glandular. And yet, as time goes by, I feel less and less confident. What if he falls for one of them the way that I have fallen for him? What if he finds that, far from being sinister social constructs, the heterosexual norm and bourgeois paradigm are expressions of a universal urge? What if he moves in with his new love and I never see him again or, worse, they integrate me into their lives, visiting for Sunday lunch like a pair of dutiful nephews? Inside this fat man there's a thin man eating his heart out.

I used to fantasise that, once I had a lover, I would be able to dispense with fantasies, but I find that I have more than ever. Julian is currently installed in his room with a man he has met in a pub or at a college disco – or worse – and all I can do is imagine them lying together, their hands charting an all too familiar terrain and yet making amazing discoveries. I wonder if the man is older than Julian or younger: English or foreign; heavy or slight. Does he have a moustache or a beard? Does the phrase *Naked Lunch* suggest to him impenetrable prose or prandial pleasure? I long to be a fly on the wall or, better yet, a flea on their bodies. I edge open the door of my room, but the only sound I can hear is my own breathing. They are as silent as teenagers pretending to study. I picture them kissing, their tongues lapping up each other's moisture . . . each other's warmth. I feel sure that this mystery man knows instinctively what is required: when to lead and when to respond; when to give and when to tantalise. He is no middle-aged adolescent worrying about the correct degree of tongue and lips and teeth.

It may be the ineptitude of my kisses that has made him turn elsewhere . . . I sound as preposterous as my mother blaming our ruined Christmas dinner on the overcooked sprouts after the dog had snatched the turkey. It doesn't take a mystic to know why he has turned elsewhere, just a mirror. His body is such a joy and mine is such an embarrassment. I used to claim that eating was my only vice, which should come as no surprise when its effects have prevented me from enjoying any other. He continues to insist that size is not an issue. 'I love your bigness,' he says, even as he struggles to encompass it. But how could anyone love something so obscene? He has two undergraduate friends, Robin and David, who pool their entire wardrobe including underwear. As they were describing it, I felt the stirrings of an erection. The only clothing that Julian and I could share would be a hat.

I long to know how he explains the light in my window as he walks up the drive. Does he claim that it has been left on to deter burglars, or does he acknowledge my presence? If the latter, does he treat me as a figure of fun – a jealous Pantaloon or, worse, a prurient Pandar – or does he dismiss me as 'the landlord', with no feelings to respect, only rules? I yearn to walk into his room and confront them, if only to stamp a definite image on my febrile imaginings. I might barge straight in, citing the absent-mindedness proverbial in my profession. Abandoning the last vestige of pride, I could go down on my knees and beg him to make love to me. 'I need you,' I would plead, 'not just in the spirit but in the flesh. I am consumed with desire. I appreciate all you said about love and sex being separate, but I belong to an older generation for whom they appear to be intertwined. My sex is my love. To pretend otherwise is to lie. And I have lied for far too long, Julian.' But I shall say nothing. I would rather have his scorn than his pity.

Instead, I abandon myself to other men's fantasies: poring (no pun intended) over pictures of Rick and Chip and Gary, in the full awareness that everything about them, from their names to their smiles to their interests, has been cynically manipulated. The flagrancy of their poses, together with the tawdriness of the experience, is perfectly calculated to neutralise my desire. I release myself into the glossy crevices of Chip's airbrushed musculature at no cost to anything but my sensitivity. I am back in the world of my adolescence, desperate to conceal my dog-eared copies of *Health and Efficiency* from my mother's unconcerned eye. Have I learnt nothing in the intervening thirty years except to find a better hiding place than my mattress? I slip the magazines back among the copies of the *John Donne Journal*. I can at least spare Julian the evidence of my degradation. And now, at last, I will be able to sleep.

Good Clean Fun

Ladies and Gentlemen, would you please put your hands together and give a warm welcome to the star of tonight's show – Mr Television himself: 'It's the way I wear them' – Harris Littlewood!

THANK YOU SO MUCH, ladies and gentlemen: thank you. All right! You can cut the cat-gut. That goes for the tom-toms too. I'm the one they've come to hear. You should know your place . . . And you should see the way they keep it: animals! No wonder they call it a pit. But enough of this idle chit-chat! Good evening, messieurs and mesdames (that's French for riff-raff). And you two gentlemen in the back row, good evening to you too. Because it's a free world, that's what I say. And we're here to enjoy it. We are. We really are . . . No! Eyes to the front! You'll give them a complex . . . It's a privilege to be with you here tonight in . . . oh me, I've a mind like a pair of fishnets (full of holes. Do try to keep up!). But it makes no difference because people are people the whole world over, whatever their colour or creed. We're all made the same, aren't we? At least most of us are . . . Have you heard the one about the transsexual? He just isn't himself these days . . . No, well, you have to laugh. Live and let live: that's my motto. And you sir – yes, you with the blind barber – you can come and live at my place any day of the week! Bring your mother . . . Oh, I'm sorry, madam. I can't see straight. It's these new glasses. I put them on and they make me come over all queer. No, but seriously – seriously! – I daren't go back to have my eyes tested. I mean who's safe with a man in the dark these days? Me . . . more's the pity! But I'm working on it. Oh, you have to laugh. The last one I saw recommended contact lenses. But I was worried they'd stick to my mascara. Tasty, don't you think? Five ninety-nine from Boots. Guaranteed not to be tested on animals. Well, that rules you lot out for a start. Riff-raff! Where was I? Oh yes, at the optician's. He advised me to try bifocals. I told him he ought to be ashamed of himself: suggesting something like that to a man my age. I'm sixty-five . . . forty-eight! Slip of the tongue, as the choirboy said to the bishop. Come on, wake up! I had more laughs from the cats in my Whiskas commercials. Am I allowed . . . oh yes, it's not the BBC . . . How are you doing out there? I can tell you I'm having about as much fun as a rabbi at the Vatican . . . Come on madam, there's no need to look so serious! You're here to enjoy yourself. And, at these prices, you might as well make an effort. Not that I see any of it. They're so tight, they'd have the rubber off your eyebrow pencil. They told me that the dressing-room had been used by Max Miller. 'Yes,' I said, 'and, by the look of them, so were the towels.' You have to laugh, don't you? Well at least you could try. Spread a little happiness: that's always been my motto.

> *Even when the darkest clouds are in the sky,*
> *You mustn't sigh and you mustn't cry,*
> *Just spread a little happiness as you go by,*
> *Please try.*

Shall I give you a twirl . . .? Thank you. You wouldn't know it but I used to be quite a mover. I still am when I'm in the wrong place at the wrong time and his wife walks in . . . No, but seriously, who has the right to throw stones? We're all the same under the skin. That even goes for you sir, yes, you in the third row with the mange . . . Goodness, but you take your time to warm up. If this is what it's like on the top of the bill, I wouldn't want to try it at the bottom . . . No, stop it! I said *at* the bottom.

At, at! Riff-raff! Never mind. Now here's one for the ladies. What are the three words you dread most when you're making love? 'Darling, I'm home . . .!' You have to laugh. No, but seriously, some of my best friends are ladies. My mother was one for a start. Well, at least she tried, which is more than I can say for you lot here tonight. Talk about common! My mother was a local landmark. Though that might have been the red light she used to stand under. I wouldn't exactly call her cheap, but she dived for pennies in the wishing-well. She was saving up for an Austin Seven. She'd put sixpence in a jar every time she went to the little girls' room. With her bladder, she should have had enough for a Rolls Royce . . . There are no refunds so you might as well make the most of it . . . She's in a home now, my mother. It's best for everyone. She didn't know whether she was coming or going. And, frankly, it was hell on the carpet. I wouldn't have cared but I'd just had the cat spayed. Don't get me wrong. I'm all for Mother Nature in her place. But, if one of us was going to be chased by a lot of tomcats, it was me . . . Tell me, madam, does your husband know you've had a face-lift or does he think your ears blush naturally . . .? It's all very well for you lot. I wish I could sit there with you and laugh at myself. I wish I could laugh at myself full stop . . . But you don't want to listen to my problems. Laugh and the world laughs with you: cry and you ruin your make-up . . . As I was saying before I was so rudely interrupted – keep up! – my health: I'm in worse shape than Madonna's mattress. Believe it or not, I'm wearing a truss. Yes, all right. I know there are those who claim that it's padding to protect me from the gay men and lesbians who object to my material, but that's nonsense. In any case, some of them are my biggest fans. They can poke fun at themselves as well as the next man – or woman. Mustn't forget the woman. Not in these days of equal opportunities. And I'm an equal opportunities comedian. I'll do anything: christenings, bar-mitzvahs, fatwas

. . . Of course they can take a joke. What's life if you don't have a sense of humour? But you have to be so careful these days, not to tread on anyone's toes. Soon the only acts left will be mimes. You daren't breathe a word about the blacks or the Irish . . . Is it better to be gay or black? Black: you don't have to tell your mother. Have you heard the one about the Irish lesbian? She liked to sleep with men . . . A good joke's universal. Laughter's what binds us together. I get letters from all sorts – riff-raff to royalty – thanking me for bringing a spot of joy into their lives. Yes, a spot of joy: that's what we all need. And, if I can't have it, why should any of you . . .! No, it's nothing to worry about, madam, I have these funny turns. I said to my doctor, 'Doctor, I keep coming over a little queer.' 'You're in the wrong place,' he said to me, 'the laundry's next door.' It's all right, sir, you're allowed to laugh. Your social worker won't catch you. She came last night. That's why the seat's still wet . . . *Just spread a little happiness as you go by* . . . The other week, I was at the tailor's having my inside leg measured by ever such a nice young man. You know the sort: trousers so tight, you can't only tell his politics but his religion . . . Riff-raff! He made me this pair specially – out of Sylvester Stallone's shirtsleeves. Have you seen the muscles on that man? I tell you, he can point his bazooka my way any day of the week. Why aren't there more like him around, eh, girls? Still, there's no accounting for tastes, as the lesbian said to the fishmonger. Oh, it's a funny old world. You have to laugh . . . though it seems you don't. Never mind, I've played to worse. Remember me? Harris Littlewood: 'It's the way I wear them.' Of course, the politically correct brigade – the tofu-eating killjoys (do you know what tofu is, madam? It's Japanese for bullshit), the sort who think it's smart to have crockery that doesn't match – would like to ban me from the stage. I get letters from them too, denouncing me as a traitor to the cause. What cause? I'm not political. I've made it my business to appeal to the widest possible audience. Not that I seem to be having much success here tonight. I feel about as welcome as a barmaid at a mosque. What's the matter with you all? It's not Remembrance Sunday . . . Have you heard the one about the two gay Scotsmen? Ben Dover and Phil MacAvity . . . A little louder, sir, please. Yes, you sir, the gentleman who laughed. I could use the support . . . There's no malice in my act. Just good clean fun. What my detractors refuse to understand is that I don't have any hidden agenda. With me, what you see is what you get. Unlike some (whose names I shan't mention) who turn up to every glitzy event armed with the statutory bimbo, I've never pretended to be anything I'm not. Of course there'd be little point, what with my past raked up every other week in the *News of the World*. If I took a cut every time some bitter queen sold a story, I'd be a rich man. But you don't hear me complain. You don't see me throwing writs about like confetti. My view is that people in the public eye are fair game. And I know you respect me for it. Why should you care what I do in bed, as long as we can all have a good laugh about it afterwards . . .? What does a gay man put behind his ears to attract his lover? His toes. What's thick, stiff and twelve inches? Nothing . . . As long as we can all have a good laugh. But it seems when they built the ring-road around this town, they bypassed its sense of humour. What does it take to get a reaction out of you? Do I have to pull down my trousers? I would only I haven't shaved my legs. My friend Bertha borrowed my razor. You remember her: Big Bertha? Yes, thank you madam. At last! I was beginning to think I'd died and gone to Aberdeen . . . Harris Littlewood: 'It's the way I wear them.' . . . We're on an economy drive so we're sharing blades. We're sharing men too, but she's had the edge ever since she started work at the abattoir. We were down at the Frog and Firkin last week – Firkin, *Firkin*! Riff-raff! – sizing up the local talent. After we'd been sat there a couple of hours, I offered to buy her a drink. 'Oh, do they sell drinks here?' she said. 'I'd never have guessed.' (She's that tight, she goes to Mass for the nibbles.) She asked for a large port and lemon. I bit my tongue while I went to the bar and then I said to her ever so politely: 'Sorry, love, they've run out of large ones, but they've put it in a saucer to make you feel at home.' Still, her heart's in the right place – which is more than can be said for the rest of her. She's never been what you'd call a shrinking violet. She did so much heavy petting as a girl that her parents showed her at Cruft's. Round our way they used to say that the one thing guaranteed to stay open when the pubs were closed was Bertha Damson's legs. Not any more. Trade is down to a trickle. Where have the real men gone? They can't all be changing nappies in Islington. I was pulled over by a patrol car the other day. The policeman was so butch. 'Wipe that smile off your face!' he ordered. 'What?' I replied. 'And ruin my make-up . . .?' Oh you have to laugh. You won't hear anything like this on the telly. There it's all 'May we have the next contestant please?' and 'I hear your granny lived in Little Midden.' But, tonight, I'm here in the flesh. And, though I say so myself, it's not bad for a man of – no, I never make the same mistake twice: I just sleep with them. Tonight, we can reach the parts that other comedians never reach – right underneath the rim. No, but seriously, the highest virtue to me has always been honesty. I've never rammed my sexuality down anyone's throat (if you'll pardon the expression), but I've never lied about it either. I lived with a man for fifteen years, and I'm not ashamed to admit it. On the contrary, I sometimes think it's the one thing I can be proud of in my entire life . . . But you've not come to hear my reminiscences. You want to be taken out of yourselves as only I can: 'It's the way I wear them . . .' There are these two gay men sitting on the beach. One says to the other, 'Shall I put the umbrella up?' 'If you like,' his friend replies, 'only don't open

it . . .' You have to laugh. Oh yes, you do. If not, you'll be shed-
ding more tears than Judy Garland. When the love of your life
dies and you find yourself turfed on to the street without even a
scrapbook. Oh, yes, you could cry then all right. But what good
would it do? Laugh and the world laughs with you: cry and you
. . . but we've been through that already. Well, I'm here to make
you laugh and I'll do it if it kills me. A young man goes into a
bar and orders six double vodkas. 'Six?' the barman asks. 'Are
you celebrating something?' 'My first blow job,' the man replies.
'In that case,' the barman says, 'let me give you a seventh on the
house.' 'No offence,' the man says, 'but if six don't get rid of the
taste, then nothing will . . .' You, sir, yes you with the stony face,
were you born like that or was the midwife's name Medusa? As
for the rest of you, the building's concrete: you're allowed to clap
. . . What's worse than your doctor telling you you've got the
clap? Your dentist   Think about it . . . But I don't have to.
See, it's second nature to me. I'm a laugh-a-minute. 'It's the way
I wear them.' I sit at home, safe behind the electric fence and
the security cameras, fairly splitting my sides. Then, always
assuming I can keep a straight face, I walk from empty room to
empty room, plumping up untouched cushions and switching
on radios simply to hear the sound of another voice. After which
I deal with my correspondence. I've already mentioned the fan
mail. I also receive hate mail. We all do – even Ken Dodd.
Though I sometimes think I get more than my fair share. I'd
like my critics to spend a day sifting through the threats of death
and damnation and then try to tell me I don't do my bit for the
cause . . . And, no, as it happens, I don't think my act gives gay
men a bad name. They've done that already for themselves: *gay*,
I ask you! Nor do I think it's insulting to lesbians. Lord knows
they can look after themselves. Have you ever seen one . . .?
What's the difference between a lesbian and a whale? About ten
pounds and a flannel shirt . . . No, no one could take offence.

I'm Harris Littlewood. At least, I think I am. I'm not always sure any more. But that's my problem, not yours. So I tell a few jokes – sing a few songs. *Just spread a little happiness as you go by.* The trouble with young men today, with their gay pride and their tasteful tattoos, is that they take themselves far too seriously . . . Have you heard the one about the gay tattooist? He had designs on several married men . . . Don't laugh too loud, you might wake up your neighbours . . . This new generation: they don't know they're born! When I was their age, we really had something to protest about. We could be flung into jail for doing in our own homes what these days you can see any Graham or Julian doing on every street corner. And, believe me, I know some who were. Such lovely boys . . . I'm sorry. I don't mean to get maudlin . . . Of course we should all have the right to be ourselves – but discreetly: there's no need to flaunt it. And, if we must talk about it, let's make light of it: show the rest of the world that we're grateful for their support by giving them a laugh . . . Did you know that seventy per cent of gay men were born that way? The rest of them were sucked into it . . . All these activists – so right-on they turn me right off – they're not just bullies, they're hypocrites. They're the first to cry foul if anyone starts to censor them. Blasphemous poems and pornographic plays: that's freedom of expression; but a well-loved entertainer, who's done as much as anyone to show that gay people pose no threat, he's treated as a pariah. The way they talk, you'd think that I'd personally polished the queerbashers' boots . . . If only Lewis were alive, everything would be different. When we met, I was just sixteen; he was thirty-four. I was apprenticed to a tailor in Soho. I expected to wind up in a gentlemen's outfitters in Jermyn Street or Saville Row, not working my tits off for the likes of you . . . Sorry, madam, you know me, mouth like the Dartford tunnel. And I've had about the same amount of traffic through it . . . No, I was such a straightforward lad. Totally on the level. It hurts to think back to it. The other day I was leafing through some old photos and I turned up one of an eighteen-year-old on the beach. So fresh-faced and innocent. And, all right, I'll admit it was me. But what's harder to admit is that I fancied him. Before I knew it, I felt something stir that I hadn't in years. But it doesn't matter, does it? Because it was me in name only. Inside we were quite different. It was as though I'd taken a suit to the cleaners and they'd given me back one with the same pattern but a different lining. I'd worn it for years without noticing the mistake . . . It was suits that brought Lewis and me together. He wanted a new one and I had to take the measurements. We knew we'd clicked the moment we went into the fitting-room. Not that we exchanged anything more than a smile. But we knew. He asked me to the cinema to see Bette Davis in *All About Eve*. She's been my favourite actress ever since. *Fasten your seatbelts, it's going to be a bumpy night.* I did her later. Oh I did them all: Judy; Joan; Marlene. It started off just for a joke at parties. I'd drag up . . . What's the most common offence committed by drag queens? Male fraud . . . That's enough! Have you heard about Ben Hur's sex change? He's now called Ben Him. Stop it please! It isn't funny . . . No, it truly isn't. But then it isn't an act, it's my life. I've been entertaining people ever since primary school. It was safer that way. The other kids could see I was different – and kids are so scared of anything different, even more than their mums and dads. If I could make them laugh, they were less likely to knock me about. And I was getting enough of that at home. With my dad, a clip around the earhole counted as a friendly greeting. And my two older brothers – my tough-nut, Jack-the-Lad brothers – passed me between them in bed. They stuffed me like a hole in the mattress. It wasn't until I met Lewis that I could call my body my own . . . Oh dear! Eyes front, Littlewood. You should see the faces back here. This isn't what they'd expected. They're wondering whether to cancel my fee or charge you extra. Is there an agent in the house. . .? Where was I? Oh yes, Lewis. He was so dignified, so cultured: a real gentleman. I thought he knew everything: which of course he didn't. But he knew about everything: which was the next best thing. He showed me how two men could be together without pain. I'm sorry. I don't know why I'm bringing this up now. I don't want to think about it any more than you do. You've come for a night out with Harris Littlewood – 'It's the way I wear them' – some old songs, some older jokes. Why do dogs lick their balls? Because they can . . . Think about it! Two gay men were watching their dog lick its balls. 'I wish I could do that,' Stanley said to Roger. 'I'm sure you could,' Roger replied, 'but you'd better stroke him first' . . . Loosen up! My job is to lift spirits not raise the dead . . . I've had my troubles too, you know. When I moved in with Lewis, not a single member of my family would speak to me – not even my mum. Oh, she wrote, saying that she wanted to but she was scared of my brothers. Imagine: a grown woman frightened of her sons. They're both long since married, with children of their own and wives who compare houses at Christmas: respectable grandfathers who tune in to men like me on the telly but wouldn't want any of us living in their street. They may even be out front now. Are you there, Brian? Are you there, Stuart? Don't be shy. Stand up and take a bow. No, they'd rather watch in the safety of their living-rooms. I wonder if they admit to the connection when they're drinking with their pals in the pubs and the sports clubs. Do they shrug off the taunts – the limp wrist and lisped catch-phrase – and bask in reflected glory, or do they sit tight-lipped whenever Harris Littlewood is mentioned? Not that anyone need know. My name is as made-up as the rest of me. I wasn't born in Westcliff-on-Sea: I created myself in Kensington when I moved in with Lewis. We had fifteen years of bliss – that's not memory talking but truth. Then, one evening when he was walking the dog, he suffered a heart attack. They took him straight to the hospital and I never set eyes on him again. For the next six days his mother and brother and sister took turns by his bedside but they wouldn't let me so much as poke my head around the door. I was the most important person in his life but I wasn't 'family'. Even now I worry that he looked for me and supposed that I didn't care. I begged his mother to allow me to share the vigil, but she refused, claiming that she couldn't make any exceptions among Lewis's friends. I was too ashamed to remind her that we'd slept in the same bed for fifteen years. She'd always been pleasant to me, not warm – that would have been too much to ask – but courteous, as if she was grateful that Lewis had found someone to love. Suddenly, all that changed. I felt a glimmer of hope when I heard his brother describing me to the porter as Lewis's 'man'. I took it to mean his lover: I was certain they couldn't keep me away after that. Then I found out it meant his servant: I might have been waiting for a tip. When Lewis died, they treated me far worse than a servant. A valet who'd worked for him for fifteen years would have been permitted a few minutes beside his body to pay his last respects, but I was barred even from that. I just wanted to see him once more. Just once. I suppose that sounds absurdly sentimental: I ought to have known what he looked like after fifteen years. But it mattered to me. It mattered more than anything ever has done before or since. At the funeral I was put in a pew at the very back of the church, behind his aged nanny and her sister, while friends who'd come to cocktails not a month before avoided my eye . . . But you didn't shell out your hard-earned cash to hear this slush! Come on Littlewood, you can do better than that . . . How do you know when you're in a gay church? Only half the congregation kneels to pray. What did the bishop do to the gay priest? He defrocked him. Do you approve of gay priests getting married? Yes, but only if they're in love . . . It was no laughing matter. I loved him and he was dead. But it wasn't just love that had been taken away from me. The house that I'd supposed was his belonged to his mother. She'd let him live there as a way of keeping him under her thumb. Furniture, ornaments, books: everything went to his family. They even preferred to give his clothes to Oxfam rather than to me. His brother came to arrange my eviction – or, as he put it, my 'fresh start'. He told me snootily that he'd like me to have a memento of Lewis and offered me his cigarette case. I thanked him even though I didn't smoke. But the cruellest thing of all was that they took Trudy. They wouldn't allow me even to keep the dog: our dog, my dog – the King Charles spaniel Lewis had bought me on our twelfth anniversary. Lewis's mother insisted she'd made a vow to him on his deathbed, which – no surprise – I was unable to chal-lenge. I begged her to think again, but the more I pleaded the more she dug in her heels. She claimed my reaction proved that I was quite unfit to look after any animal: I was displaying the hysteria typical of men of my kind . . . Very wise, sir, madam; I'd have walked out on me long ago. Don't worry about disturbing the rest of them. They're obviously gluttons for punishment . . . You may wonder why I didn't put up more of a struggle but, when Lewis died, the spark went out of me. What's more, the memory of Trudy curled up between us on the bed is why I've never been able to have a dog – or a lover – since . . . But I'm not here to set the world to rights, simply to tell a few jokes. Have you heard the one about the man whose lover did it in the doggy position so often, he had to tie him down to stop him chasing cars? Why do dogs lick their – oh, we've done that already. Two gay men were watching their dog lick – and that too! Are there no jokes left? There is one: the biggest and sickest of them all: me! I wish I could laugh at myself but I can't, so I let you do it instead . . . Some of Lewis's friends remained loyal to me. One

with theatrical contacts persuaded me to flesh out my imper-
sonations until, gradually, what had begun as a party-piece
turned into a career and I became the Harris Littlewood you see
before you tonight: veteran of two Royal Variety Performances;
three times runner-up as TV Times Personality of the Year. So
why should I care what my critics say? Just because they lack
any sense of humour, do the rest of us have to be miserable?
Take it from me, there's no broken heart – no bruised spirit –
that can't be healed by Dr Laughter . . . What did the gay captain
give his first mate for Christmas? A tug. Where did the gay
bank-robber fall down? He tied up the safe and blew the guard.
How can you tell if a house is owned by a gay man? The
welcome mat reads 'Please wipe your knees' . . . That just about
rounds off the proceedings, ladies and gentlemen. I'd like to
thank you for being such a wonderful audience. I'd like to, but I
can't. Yes, the old ones are the best – as the judge said to the
rent boy. But, seriously, ladies and gentlemen, I think we can
truly say that, tonight, we've shared something very special. So
let's thank the Lord for his precious gift of laughter

> *Even when the darkest clouds are in the sky,*
> *You mustn't sigh and you mustn't cry,*
> *Just spread a little happiness as you go by,*
> *Please try.*
> *What's the use of worrying and feeling blue?*
> *When days are long, keep on smiling through,*
> *And spread a little happiness till dreams come true.*

There's no more pressing task, ladies and gentlemen, in this
funny old word of ours than to spread a little happiness. So,
thank you for giving me the opportunity to spread the Harris
Littlewood brand of happiness here tonight: 'It's the way I wear
them.' I'd like to leave you with a final thought. Have you heard
the one about the gay deaf mute? No. And neither has he.

The Night Out

'HAVE A GOOD WEEKEND,' Roy called as he disappeared through the vast swing doors that led from the library. 'Don't do anything I wouldn't do.'

'I won't,' Jeremy called back, more from politeness than enthusiasm. He liked Roy, whose kindness was genuine, but he sometimes felt, when they were standing together at the Admissions Desk, that he was being haunted by the ghost of things to come.

Roy was what Jeremy might turn into if he let the workaday world engulf him. He was the Senior Library Assistant: a position to which Jeremy himself had once aspired, until he realised the pettiness of such aspirations. He also had a lover, Clark, of whose existence Jeremy had been madly jealous until the previous month, when Roy had invited him to Stanmore for dinner. 'Nothing fancy. Just the three of us. To sample Clark's famous chilli.' Clark, who was a clerk in the Civil Service (a verbal association he treated like an act of fate), was ten years younger than Roy, yet he managed to look like him, turning even his premature baldness into a badge of sympathy. They had a cat called Bangkok ('though she's not Siamese'), a joint mortgage, and spent Christmas quietly at home with their two mothers. And, although that made a part of Jeremy feel cosy, the rest of him seethed with scorn.

He looked around and, as there was no one in the vicinity, he grabbed a small pile of books and headed for Performing Arts. At last he was where he belonged, safe in that bay of wonders full of cinema, theatre, opera and ballet – in particular the last. He lovingly picked up his most treasured volume: a folio study of the male classical dancer, which he had deliberately shelved under Stage Management, in the hope that it would be hidden from idle hands. It fell open at his favourite double spread, in the way that the Oxford Dictionary at school had always done at the page for *cunnilingus*, and for much the same reason.

There *he* stood, soaked in sweat, drinking up the applause. His Tartar cheekbones displayed a woodcut simplicity. His taut chest evinced a marmoreal strength. And his thighs . . . oh those thighs, each one of which was thicker and more powerful than Jeremy's waist. Jeremy had read of men who could crack nuts in their armpits; well, he could have crushed every bone in Jeremy's body between those thighs. And he gazed, awe-struck that a man could manifest such animal vigour and yet such delicate artistry, that he could revel in his own energy and yet achieve such perfect balance, that he could strut and leap and make violent love to his audience and yet remain inscrutable. It was from such paradoxes that Jeremy's passions were born.

'Penny for them!' Jeremy was startled by the practised bonhomie of the Chief Librarian.

'I was just reshelving. Someone left something sticky – I think it may have been chewing gum – in the pages of this book.'

Mr Mitchell smiled, as though no stranger to the readers' foibles.

'Good for you. We can't afford any replacements. Not these days.' His face assumed the expression of beleaguered decency which always accompanied any mention of budget cuts. 'I don't know. The Library Service used to be such a worthwhile profession. It's all very well for me. Only three years to go. It's young men like yourself I feel sorry for.'

Jeremy was torn between the desire to disabuse him and the risk of causing offence. There was no way that he was going to spend his life in a library, only to end up like Mr Mitchell, as spineless as a vandalised book. He would make a career in the Arts. His present position was just a stop-gap until he determined the exact branch for which he was suited. Even in his best moments, he was uncertain how precisely to marshal his talents while, in his worst, he was uncertain that he had any at all. But he quickly dismissed a pessimism which would threaten his entire existence.

'Why don't you collect your things and put your coat on? Harry'll be shutting up shop in five minutes. I'm just about to ring the bell.'

'Oh, thank you,' Jeremy said, edging away. The five-minute respite made him feel unduly grateful.

'Doing anything special this weekend?' Mr Mitchell asked.

'Well, I'm seeing some dance tonight. I managed to get tickets.' The fanciful plural stuck in his throat.

'Sounds fun,' Mr Mitchell enthused. 'Where's it on? Covent Garden? Sadler's Wells?'

'The Rhombus in Clapham, actually. It's Brian Low and company.'

'Oh yes. I saw the article in the *Guardian*. They're the new punk group, aren't they?'

'Post-punk,' Jeremy replied smugly.

'I'm afraid it's pretty much of a muchness to me. I'm sure it's all very clever and apropos, but give me a good *Nutcracker* any day.' Mr Mitchell smiled, misconstruing Jeremy's shudder. 'Anyway, enjoy yourself. I'll look forward to a full report on Monday.'

Now it was Jeremy's turn to smile, as he anticipated how much he would have to censor. He hurried to the staff cloakroom, which smelt even mustier than the books. He shrugged on the heavy tweed coat which his mother had bought him 'almost new' from her local Oxfam shop. He trusted that people would realise that he wore it in a spirit of irony. He was so absorbed in assessing his appearance that he missed his bus and was forced to wait half an hour until a whole convoy arrived.

He reached his digs and, after a meagre lunch, went downstairs to run himself a bath. He had camouflaged his contempt during sufficient conversations about football to have calculated correctly that none of his fellow lodgers would be hammering on the door on a Saturday afternoon. The room filled with steam. He stepped into the tub. In the heat, his skin puckered like a plucked chicken (he dismissed the resurgent image of his mother). He savoured the oil which smelt satisfyingly like incense as he scoured every lingering impurity. He wanted to sing – something brash and upbeat from a Hollywood musical, but the song that stuck in his mind was *I'm going to wash that man right out of my hair*, which was irritatingly inappropriate on a day when he was determined to let somebody right in.

He quit the room after rigorously scrubbing the bath. His own discreet notes about tide-marks having been studiously ignored, he was anxious to leave no telltale traces on the rim. He stood in his bedroom, regally cloaked in his towel, and primed himself for action. He removed various packages from their hiding places and laid them out on the bed. Every nerve in his body tingled at the prospect of transformation. This was the moment he had waited for ever since his chance visit to the Rhombus last September, when Brian Low had been no more than a name in a newspaper review. The experience, both on the stage and in the audience, had been overwhelming. Although Jeremy was a devotee of classical ballet, he knew little about modern dance and still less about its fans. At the Rhombus, he could not even be sure where the performance ended and the audience began. He sat alongside women coated only in red, white and blue paint, and men whose skirts would be even more offensive to true-blue patriots. A group of women had hair shaped like ice-cream cones, but it was the men for whom he hungered. It was a far cry from the amphitheatre at Covent Garden. He himself was wearing a sports jacket and cords: it was no wonder that no one looked twice at him. He might as well have been an usher. He was desperate to tear off the mask of respectability and reveal the rebel underneath.

He entertained some reservations about the dancing. To his own chagrin, he still preferred a line of melancholy swans or wistful Wilis to a pair of gyrating punks. But the performers were far more than their steps. He felt liberated by their antics: the split pants and high-heeled shoes; the painted faces and naked flesh. Never before had shamelessness struck him as such a virtue. He swore then and there to banish all his inhibitions. But his resolve required the stimulus of the company's return visit and so, as soon as flyers for the new show arrived at the library, he had embarked on a plan of campaign. Inspired by music papers and fashion magazines, he meticulously created his image. He experimented with make-up and clothing. He trawled the King's Road and Camden Lock for accessories. At last it was time to put his new self to the test.

He decided to start at the top. Having never previously dyed his hair, and afraid of an adverse reaction, he had opted for food dye on grounds of safety. Tufts of pink emerged with gratifying speed from the mud-brown of his curls. He waited the requisite two minutes before tentatively blowing them dry. The colour had stuck, the mottled look merely adding to the carnival spirit. If only Mr Mitchell could see me now, he thought. *Nutcracker* indeed! But he was too busy to gloat. He plucked what remained of his eyebrows. The pain gave him a perverse satisfaction. It seemed right that he should suffer for his art. And, if the effect were not perfectly symmetrical, he would concentrate on presenting his profile. He set about painting his nails (cerise, which he had chosen as much for the name as the colour) and tried not to hate his squat, stubby fingers which had already punctured one dream when, years earlier, they had prompted his banishment from piano to percussion. Still, no one would notice such details if they were sufficiently dazzled by the whole.

He wafted the varnish dry and picked up his clothes. He called them clothes because he was afraid to tempt fate with the word *costume*. He was amazed at the depth of feeling that the material could inspire. Jeremy had no ambitions as a transvestite. He had only ever worn women's clothing on stage at school, but he would never forget the excitement of stepping into Olivia's farthingale. Such unconstrained joy was an emotion that he longed to recapture. It was time to kill off the mild-mannered librarian, whose life was as second-hand as his coat, and explore fresh possibilities, although he remained uncertain as to precisely what these were, let alone the best way to set about finding them: a confusion that was reflected in the mishmash of his outfit – which was also a statement of sorts.

He wriggled into a *Safe Sex* T-shirt which, even if the admonition were depressingly academic, he still regarded as valid. Responsive but responsible was a crucial part of the image that he wished to convey. He wondered whether to add a fashionable rip, but was afraid it might send a mixed message. Besides, the first and last letters disappeared when he put on his Afghan patchwork leather waistcoat (which was so authentic that it smelt like a ham). He then directed his attention below the waist and unwrapped a black male-miniskirt, lifting it from its layers of tissue paper as reverently as a priest revealing a relic. He had devoted considerable time during several dress rehearsals to learning how to manage the buttons so that they now felt as natural as a fly. He paused for confirmation from the wardrobe mirror and shuddered with delight, anticipation and fear.

He began to apply the make-up. Such an unremarkable face required contrast, so he covered it in powder before highlighting his cheekbones and painting his lips. He smeared kohl around his eyes and watched as the mirror became the frame for an Egon Schiele portrait. He seized on the phrase 'his own mother wouldn't know him' and saluted his metamorphosis. Then, although he knew that it was foolish, he could not resist going further, stepping up to the glass and planting a kiss on the inviting lips. He quickly looked round, but there was no one to see him aside from his own reflection, which flashed an encouraging smile. They might have continued to smile at each other all evening, but the kiss had been cold and hard and lonely: Jeremy longed for the tender endorsement of another man's flesh.

Jeremy was a virgin. He was in no doubt as to where his sexual preferences lay but, like so much else in his life, they remained dormant. He had always been too frightened to commit himself to somebody else, not just of losing control but of losing face. He had once heard a friend remark, 'Oh, Jeremy, he's not interested in men, women or dogs,' and, for reasons he had not cared to analyse, it had pleased him. From then on, he had striven to cultivate an austere, monkish persona – which was doubly destructive outside the fellowship of a monastery. The pain of his isolation was almost unbearable. He was desperate to find a like-minded man, although that epithet too was a prevarication, for what he really wanted was a like-bodied one: someone who would gather all his complexes and complexities and make of them love. That was unlikely to happen in the library (he thought scornfully of Thelma making sheep's eyes at Roy over the large-print books), so he had to branch out. He would make a strength of his ambiguity: no longer asexual but androgynous.

He patted the pleats of his skirt. The gas meter had run out and there was a nip in the air. He knew that he ought to wear a coat but refused to compromise the effect with Oxfam. Even blue legs would be preferable to shapeless shoulders. Besides, he had booked a taxi: his new-found sense of adventure stopped short of braving the streets. So, after tucking his handkerchief into his pants (a tip he remembered from nursery school), he went down to wait in the hall.

The cab was late. As he peered through the frosted glass, his landlady's granddaughter dashed out of the sitting room. She saw him and burst out laughing, before running back with a shout of, 'Nana, nana, come and look!' Mrs Sage hurried into the hall. Her eyes opened wide in amazement.

'Why, Mr Rowan, whatever do you look like?'

'I've been invited to a fancy dress party, Mrs Sage.'

'Thank the Lord for that. You gave me quite a turn. You look like that Boy George.'

'Do I?' Jeremy asked with a shudder. He was yesterday's news: last year's fashion. But that should come as no surprise. Mrs Sage could hardly be expected to keep abreast of the times. He must be one of the few counter-culture figures of whom she had heard: a reassurance that fell flat when he realised that he was one of the few of whom he had heard himself.

'You just be careful where you go, dressed like that.'

'Don't worry, Mrs Sage,' Jeremy assured her. And, although he sometimes felt warmed by his landlady's prattle, it now threatened his resolve. At that moment, the doorbell rang and he disengaged himself.

'That'll be me,' he said.

'Enjoy it. Make sure you bring home a prize.'

'I will,' Jeremy promised as he walked out. He would bring home the biggest prize of his life.

He stepped into the cab, uncertain whether to feel relieved or disappointed by the driver's lack of interest.

'It's Clapham you want, son?'

'Yes, please. The Rhombus Arts Centre.'

Further conversation was forestalled when the driver shut
the partition between them as emphatically as if he were a sani-
tation officer. Jeremy reviewed events so far. He cursed himself
for his cravenness before Mrs Sage. Instead of all the guff about
fancy dress, he should have told her the truth – that he was off
to the ballet that would change his life as dramatically as the
ball had Cinderella's. He began to speculate on the identity of
his prince. It might be one of the audience. It might be one of
the dancers. It might even – he took a deep breath – be Brian
Low himself.

His reverie was punctured by car horns. He cursed the traffic
which cut into the time he had set aside for mingling before the
show. When the driver at last pulled up, Jeremy gave him an
ostentatious tip. That night he wanted everyone in London to
love him, and he refused to be cast down by the lack of response.
He walked into the foyer with its café and bar, its whitewashed
walls hung with embroidered collages, and was struck by an
immediate sense of belonging. He tried to insinuate himself into
the general mood but everyone appeared to be engrossed in
private conversation. He felt tongue-tied, in spite of not having
been asked to speak, and wished that he had invited a friend to
accompany him, although, leaving aside the lack of any obvious
candidate, that would have defeated his entire purpose. The
least hint of a couple would have scared off any suitable man.

He scanned the room with a deepening sense of unease. He
felt as out of place as he had done the previous year, although for
the opposite reason. Then he had resembled a bible salesman
who had stumbled on a saturnalia; now he resembled a
pantomime dame who had wandered into a serious play. The
audience was young, smart and painfully attractive. But where
were the peacocks? Where were the punks? The men were
dressed in black or grey with jeans turned up to reveal
workmen's boots. A few were wearing T-shirts, but the only

identifiable slogans were in Russian – he drew his waistcoat as far as possible across any hint of sex. There was no anarchy: no androgyny. They sat, with hair as square-cut as their jaws, secure in their own masculinity. He longed to know where he had gone wrong. He had planned everything so meticulously. Had he visited the wrong shops? Had the magazines he studied been out of date? He wanted to crawl to the door, hail a taxi and hurry back to his digs, where he could tear out his hair or at least wash out the dye. But he was obliged to stay. There was so much at stake.

He ambled casually to the bar. No one caught his glance, but he could tell that all eyes were upon him. At every table he passed, the occupants began to chatter with forced animation. He searched vainly for an empty chair. Sitting down, he would at least be less conspicuous. There was a time when he had prized his individuality. Now he longed for nothing more than to be a face in the crowd.

The auditorium doors opened. He seized the opportunity and made straight for his seat. With dreadful predictability, he had been placed at the end of a row. It felt as if half the audience were required to squeeze past his skirt. Nevertheless, he refused to despair. It was essential to guard against self-pity which, on a recent questionnaire, he had named as his most characteristic vice. He had made a simple – and understandable – error of judgement. Fashion was not for the dilettante. Like any other art, it required work. Besides, he should have been as ashamed to assume someone else's look as to plagiarise a poem. Honour required that he create one for himself – one that was a genuine reflection of who he was – even though, right now, the *who* felt more like *whoever*. Meanwhile, he vainly pushed his hair behind his ears and licked his lips to tone down the red.

The performance began. It, too, stood in stark contrast to the previous year. Then, the keynote had been dissonance. Much of the movement had been wilfully ugly. Whenever a moment of tenderness loomed, it had been literally stamped out. Now the stage was suffused with lyricism. The dancers had not entirely abandoned their pasts. The extravagant costumes and expressionist make-up remained, albeit muted, but the choreography was instilled with a new-found warmth. It was when Brian Low himself appeared that the change was most marked. He partnered one of the women in a duet of such poignancy that Jeremy completely forgot his humiliation. Personal concerns were transcended by the display of elegance and passion. At the end, he joined in the thunderous applause, even jumping up for the standing ovation, giving no thought to his legs.

Until then, Jeremy had considered the dancers almost incidental to the event. They provided a pretext for the audience to assemble and sparkle. He was unable to hold them in the same regard as their classical counterparts. But the new vein of emotion that they had tapped had profoundly moved him. It was clear that Brian – and Brian alone – possessed the answer to his problems. He would point the way through the labyrinth of fashion as though it were as straight as the Mall. He would identify the inner Jeremy, teaching him how to be both true to himself and irresistible to others. He would show him the nakedness that shone through clothes.

Jeremy waited for the audience to file out and then followed. He spotted an usherette who returned his glance warily, although, with his fresh sense of confidence, he no longer cared what anyone thought.

'Would you tell me where to go for a word with Brian?' he asked, with the air of one to whom surnames were superfluous. 'I'm writing a piece about the latest directions in dance.'

'Really? What for?'

'A new magazine: *Conundrum*. We're currently pasting up the first issue.' He hoped that he had hit on the right term. 'I cleared it with the PA . . . PR. She . . . they said to make myself known after the show. So here I am.' He wondered whether she might show him straight into Brian's dressing-room. He had slipped into the role so easily that he felt sure he could carry it off. But she told him to wait in the foyer. The company always gathered for a drink after the performance. The thought of such a routine depressed him, but he thanked her and made his way to the lavatory, for which he felt an urgent need.

He nudged open the door. He pictured his own misgivings if a man in a mini-skirt were to join him at a urinal. Of the three stalls, only the central one was free. Worried that waiting might create the wrong impression, he decided to brazen it out. As he lifted the skirt, he heard a husky chuckle to his right. He felt too nervous to pee.

'You're in the wrong place, man,' his neighbour informed him. 'The ladies is next door.'

Jeremy smiled thinly before realising that it too might be misinterpreted. He remembered that there was a reggae band playing in another part of the Centre and wondered whether it would be best to go straight home.

'What you look like that for? You a batty boy?'

'Who, me? Ignore the costume. I've come from the dance and I'm going on to a fancy dress party. So I thought I'd kill two birds with one stone.' He laughed at the joke, even though it undermined his whole identity.

'You'll kill all the birds I know stone-dead,' his tormentor replied, while his companion chortled. Jeremy looked down at the floor. Fear was supposed to cause incontinence but it was having the opposite effect on him. He kept his eyes carefully lowered. He caught the sound of zipping flies. He prepared himself for the knee in the kidneys . . . the knife in the ribs. But the men just guffawed and moved on. The slamming door provoked a torrent that afforded him legitimacy, if little relief.

He hurried back into the foyer, but the two men were nowhere to be seen. Stray members of the audience lingered at the tables, while a trio of dancers queued for food. He searched for Brian and found him, a far slighter figure than he had appeared on stage, standing alone at the bar. Jeremy took heart from their shared isolation. Banishing diffidence, he headed straight for him but, at the last moment, his courage failed and he called to the barman for a drink.

'All in good time, mate,' the barman replied. 'Can't you see I'm serving someone?'

Jeremy's embarrassment intensified when he saw that the someone was Brian. Mr Reticent had turned into Mr Pushy, the very opposite of the image that he wished to convey.

'I'm sorry,' he said, 'I'm short-sighted.' And he bit his lip twice: first, for coming up with such a lame excuse and second, for drawing attention to a defect. In desperation, he tugged at Brian's sleeve, forcing him to swing around, a glint of consternation in his large, limpid eyes.

'I want to tell you . . .' he faltered, 'how much I enjoyed the performance.'

'Good on you,' Brian said with a smile. 'You were a brill audience.'

'It was fantastic . . . absolutely fantastic.' Jeremy searched vainly for a critical term with which to establish his credentials.

'Thanks,' Brian said, showing himself as succinct with words as with steps.

'I've been waiting to see you all year. I came last September and it changed my life.' He wondered whether Brian were smiling at him or at the barman from whom he was collecting change.

'That's great! So what do you do then?'

'I'm a model.' He gulped. Then, afraid that Brian was looking sceptical, he added quickly, 'And a poet.' He did not want him to think he was just a pretty face.

'That's cool,' Brian said, juggling three pints of lager. 'Now I'd better split. There are two very thirsty dancers back there who'll be after my blood.'

'Yes, of course,' Jeremy said, terrified that the moment was slipping away. 'I wonder – '

'Yes,' Brian turned back. His smile was beginning to fray.

'Do you think you . . . do you think I could have your autograph?'

'Sure.' Brian sounded weary as he put down the beer. He took a pen from his trouser pocket. Shaped like a penis, it seemed to capture the essence of the man.

'Well, do you have something for me to write it on?' Brian asked. At which point, Jeremy realised that he had left his programme in the lavatory.

'How about my hand?'

Brian looked uneasy but he was prepared to oblige. 'Whatever you say!' He tried to write but the ink dissolved in the sweat on Jeremy's palm. 'Sorry, but it doesn't seem to be working. Save it till next time. OK? Now I really must dash.' His companions were beckoning him across the foyer as if he were a waiter, not a star. Jeremy felt the slight personally. He grabbed hold of Brian's arm. 'Hey, what is this?' Brian tried to shake him off without spilling the drink, but Jeremy held fast and then, with a spontaneity that had previously eluded him, pulled Brian forward and kissed him full on the lips.

'For fuck's sake!' Brian shouted, pushing him off. Jeremy heard the crash of broken glass and felt the splash of beer around his ankles. 'You twat!' Brian spat out the insult as he wiped the saliva from his lips. 'What the fuck's your game?' Jeremy stared at him blankly. He became aware of a circle forming around them: dancers, spectators, the usherette. The barman came out from behind the bar. Unlike Brian, at close range he looked bigger. One of his fists was clenched, while in the other he carried a brush.

'What does the little toe-rag think he's up to?' he asked.

'No sweat,' Brian said, still spitting into the tissue, as though sickened by the slightest taste of him.

'Are you all right, Bri?' A woman put her arm around his neck. Jeremy recognised her as Brian's partner in the duet. From the look that passed between, it was clear why their dancing had exuded such power. He watched in torment as she rested her arm on the back of Brian's shirt . . . her hand in the heat of his back. He wanted to shout 'No, it can't be! What about all the costumes and make-up? Were they just a fashion too?' Instead, he babbled an apology – a mere form of words – when it was they who should be apologising to him.

'Are you sick or something?' the woman asked.

'Let's drop it, Kathy,' Brian said. 'No harm done.'

'How can you know? With everything going around, who knows what he's got? Jesus!' The wording was vague but the meaning was unmistakable. Jeremy was horrified. He wanted to assure her that Brian was the first man he had ever kissed. But he was afraid that they would despise him even more.

'Come on, Bri, let's sit down. I got you some food.' The woman took Brian's hand with a sense of perfect propriety. Jeremy rattled the bars of his solitary confinement. Brian turned to him as he walked away.

'Look, no harm done. But you should take care what you get up to in the future. You can't just go hitting on total strangers. Some blokes might cut up rough.' Jeremy longed to explain that Brian was not a stranger but a soul mate. He knew everything about him. Then he watched him put his arm around his girl-friend and realised that he knew nothing at all.

He stood in limbo as the company closed ranks. Then,

salvaging the remnants of his dignity, he left. His legs wobbled as though on stilts. He passed a pair of dancers who gave him a slow handclap, and he winced at the irony of their reversed positions. He emerged into the brittle air and walked through Clapham. In despair of finding a taxi, he headed for the Tube, hotly pursued by a horde of phantoms. By now he took his appearance so much for granted that he was startled by the odd hoot of derision. He made his way to the platform through a tunnel that smelt suitably sour, where he met an old woman, dressed in a coat the colour of his nails, who was leading a young boy by the hand. The boy gazed at him wide-eyed and directed his grandmother's attention to his skirt.

'Don't stare,' she ordered, 'and don't dawdle.' Then, as if over the tannoy, she announced. 'It's no wonder the streets aren't safe. In my day, he'd have been locked up.'

To his surprise, Jeremy found that her words roused him to a response. 'You needn't worry, madam,' he declared, in his best Enquiry Desk voice, 'I usually am. I was allowed out for an evening to go to a Fancy Dress Party. I went as Last Year's Fashion. I didn't win a prize.'

The Pillar of Strength

I WAS TWENTY-FOUR when I married and naive as a girl of twelve. George had wanted to elope but, as an only child, I was loath to cheat my parents out of a wedding. Besides, although my churchgoing was primarily social, I placed a superstitious trust in vows made at the altar. So we stood before God and the congregation of St Mary's, Bourne Street, pledging to love one another for better for worse . . . although I had no idea quite how bad worse could be.

On the night I found out, George was at a reception – something East European: no wives. I can't say that I was sorry. Since leaving London eighteen months earlier, I'd become increasingly reluctant to return. My disillusion with the metropolis had grown through the years of battling in bus queues, sidestepping drunks and paying unofficial tolls on the pavements, but what had finally tipped the balance was George's mugging. He was beaten up one evening on the towpath of the Regent's Canal. He wasn't seriously injured – thank God – but he was so badly shaken that, when the police produced a suspect, he failed to identify him. That was the first indication of the personality change that was to come. Although, given what occurred later, I can't help wondering whether he might not have provoked the attack. Which is what's so hard about the whole business. It not only alters the future but the past.

At the time, we had been married for thirty-nine years. Our one great sadness was that we had no children. We tried for far longer than was sensible, enduring a host of humiliating tests and treatments that played havoc with my hormones. For a while, my infertility cast a shadow over our lives but, in the end, it seemed to draw us closer. Not, perhaps, in every respect. For George, bed was forever tinged with failure. I even speculated that the flawless bodies in the magazines he was given at the clinic had spoilt him for mine. Yet sex for its own sake played such a small part in our relationship that its absence caused me barely a pang. Moreover, parenthood no longer appeared to be an unmixed blessing. I had been outraged at the mothers of my acquaintance who looked with envy at me, comparing my freedom with their constraints and hinting darkly at divided loyalties. But, as more and more of their marriages broke down, I was struck by the irony that, for George and me, our greatest sadness was also our saving grace.

The new house was far too large for our needs, but we fell in love with it and, as George said, we had to put our money into something. He took the train up to town every day (although his plan to use the time for reading collapsed when he made friends with the fellow-commuters in his carriage). Whenever he had a late dinner or a breakfast meeting, he stayed at his club. Besides, after a lifetime at the Department of Trade, he was within a whisker of retirement. I work from home – or, more accurately, from an old outhouse which we converted into a studio. I'm a picture restorer or 'scrubber and dubber', as less reverent souls would have it. I long since acknowledged that I would never be Picasso but, even after thirty years, I find something uniquely satisfying about bringing a painting back to life: revealing it in its true colours. My friends issued dire warnings about my safety in such an isolated spot, but I felt no qualms – and, besides, I had Wellington, our aged golden retriever. Whenever George was away, I dragged his basket up to the bedroom. I found his presence just as comforting as his master's. For a start, he was a good deal less deaf. On the night in question, it was his barking that alerted me to the phone.

I looked at my watch. It was two-thirty. I presumed that it must be a wrong number or a heavy breather . . . or both. Steeling myself, I picked it up. To my amazement, it was George. His voice sounded pinched. 'Elizabeth,' he said, 'I'm sorry to wake you, but this is serious. Would you look up Jerry Stirling's number, ring him and ask him to meet me at Bow Road Police Station as soon as he can?' The lateness of the hour combined with the shock of the call to fill me with a sense of unreality. I fired off a series of questions, which he brusquely dismissed.

'Just do it. Please.'

'But it's the middle of the night. He'll be asleep.'

'That can't be helped. Bow Road Police Station. It's a matter of some urgency. I'd have done anything rather than involve you, but I don't have his number and he's ex-directory.'

As I replaced the receiver, a range of conflicting possibilities raced through my mind. The strongest was drink. Quite apart from the official toasts, he was dining with East Europeans. He must have been picked up drunk. – or disorderly – perhaps even while he was driving. The limit had been set so low and the police were so zealous. By the time I found Jerry's number, I was full of rage at their over-reaction and determined never again to buy tickets for their Benevolent Fund raffle. Trembling, I dialled, while perversely hoping that the phone might be off the hook. At least it was Jerry who answered and not Ruth. He appeared neither surprised nor annoyed by my call and agreed to go down to the station straight away. His imperturbability restored my hope. Nevertheless, I made myself a second mug of cocoa before returning upstairs. I fretted that George's drinking might have deeper roots. The mugging was one possibility; the prospect of retirement another. His work gave him both satisfaction and status. As someone who had known the terror of the blank canvas, I understood his alarm at the thought of the emptiness ahead. I blamed myself for having done too little to reassure him. When I climbed into bed, even Wellington flashed me a look of reproach, although it melted as soon as I patted an invitation on to the covers. He seized his special licence with alacrity, leaping up for a cuddle. In some ways, I had come to prefer his cuddles to George's. Perhaps, after all, it was my fault . . .

I woke up so late that my guilt was redoubled. My mind preyed on the phone call, which was the first that I could remember receiving from George after midnight . . . at least since our engagement when he'd been so desperate to hear my voice that he'd reckoned without hearing my father's, which had been far less cordial. By ten o'clock I could no longer contain my unease. So, against my better judgement, I rang his office where his secretary informed me in her familiar trill that George was in a meeting with Sir Neville and would not be back all day. Which was just as well, she added, since she had been up half the night with cramps . . . a confidence I resented from a woman I had never met. Unwilling to feign nonchalance in a call to Jerry, I tried to work. But my mind was elsewhere and, after a mishap with a tube of carmine that threatened to restore the Magdalene to her former profession, I returned to the house. I mulled over various scenarios and, by noon, I had settled on a Whitehall corruption scandal that George had single-handedly brought to light. I cried off lunch with Peggy Lincoln, coupling an unconvincing excuse with the hint that she might discover more when she looked at the papers . . . words I would live to regret. I was sitting down to some cheese and an apple, when George arrived home.

My first concern was that I had nothing to give him to eat. He took the rabbit's food view of salad and the doctor had proscribed eggs. He insisted that he wasn't hungry. I was dissuaded from arguing by the grim expression on his face. And, although it was only half-past one and he had always been a dram-before-dinner man, I offered to pour him a drink.

'I was drunk. That's why I did it. I swear I shall never touch another drop again.'

Shock at his admission vied with satisfaction that my instincts had been correct. But I told him that I had already decided to forgive him.

'What? How do you know? Has Jerry spoken to you? He gave me his word.'

'Jerry? About what?' A trickle of sweat issued from nowhere. 'You didn't hurt anyone, did you?'

'What are you talking about? What do you mean?'

'Last night, when you were drunk.'

'Drunk? Who said so?'

'You did. Just now.'

'I've never been drunk in my life.'

I decided to pour that whisky after all.

'George, dear . . .' My voice seemed to come from a mirror. 'Please tell me in words of one syllable, because I'm rather confused. What's happened?'

'You won't understand. Not at all.'

Perching on the arm of his chair, I gave a wobbly show of support.

'Let's go abroad, Elizabeth,' he said. 'Let's leave this wretched country once and for all.'

'Forever?'

'Perhaps. Why make plans? We're both free.'

I was incredulous. The George I knew had been replaced by a hippy.

'Of course we're not. You have your work and I have mine. And what about Wellington? And our friends? George, are you ill?'

'Yes, that's what they'll say. I'm sick. Sick!'

It was then that it started to come out, in dribs and drabs. Incoherence is doubly disturbing in a man with a first-class mind. He began by announcing that he had resigned from the Ministry. He went on to tell me the reason.

'I was arrested last night.'

'Arrested? Don't you just mean picked up?' I clung to the colloquial.

'I was arrested, Elizabeth.'

'But why? What for? What were you doing?'

'I'm not sure what I'm doing any more.'

'Don't play games with me!'

'I'm sorry. This is hard . . . so hard.'

He was right. It was so hard that I had to ask him to repeat every other word, which only made it harder. The simplest sentence fell apart in my brain.

'I was at the Bill Sykes pub in Stepney.'

'Bill Sykes? Is it something to do with Dickens?'

'No. Not exactly. Not at all. Please let me speak!' I was shocked by his tone since that was precisely what I had been asking. 'It was full of men. Only men. I'm so sorry. I must have been out of my mind. How could I do it to you?' But he had done nothing to me – nothing at all. What I wanted to know was what he had done to them. He began to elaborate. 'It was all a mistake . . . a complete misunderstanding. You must believe me.' I assured him that I did. But he saw through my pretence as clearly as I saw through his. Deception enveloped us like a double bed.

Gulp by gulp, he told me the story. 'They were half-naked. It was an underwear night.'

'But I buy your underwear. If you needed new ones, why not ask me?'

Thirty-eight years of scrutinising Marks and Spencer's menswear, of choosing between Y-fronts and boxers, of daring to vary the whites with a dash of paisley, stoked my resentment. He had no need to search for bargains in an East End pub as though they were stolen videos.

He explained that they were wearing the underwear, not buying it. The pub was full of men parading in their pants. My first thought was to hope that they were clean.

My humiliation increased as I realised that, while he relished the sight of their underwear, he had avoided the least glimpse of mine. For years, I had sat at my dressing-table with impunity. But what I had taken for discretion turned out to have been disgust. Far from sparing my blushes, he was saving his glances for boys.

'It wasn't just boys; there were all sorts.'

'I don't care.'

'A party night for "older men and their younger admirers".'

'A fine sight you must have looked, all prancing around with your paunches.' I pictured George, with his Buddha-breasts, emerging from the bathroom and felt a surge of revulsion.

'I wouldn't know. It was too dark.'

I saw that, if he had been sleeping with a stranger, so had I.

'What about the police?'

'They turn a blind eye.'

'Why? Don't we pay taxes?'

'They turn a blind eye to the . . . men. But not to the drugs.'

'Are you telling me you've been taking drugs as well?'

'No, of course not.'

'There's no "of course" about it; there are no "of courses" left.'

'What I meant is that they'd had a tip-off that drugs were being sold. They raided the pub and I was caught in a corner.'

'What's wrong with that? What sort of corner?'

'It was more of a cubicle.'

I knew what he meant, although I had never entertained

such thoughts about anyone, least of all George. Suddenly, I had an image of the kind of cubicle in which he had been caught with one of his undiscriminating 'younger admirers', causing the policemen's sight to be spontaneously restored. I felt sick and walked haltingly from the room, placing one foot in front of the other like a child. I felt as if I had drunk from a bottle marked 'Drink Me' and shrunk to a fraction of my former self. I was afraid to bend over the lavatory for fear that I would be sucked into the bowl, to find all the filth which was engulfing me made real. Then I was sick, which somehow calmed me. Even the smell was consoling. It was a normal human response, something to keep hold of. I walked back into the drawing-room and faced George.

'Are they going to charge you?'

'They already have. Jerry pleaded with them but without success. I went before the magistrates this morning. As you see, I was given bail. Though I'm more determined than ever to elect for a jury trial.'

'You mean other people?' It was then that I realised it wasn't just a matter for George and me, and Jerry and Ruth (the thought of Ruth appalled me); it would become public knowledge. George seemed to read my mind.

'How can I live with the shame: the sniggers; the scorn; worse, the disillusioned sympathy? Everyone claiming the right to play judge. To say nothing of the papers.'

I think that that was the very worst moment of all, when I had a vision of breakfast-tables across the land sinking beneath the reports of gross indecency. For that was what it was. Moreover, it was grossly inconsiderate. He talked of not being able to lift his head, but what about mine? We were husband and wife – one flesh – and half of me was putrid. I felt full of hate.

'Has this happened before?'

'Why torture yourself?'

'Just answer me!'

'It does no one any good.'

'So, all the times you were allegedly staying at your club, you were actually sleeping with boys?'

'Try to understand.'

'I suppose I should be grateful. At least there's no danger of your having given me some dreadful disease.'

'We're both suffering from the same disease; it's called loneliness.'

'I am not lonely! I have my friends. My colleagues. Surely a man of your intelligence can appreciate the distinction between loneliness and being alone?'

'I'm sorry. I didn't mean – '

'Thank God, at least, that we have no children.'

'Please don't say that.'

'What kind of a father would you have been?'

'Who knows? Maybe the father would have given the husband strength?'

'So you blame me?'

He made no attempt to deny it, for he had no need. I knew, as I spoke, that he never had reproached me and he never would. I was simply trying to find some coherence: to fit the aberration into a pattern I could understand.

I asked him what he wanted me to do and he said that the decision must be mine but that he would respect it either way. Which sounded much more accommodating than it was. He professed to be giving me the freedom to choose when, in fact, he was using it to make me feel obliged. Of course, there was no question of my asking him to leave. If the wives of serial killers could stand by their husbands, then I could stand by him . . . although I knew to expect similar censure from the world at large. Instead of complicity, I would be charged with frigidity – or worse – by people convinced that they knew their partner's every move. Even so, I never wavered in my support, except to impose one condition: that there be no attempt to dignify what he had done with explanations. I refused to disinter a past that was neatly buried in photograph albums and then point the finger at his mother or nanny or school. After all, a hit-and-run driver did not blame the instructor who had helped him pass his test.

As the days wore on, my pain gave way to resentment. I made lists of all the things that I'd never done – things that had merited nothing more than an amused or baffled glance when I'd heard about them from other people, but which now appeared to be pivotal experiences for which no British Museum trip to Kurdistan or Swan Hellenic cruise of the Baltic could compensate. I had never made love with food or out of doors or even downstairs. I had never encountered an orgy except on canvas. A neighbour's daughter in Camden once interviewed me for a project on the Sixties. 'Were you really there?' she asked, as if my mere presence ensured that I must have rubbed shoulders with the Beatles. 'Yes, of course,' I replied, but it was a lie. I may have lived through the decade but I never lived through the *Sixties*. Everything but the chronology passed me by.

Although his sexuality had come as a shock, it was his deceit that really shook me. His need for concealment stood as a savage indictment of our marriage. He insisted that he had been trying to protect me. 'You've always said that, in your work, the key is to know when to stop. Just as a patina can enhance a painting, so an illusion can sustain a life.' Far from consoling me, his words were a graphic reminder of my failings. For all my skill at detecting defects on canvas, I had been blind to the discrepancies in front of my eyes. Desperate for reassurance, I recalled his response when a group of gay soldiers had claimed compensation for their dismissal. I found it incomprehensible that they should ever have joined up, but George stated – curtly, it seems to me now – that they had been very young and may still have been confused about their natures. I wondered whether the same might be said of him. Had he been unaware of how he felt when he proposed, or had he known and looked to me to convert him? Worse, had he used me cynically, as a decoy? He ducked all my questions, swearing that what had happened in the pub had nothing to do with us. But he was wrong. If it were to do with him, then it was to do with us – unless my entire existence had been a sham.

I held that he had been extremely rash to have handed in his resignation and that, given his vulnerable state, Sir Neville had been wrong to accept it. But, when I rang him at home one weekend and put to him that even cabinet ministers were now openly gay, he replied that, as far as he knew, none of them had been caught with their trousers down in an East End pub. To which there was no answer. My own solution to George's change of circumstances was to think of it as early retirement. If it were not quite such a rosy one as we had planned – if the leaving-card contained fewer signatures and the ice-bucket were less heavily subscribed – then so be it. The one thing that I did not regret was the loss of his *gong*. I watched blithely while my crested writing paper went up in smoke. I'd long dreaded all that 'well done, thou good and faithful civil servant'. This ladyship was one might-have-been who had never wanted to be.

Meanwhile, my fears that George's daily presence would become an irritant turned out to be unfounded. Not only was I forced to spend more and more time in the studio but, even in the house, he rarely obtruded. Despite having put on an alarming amount of weight, he seemed to take up less and less space. The faint burr of the television was often the only reminder that he was there. I saw no cause for alarm, for I knew it was a period of adjustment. His old vivacity would return after the trial.

Unfortunately, it was not to prove so easy. For, with the trial, came the press. The combination of top civil servant, drugs and illicit sexuality was too potent for them to resist. The *Standard* located Shame in the Corridors of Power; although it seemed to me that both power and shame resided elsewhere. George's face looked even more strained in the photographs than it did in court. I felt great tenderness towards him and equal bitterness towards the journalists. There were wars going on, bombs going off, wives being battered and children being abused, but they deemed that my husband's petty indiscretion took pride of place. To the accompaniment of finger-wagging from the judge and tittering from the public gallery, he was fined £500 with costs. The judge then directed some words at me, although I was smiling too intently to listen. It was only on reading the reports that I learnt he had described me as a pillar of strength. Looking back, it felt more like salt.

I was determined to strike a balance between courage and defiance and, after a considered interval, I began to contact friends. I reminded them of the weekends that they had promised to spend with us when we moved. But the snag with knowing such busy people was that they had such full diaries. Time was so pressed that they never even managed to ring back with dates. I understood. George's sexual impropriety was a minor offence compared to his breach of the social code. He had let the side down – and the side would not readily forgive him. So I gave up. Besides, I wasn't convinced that he was fit company. He had grown morose, rarely leaving the house or even stirring from his chair. He spent the day slumped in front of quiz shows, noting down facts which were of interest only to would-be contestants. He neglected to dress or shave and displayed an increasing indifference to soap. He even stopped going to church. And, although the vicar came in person to invite him, I detected a distinct relief when I walked to my pew alone.

I tried to shake him from his lethargy. I stressed that his career might have ended but he still had a life. Given his health (and his pension), he was ideally placed to take up all those activities for which he had never before had the time. He listened to me as though I were a budgerigar. I suggested that we went on holiday, countering his resistance with a reminder of how, when he was first charged, he had talked of settling permanently abroad. 'It was different then,' he said. 'There was still hope.' That, I declared, was precisely the kind of self-indulgence which proved my point. He shook his head as if to imply that I could never understand his pain; which was particularly hurtful given that it was self-inflicted. I had been scrupulous about not pressing my advantage, neither engaging in recriminations nor laying down rules for the future. And, although I had roundly dismissed all the unsolicited advice to leave him (not least from my sister, who felt that her own failed marriage had been vindicated by mine), I knew that I deserved better than this.

'We have to make the most of the hands we're dealt,' I said. 'There are millions of people worse off than us. If you want to spend the rest of your life feeling sorry for yourself, that's your funeral.'

My flippancy has haunted me ever since. I gave way to it one morning when I was going into Guildford to shop. I had put off the trip for weeks in deference to his mood, but I needed a break and, besides, I'd promised to be back for dinner. It was one of those crunchy autumn days, free from the complications of spring and the intensity of summer, that lift the spirit. As I walked up the drive, clutching an array of bags filled with that mixture of treats and bargains which is the essence of successful shopping, I felt at peace for the first time in months. But the moment I entered the house I sensed that something was wrong. Wellington was yelping in the kitchen. I let him out with a bitter rebuke for having made a mess on the floor. I was even

angrier with George for ignoring him . . . an anger which intensified as I hauled the packages upstairs on my own. Wellington
bounded in front and stood scratching and barking at the bathroom door. I opened it to the sight of George sprawled on the
lavatory, the left side of his face sunk into his neck. I wanted to
scream but produced only phlegm. I wanted to drop my bags,
but they seemed to be clamped to my hands. I stumbled towards
him. He was still warm. A faint memory of a first-aid manual
impelled me to massage his heart. My fingers felt cold against
his chest.

Instinct guided me to the phone and sustained me on the
journey to hospital. Panic set in once he was whisked away by a
medical team more suited to a major emergency. I waited in the
corridor like a schoolgirl, until I was summoned to see a doctor,
who explained that they had placed him on a ventilator. He
promised me that he was out of danger and advised me to go
home and rest; I could do no good by waiting. They would take
care of George.

Rest was fitful. Not even Wellington's stertorous breathing
brought any relief from the twin scourges of anxiety and guilt.
The latter was alleviated only by the knowledge of the presents
that I'd bought him earlier in the day. I stroked the new pyjamas
that I'd laid out royally on the bed. At the end of a turbulent
night, I returned to the hospital, where the doctor led me into
his office. I could see from his face that it was bad news and my
first thought was to wonder whether I had sufficient black. He
assured me that the prospect was not so grim. George had
suffered a massive stroke. It was impossible to predict the long-
term effects but the disruption to the blood supply had left him
with permanent damage to his brain and his sight.

Death, by comparison, was easy. Death was sharp and
unequivocal, whereas George's whole existence would be
blurred. How would he cope? How would I cope? The doctor

promised that the medical and social services would provide me with every assistance. I felt like a one-parent family. Which, in effect, was what we were. I was no longer his wife but his mother and father. I had wanted his child; now he had become mine. The irony made me laugh, which the doctor mistook for hysteria. He called a nurse to make me a cup of tea which, for form's sake, I drank. He then escorted me to the ward. I was heartened by George's appearance of normality, until I saw the look – or rather the non-look – in his eyes. He showed no sign of recognition of either my voice or my touch. 'I'm very sorry,' the doctor said, as we moved outside and the tears strained against my eyelids. 'But it's early days. Only time will tell.'

It did, confirming their worst prognosis. George would never improve. He was discharged from hospital with his mental and physical ages at permanent odds. He could not speak but emitted an unremitting bleat to which, after a while, I grew as inured as to the noise of planes taking off from Gatwick. He was incontinent and had to wear pads. I would remind Wellington, whenever he had an accident, that it was far worse now I was cleaning up after two. He, at least, had the grace to hang his head. My biggest regret was having to turn down work but, although the doctor proved as good as his word and I was allocated help, caring for George took up all my time. Not that my friends neglected me. Some days, the phone barely stopped. 'I had to put you on ring-back,' people would say with a hint of reproach. And the calls were reinforced by invitations. I was under no illusions. I knew that George had become acceptable once he could not be held responsible for his actions. He was no longer an embarrassment, he was a tragedy; just as I was no longer a victim, I was a saint. Everyone said so. To have kept him at home with me . . . to nurse him twenty-four hours a day. And it was as if they were adding a rider under their breath, 'especially in view of everything that has happened'. What they failed to understand was that it was only by keeping him at home that I could prove to the world that nothing had happened. It was only by keeping him at home that I could prove it to myself. The incident had been an anomaly. What mattered . . . all that mattered was that we had been married for forty years.

'You're one in a million, Elizabeth,' my old schoolfriend Laura declared.

'Not at all,' I replied, as I excused myself to go upstairs and change him. 'I'm just an ordinary loving wife.'

Contentment

HIS NAME WAS Gabriel. Richard met him in the Rat and Parrot in Soho, a pub where he had once received a round of applause merely for walking down the stairs. But that had been many years ago when he had been as young and fresh as Gabriel was now. The memory disturbed him and he retreated to the safety of a world in which he was one of the admirers rather than the admired. There was no in-between, not in the Rat and Parrot. He cast an appraising eye over the clientele. Mammon, rather than Cupid, lay behind the pervasive pairing of teenage boys and middle-aged men. He, however, felt at ease. He had always used prostitutes. His family's wealth allowed him to satisfy desires which its disapproval ensured that he kept hidden. So, flexing his financial muscle, he made the first move.

'That's a big glass,' he said, as Gabriel drank a pint of Newcastle Brown. He fed him an obvious line which, to his consternation, Gabriel ignored, saying simply, 'Yes, I've got a big thirst.'

'Then may I buy you another?'

'All in good time. What's the rush?'

He was even more confused. He had never known any of them to refuse a drink. He stared at Gabriel who, knowing that he was being perused, lowered his eyes in his one concession to work. Richard was smitten, although the boy was not at all his usual type. As if to compensate for his attraction to men, he preferred them to be overtly masculine: the square-cut jaw, the five o'clock shadow, the home-made (or preferably cell-made) tattoos. Gabriel, on the other hand, was slight. His hair was a packet russet. His eyebrows may have been plucked, although it was hard to tell underneath the freckles. His slightly fey gestures would normally have deterred Richard from giving him a second glance but, despite himself, he was transfixed. Fearful that Gabriel might be distracted, he placed a proprietorial hand on his arm. He was determined that there should be no misunderstanding over the sleeping arrangements for the night.

He waited while Gabriel finished his beer.

'Now may I get you that drink?'

'Why not? I'll have a lager and blackcurrant.'

He had to restrain a smile. He was on familiar ground. Changing his drink was a classic whore's trick. 'I don't know your name,' he said.

'Gabriel.'

'Like the angel,' he said, and then regretted it.

'Oh me. I'm a little devil, me,' Gabriel said. 'A real bad lot.'

'I hope you are,' Richard said. 'I really hope you are.'

'What's your name then?'

'Richard.'

'Nice to meet you, Richard.'

'Nice to meet you, Gabriel.' Richard stood as if in a daze.

'Go on then. Get them in.'

Richard hurried to the bar, where he felt his customary resentment at being ignored. He failed to understand why he was always the last person to be served. He did not look insignificant. He was tall and broad and had once rowed for his college – although that was an even dimmer memory than his entrance applause. He wondered whether he gave off an air of desperation that brought out every barman's worst instincts. Then, worried that Gabriel might be judging him, he abandoned all restraint and elbowed his way to the front. The injunction to 'Wait your turn' left him shamefaced, a sensation that placing the order did nothing to relieve. The very words 'lager and black-currant' sounded compromising, and he stammered his own request for a straight scotch. He flirted with asking for a double but opted for a clear head. He returned to Gabriel, who was leaning against a fruit machine talking to a young man. He experienced a pang of jealousy that was frightening in its ferocity, even though he realised on introduction that it was groundless.

'This is Richard, he's a mate of mine.' Richard tried to still his exultation at what he knew was sales talk. 'Richard, this is Mona. She's one of the girls.' Mona's smile revealed a mouth in need of extensive dentistry.

'I'm really not keen on the practice of calling men by women's names. I find it degrading.'

'Oh, pardon me for breathing.' Mona pouted.

'Believe me, it's nothing personal.'

'Don't worry, Richard,' Gabriel interjected. 'Mona, or should I say Melvyn, was on his way out. He just came over for a quick goss.'

'Yes, I must click my heels and disappear. You wouldn't have the fare for a cab to Brixton? I've sprained my ankle.'

'Of course,' Richard said, considering it a small price to pay to be relieved of Mona-Melvyn's company.

'No, he has not,' Gabriel said, putting a restraining hand on Richard's wallet. 'You can take the bus like anyone else.'

'But my foot!'

'Then hop. Now be a good girl and scram.'

'Ooh, someone's got her rag up,' Mona said, investing the words with a surprising degree of affection as he walked away.

'I'm afraid I was rather sharp. I hope I didn't offend him.'

'Forget it. It'll take more than a few home truths to offend Mona, sorry Melvyn.'

'Thank you.'

'You know, you have gorgeous eyes. Has anyone ever told you you have the most gorgeous green eyes?'

'It's the Celt in me.'

'I've had quite a few Celts in me but they haven't turned me green. Black and blue perhaps . . . sorry.'

'There's no need.' Richard was suffused with happiness. Every patch of his skin tingled. In answer to Gabriel's question, no one had ever complimented him on his eyes, but then he had never given anyone the chance. His was a world devoid of intimacy. At the age of forty-two, he lived with his parents. Their house was large enough for it to seem a privilege rather than a penance (he had his own entrance to his own set of rooms), but the key was as symbolic as that on an old-fashioned twenty-first birthday card. His independence was one of many carefully fostered illusions, among them his mother's claim merely to be looking after him until he met the right girl, and his father's pledge to be planning the retirement that would leave Richard in charge of the firm. He had nothing to call his own – apart from secrets, of which he had plenty, hidden like magazines in the back of drawers, secrets with names like Todd and Shane and Dean. But none of them until Gabriel had ever told him he had gorgeous eyes.

'Could you buy us twenty Silk Cut?'

'What? Yes, of course.'

'They don't come round with a tray. You have to ask at the bar.'

'Oh, right. Sorry.' At a stroke, his elation vanished. Of course he had gorgeous eyes. They blinked like cash registers.

Overcome by a sudden sadness, he made his slow way to the bar. He knew now that he had no need to impress: he had no need to do anything but pay. He had turned sex from an attraction into a transaction. The pattern was predictable. He came to

London, did business for his father, ran errands for his mother, rounded off the trip in a bar and bedroom, and then returned to the north where he lived off the memory for the next few months. Life did not have to be like this. He was not bad-looking (the grudging avowal being his sole concession to self-esteem). It should be possible to meet someone who would want him for himself. And yet the implications, on every level, were too daunting. What's more, his desires seemed to have been shaped in another age. His would not be a smart cocktail-party coupling of 'my boyfriend, the lawyer,' or 'my lover, the banker'. He favoured working-class boys who were the opposite of him in almost every respect (including, at times, sexual taste).

He dismissed any suggestion that they might want him for something more than what he had in his wallet. Few, if any, of them did what they did out of choice. They didn't know him and he didn't have the time to get to know them. Theirs was as much a business relationship as all the others on his trip. Nevertheless, over the years, he grew increasingly despondent at the cynicism of the encounters, whose chief effect was to increase his isolation. What's more, they came to colour his daylight attitudes, confirming his place in a world where every-body had his price. On each journey home, he swore to himself that he would never again give way to temptation. Then, on each return trip, he would find himself heading back to Soho and a pub such as the Rat, where the quick drink he had planned turned into two or three, as he prepared to slake an ever deeper thirst.

He bought the cigarettes and returned to Gabriel, who ripped open the packet with a craving as intense as his own lust.

'So what do you do then?'

'I'm in publishing. Provincial newspapers.' He took care to say nothing that might identify him the next day.

'Really? Can you make me famous?'

'There was an American artist who said we were entering an age where we'd all be famous for fifteen minutes.'

'That'd be no good. I wouldn't have time to put my slap on.'

'You're making yourself cheap again.'

'Sorry I spoke.'

'No, I am. I've no right – '

'But then you're all butch on newspapers. Biceps like Australians.'

'How would you know?'

'I've had a few in my time.'

'Newspapermen or Australians?'

'Both.'

'I haven't asked you yet what you do.'

'Isn't it obvious? I'm for rent.'

'Yes, I suppose so.' Richard's relief that the evening would be proceeding as planned was tinged with regret that his intuition had been correct. 'May I ask how much?'

'Sure. Sixty quid for a full service. Eighty if you want to stay the night. Bargain basement me.'

'I'm not rich.'

'No one ever is. It's the story of my life. If I got to meet George Michael, he'd have been wiped out the day before.'

'If you're not careful, I could end up falling in love with you.'

'Don't be so fucking stupid!'

'I'm sorry. I don't know why I said that.' Richard blushed. He knew the reason all too well, which was why he must be sure not to lower his guard. He said things that he did not mean, or rather that he did not mean to say. He felt like a young Hare Krishna professing indiscriminate love the length of Oxford Street. He was addressing a prostitute. He might as well have claimed to be in love with his accountant . . . But that was the problem: he sometimes felt he could fall in love with any man he met solely on the grounds of his gender. He, who had always been so fastidious, had lost all discrimination. The solution might be to abandon the world and become a monk. But monasteries were made up of men.

His train of thought sickened him. Gabriel's interruption was doubly welcome. 'Shall we make a move?'

'Fine.' Richard gulped down his drink and was rewarded with a fit of hiccups as they made their way to the Tube. He came from a long line of hard-headed businessmen and the guilt that followed each of his encounters was compounded by the outlay of so much cash. He was determined not to add to it by taking a cab. They arrived at Piccadilly Circus station and reached the platform just as their train was pulling in. Fate, Richard said to himself, and Gabriel's laugh echoed it. They sat in an almost empty carriage on an otherwise crowded train. As they moved off, the anomaly was explained by the rancid old man sprawled across a seat. Richard wanted to escape at the first stop, but Gabriel was worried that it would hurt the man's feelings. Richard was startled by the display of sensitivity, which filled him with both hope and alarm. All at once he wanted to know everything there was about Gabriel, not just to shape him to the blueprint of his own desires. But he needed to be circumspect. Gabriel might have secrets to guard too.

Richard's watch showed ten to midnight when they arrived at Ladbroke Grove, but the vibrant streets suggested that the majority of the residents had their body clocks set to Caribbean time. Families were parading and friends were meeting. Young children were skipping and older ones skateboarding. Blasts of music greeted him from passing cars. A sweetish, smoky, student-room smell emanated from a group of rastafarians. Such a show of exuberance left him feeling very grey. He strove to keep pace with Gabriel. With any other guide, he would have been unnerved by the ill-lit side-streets. His usual practice was to take the boys back to his hotel. Even braving the night porter's sneer was preferable to risking a psychopath's knife. But Gabriel had given him confidence. Moreover, he welcomed the chance to see him on his home territory. They entered a pocket-size garden, where a few shrubs thrived with cactus-like tenacity in an otherwise metallic landscape, and descended a flight of narrow steps to the basement flat. The peeling paint smacked of transience, an impression confirmed when, after grappling with the warped door, Gabriel led him inside.

The hall resembled an experiment in how to fit the greatest number of doors into the smallest possible space. Richard trusted that it would have the benignity of a farce and not the menace of a maze. Gabriel led him into what, given the sofa, seemed to be the sitting room, although it made few other concessions to either function or decor. There were no pictures, no ornaments, no plants, no books. He struggled to escape the stream of negatives. Stacked against the wall were three large boxes that looked to have come straight off a removal van or, perhaps, to have been prepared for a swift escape. The floor was thick with rubbish: half-filled cups of coffee; half-finished plates of food; cigarette boxes; crisp packets; magazines; underwear. Gabriel swept the sofa free of clutter and invited him to sit. He accepted warily, wondering how his mother would respond to an infestation of lice.

'Would you like a coffee?'

'Thank you. Milk, no sugar. On second thoughts, make it black. I want to keep awake.' He wanted even more to avoid botulism. While Gabriel disappeared into the kitchen, he examined the discarded clothes. He had just returned to the sofa when Gabriel brought in the cups.

'Do you live on your own?' He doubted whether anyone else could stomach the mess.

'No, I share with a mate. But don't worry. He's away tonight.'

All Richard's prurience was aroused as he speculated on the nature of their relationship and whether Gabriel's 'mate' pursued the same line of work. He tried to bury the thought in a burst of inconsequential chatter. He felt reassured by Gabriel's casualness. Intensity about sex – as about so much else – was something he preferred to experience alone. He felt equally reassured by the boy's air of innocence. That he had remained, to all appearances, unscarred and unsullied by the squalor of his life boded well for their own encounter . . . He was suddenly struck by a terrifying thought.

'How old are you?'

'Old enough. What's it to you?'

'Curiosity. I'm hopeless at guessing.' He wondered why that should be, given his unbroken record at the village fete.

'Depends who's asking. I'm nineteen if you want the truth. All legal and above board.'

'So young.' He was starting to feel guilt of an unexpected sort.

'Believe me, you're not taking my cherry. I lost that a long time ago.'

'I was twenty-two when I first had sex, and that was with a woman.'

'What do you want? Violins?'

'I kept my integrity . . . my self-respect. Whereas these days it's more like another O level.'

'GCSE, mate. Times have changed.'

'Were you abused as a child?'

'Fuck off, can't you? Just fuck off.'

'What else can explain your going to bed with men you've barely met?' Richard broke off in confusion.

'I'm on top, mate. Even when I'm underneath, I'm on top. I know what I want and I get it. And I get paid for it, too.'

'But don't you feel degraded?'

'Why should I? I might do if I was the one who was paying.' He smiled pointedly at Richard. 'It's a question of making the most of what you've got. You with your newspapers. Me with my arse.'

'There's no call to be crude.'

'Come off it! You're not here just for the coffee. Blokes like you really piss me off. You feel bad about yourself, so you want everyone else to feel the same. Well, tough! I feel good about myself. Bloody good. And I give a bloody good service. I want you to feel good about yourself, too.'

'I don't doubt it. It's sound business: a satisfied customer is more likely to come back.'

'Look, if you want to leave, there's nothing to stop you. The door's not locked. You can get a cab at the end of the road or, if you're still too fucking tight, there's the night bus. What are you afraid of? That I'll call up some mates and have you duffed up?'

'I'm sorry. I didn't mean to offend you. I'm just nervous.'

'I can do without this. I really can.'

'I'd like to stay. Please let me stay. I need you.' Gabriel smiled, as if he had spoken the magic word.

'Well, if you're going to stay, we'll have to start again. What's your name?'

'What?'

'Your name?'

'But I've already told you. It's Richard.'

'Pleased to meet you, Richard. I'm Gabriel.'

'Hello, Gabriel.'

'Sorry this place is such a tip. My flatmate's a slut.'

Richard swallowed. 'I like sluts.'

'You see. You're getting the hang of it already.'

Richard was suddenly filled with apprehension that he might say the wrong thing.

'May we go to bed? I don't mean to pressurise you, but I'm exhausted and I have meetings all day tomorrow.'

'Yes, of course. Won't be two ticks.'

'Which way's the bedroom?'

'You're looking at it.'

'I am?'

'This couch does amazing things when it flips its cushions.'

'I can't wait. May I use the bathroom – or do you need some help?'

'Be my guest. First door on the left. Take the blue towel.'

Richard returned from washing to find that Gabriel had effected the transformation.

'There's an awful lot of make-up in the bathroom. Your flat-mate?'

'Yes. He's heavily into drag.'

'I see.' He tried to keep his voice neutral. 'What about you? What are you into?'

'Oh me, I'm into pretty much everything. Cos I'm into people.'

Richard felt a glow of reassurance. If he were into everything, he might even be into him.

Gabriel rolled down the duvet and Richard, who was determined to find a deeper meaning in every action, saw it as a sign that their encounter would not be confined to the surface. He stripped to his underclothes and slipped into the left side of the bed, only to slide across to accommodate Gabriel's prior claim. Gabriel, who appeared to have no qualms about nudity, leant over and began to nuzzle his neck when Richard, apologising for his inhibitions, asked if it might be possible to turn off the light. Cursing himself for his discourtesy, Gabriel leapt out of bed and dashed to the switch: a move that allowed Richard to scrutinise his body. The wiry chest and hairless flesh reassured him about his own imperfections, and he tore off his vest and pants. To his surprise, he found that his penis had anticipated any touch.

They tentatively mapped one another's bodies. From the start Gabriel took the initiative. He teased. He tongued. He stroked. He caressed. He sucked. He kissed. He blew. Richard was amazed. He was accustomed to making all the effort: to being with boys who could not do enough for him until it came to bed, when they no longer did anything at all. They seemed to feel that they had done him an enormous honour simply by taking off their clothes: anything else was up to him. So he was left to arouse both himself and his partner, while concluding that he would have been better off on his own. But, with Gabriel, he experienced genuine passion. For the first time he felt that making love was not a misnomer: something new . . . something honest and beautiful had emerged from their coupling. Everything about him moistened, from his eyes to his lips to his penis. He came with rare intensity. He was so wet, so weak, but so strong. Gabriel matched him, which was also unexpected. Most of the boys held back, as if pleasure were an affront to professionalism. Gabriel, however, was as generous with himself as he was with his client.

They lay back on the pillows, the moonlight marbling their skin. Gabriel offered him a cigarette.

'I don't smoke, I'm afraid. Although, for the first time, I wish I did.'

'Why on earth? It's a filthy habit.'

'Because it would be something else I could share with you.'

Gabriel kissed him on the nose, which made him cry.

'I'm sorry. You should have warned me. Is it sore?'

'Not at all. I'm just happy. Everyone cries when they're happy. It's a sort of insurance for when they're sad.'

'That's too deep for me. I'm only a whore.'

'Don't say that. Please don't ever say that again.' Whereas

Richard had previously aimed to spare himself guilt, he now felt genuinely concerned.

'You're a real case.' Gabriel nestled his head in the crook of Richard's arm, while Richard gently stroked his hair.

'You're far too nice to be doing something like this.'

'What do you mean? How else would I get to meet such nice people?'

'I was right,' Richard said. 'Gabriel like the angel.' And he fell fast asleep. He awoke soon after eight, with the sun in his eyes and a weight on his chest, which he joyously identified as Gabriel. He gazed at him with infinite tenderness. He was conscious of instincts he had only read about in stories: he wanted to lift him out of his basement life and into a world of luxury; he wanted to give him all the advantages of which he had been deprived. First, however, he would give him breakfast. He knew that it was not the usual procedure, but he felt that the rules had changed. This would be confirmation. He crept out of bed, desperate to make no noise. He kicked away the pile of underclothes and gloried in his new-found nakedness. He tried to make sense of the myriad doors, sure that one of them must lead to the kitchen. He smiled as the first attempt brought success.

His hand flew to his groin, although not fast enough to avoid embarrassment. Sitting in a fug at the kitchen table was a woman. His eyes glazed. All he could see was a shock of hair coloured from the same packet as Gabriel's. His sense of euphoria vanished. He thought . . . he prayed that he must be still asleep. A swarm of questions stung his brain: who was she? where was he? was he the victim of a practical joke – or, worse, something more sinister?

'Don't mind me, love,' she announced with a bored smile. 'Help yourself.'

The vagueness of the invitation added to Richard's discomfort. His nakedness hung as heavy on him as a winter coat. He edged to the door. 'I'm sorry to have disturbed you. I'll just . . . I'll just . . .' He pulled at the handle. It was a broom cupboard. A mop-head poked him in the small of the back with Marx Brothers timing.

'It's the next one along. Easy mistake.' The woman smiled and gazed back at her cup of tea. 'Can I get you something, love? It's that Gabriel. I call him Weary Willie. He's a lazy sod.' The easy familiarity with which she said his name spoke of conspiracy. Richard had to escape.

'No! No thank you. I'm just . . .' At a loss for words, he gratefully grabbed the correct handle and hurried back to the bedroom, as sickened by his own gullibility as by the trick that he had been played. He threw himself on to the bed and shook Gabriel awake.

'What the . . . Here, hang on a minute. Where's the fire?'

'Who's the woman in the kitchen?'

'What woman? Look, keep your hair on. Where's my fags?'

'Don't . . . don't talk to me about cigarettes!' There was a moment when composure became callousness. It was one that Gabriel had reached. 'There's a woman in your kitchen.'

'Oh!' Gabriel said without surprise. 'I expect it's my mum. Now would you mind shifting your arse? My leg's numb.'

'Your mother?' Richard reeled. Soho apart, his life was strictly conventional. This was too weird for him to comprehend.

'Yeah, you know. The woman who found me under the gooseberry bush.'

'Stop it, Gabriel,' Richard pleaded.

'Sorry, I thought you wanted to know.'

'But what's she doing in your flat? Does she have a key?'

'I should hope so. She lives here too.'

'Then she's your flatmate?'

'Fraid so.' That at least explained the make-up. Richard

found the perversity of the arrangement was starting to set its own rules.

'You should have told me. You shouldn't have let me go barging in.'

'Excuse me? How was I to know you'd get up at the crack of dawn?'

'It's half past . . . that's not the point. You should have said.'

'Why? You're not my boyfriend. You're here for a fuck, that's all. Which reminds me: you owe me eighty quid.' Richard sank dejectedly on to the bed. 'Look, it's no big deal. I didn't say because it didn't seem to matter. She shouldn't have come back last night. She was supposed to be staying at her mate's. If I told you, it might have freaked you out.'

'Too true,' Richard said, as his attention was diverted by a steady tapping.

'Are you decent?' A woman's voice was swiftly followed by a russet head at the door.

'That's OK, Mum,' Gabriel called from the safety of his duvet, leaving Richard fully exposed on the bed.

'Don't mind me, love,' the woman said. 'But I know what it's like first thing in the morning when you're gasping for a cup of tea. I reckoned it knocked the stuffing out of you seeing me in there. You blushed right down to your dong. So I brought you some in myself.'

'Ta, Mum,' Gabriel said and stretched out his hand for a cup. Richard did not have one free. He bent forward, as desperate as a drag queen to conceal his penis. At the same time, he strained to come up with a convincing explanation for having spent the night with her teenage son.

'I put two spoonfuls of sugar in, love,' the woman was saying. 'I find most men like it sweet.' Richard tried to disentangle her innuendo from his paranoia. He swore to himself that he would never go home with a stranger again.

'Thank you,' he said, leaning discreetly to accept the cup. There was nowhere to rest it but his lap. He hardly dared breathe for the risks. He listened to Gabriel slurping tea, apparently oblivious of his discomfort, before turning to the woman, his story as honed as circumstances would allow. 'It must look strange, I know. But your son did me a good turn last night. I'd locked myself out of my flat and he said I could sleep on the floor till I got hold of the alarm people in the morning. He has a heart of gold,' he added, to his immediate regret.

'Christ, what a performance!' Gabriel said, between slurps.

'What?' Richard was amazed at the lack of support.

'Leave it out, Richard. My mum wasn't born yesterday.'

'Don't worry, love,' she said, moving to the door. 'You drink your tea. Don't mind me.'

'But . . .' The truth was more vicious than anything he had imagined. 'You mean you know what he does?'

'He hardly keeps it a secret.'

'But he's a prostitute.' Richard felt a chill fall over the room.

'You were pissed off when I called myself one before.'

'It's too late to pussyfoot around. He sleeps with men for money. And I don't suppose I'm the first.'

'No,' she said very quietly. 'He had his first when he was fourteen.'

Richard thought he saw pain in her eyes and wanted to add to it. He was eager to punish her for her connivance.

'How could you have allowed it?' he asked. 'He was just a child.'

'He's not exactly Old King Cole now.' Richard recognised the threat in her tone but resolved to disregard it. As Gabriel's mother, she was the one with the most to fear.

'Granted. But fourteen to nineteen is a big difference.'

'Oh, sure.' He flinched from the crudeness of her irony. 'A difference big enough for you to squeeze yourself in – and out.'

'Don't, Mum . . .'

'They're all the same, don't care where they draw the line just so long as they're behind it.'

'That's not true.'

'Mum, what's the point?'

'The point is that it's your body, your life. Not his or anyone else's.'

'Or yours for that matter,' Richard interjected.

'No, nor mine neither. Not any more. That's why, when he told me, I didn't throw a fit. Oh, I tried to stop him. As God's my witness, I did everything I could. But he was dead set. And I reckoned, if anyone could take care of himself, Gabe could. After all, he's lived all of his life with me.'

'You mean . . . you too?'

'Is something wrong, love? Do you have a stutter?' As she laughed, Richard realised that, for all his boys, he had never before met a female prostitute.

'Do you have no shame?'

'No, love. Why, would you like to give me some of yours? There's no shame because we're honest with each other. I can talk about my blokes and Gabe can talk about his.'

Richard found himself locked in a recurring nightmare. His name leapt out at him from a newspaper headline which, when he looked closely, he recognised as one of his own.

'But you're his mother!'

'That's why we can talk to each other.' Richard failed to follow the logic. He never discussed anything important with either of his parents. Evasion and subterfuge were the cornerstones of family life. 'We do all right, don't we love?'

'Course we do, Mum.' Gabriel slipped out of bed and stood with his arm on his mother's shoulder, as naked as the day she had borne him. Their very naturalness accentuated Richard's unease. 'I enjoy what I do. It's a living. Lots of blokes go into their dad's business. Well I went into my mum's.'

'It's hardly the same!' Richard pictured his father's office, where five generations of publishers stared down at him from frames as solid as their lives.

'Why not? Don't you believe in making people happy?'

'Yes, of course,' Richard said, feeling more miserable than ever.

'Well, my mum does that better than anyone I know.'

'Thanks, love,' she said, flashing him a smile of unexpected vulnerability. 'But there's no need.'

'Isn't there? Tell him about the blokes that have come to you for fifteen years and more. Tell him about the couples you've kept together when, left to theirselves, they'd have split.'

Richard dismissed Gabriel's speech as special pleading but, on looking at his face, he was no longer sure. Of course he was trying to justify his life: it was only natural. He did the same thing himself every day. The difference was that Gabriel was trying to justify the pleasure he gave, whereas he tried to justify the pain. He watched as Gabriel flung his arms around his mother and hugged her tight. The sight of the naked man and the clothed woman put him in mind of a Pietà, and he felt both strangely moved and achingly, unbearably alone.

'Right then, love. I'll leave you to make yourself respectable. You'll want to be off.'

Richard realised with a jolt that he too was naked, but he no longer felt ashamed. He was anxious to prolong the moment and avoid the need to dress, which would be like a snake slithering back into its sloughed-off skin. He yearned to be free and natural and unconstrained. Last night he had embraced Gabriel's nakedness, now he wanted to embrace his own.

'No. The last thing I want is to be respectable. I can't step back into my old clothes. They'd feel all wrong.'

'But you'll have to wear something,' Gabriel said. 'My gear'd be too small. I suppose you could try something of Mum's. She's a size sixteen.'

'Cheeky monkey!'

'Only you're that keen on drag.'

'I'm not . . . I wasn't. But I might change. Who knows how much I might change if I had the right teacher.'

'Is that so?' Gabriel smiled mischievously. 'Well, I have been known to give tuition.'

'Good Lord, no!' Richard recalled the advertisements in certain specialised magazines. 'I wouldn't want anything like that.'

'Don't worry. I'm being wicked.'

'I thought we'd already established you're on the side of the angels.'

'Nah, far too boring. All that listening to prayers and stuff. I just want blokes to have fun.'

'Will you help me to have fun?'

'It all depends what you have in mind.'

'I don't live in London.'

'You said.'

'But I come down fairly often. I could arrange to make it more.'

'Whatever you like. It always helps to have a few regulars.'

'Is that all I'd be? A regular?'

'We'd have to see. It's a question of give and take.'

'I can give you anything you like. I'm a rich man.' He saw Gabriel's face fall and wondered whether he had once again misjudged him. 'I'm sorry. I didn't mean to insult you.'

'Don't worry. You can't insult a whore.'

'Oh yes you can, love,' his mother interjected. 'You should know better than that.'

'I knew that Gabriel didn't mean money,' Richard said, 'but it was easier to pretend that he did: that it's the one thing I have going for me.'

'In that case, love, Gabe would never have brought you here. Believe me, it's not many that gets past this front door.'

Richard began to feel uneasy. 'But it's his job.'

'That doesn't mean he brings his work home with him.'

'Don't tell him that, Mum. Look, he's trembling. He wants to think he can have everything – and everybody – so long as he pays enough. It's the only way he can feel in control.'

'How little you know! I don't feel in control of anything.'

'Not now, no, because your cover's been blown. But before . . . Tell me, where do you keep your wallet? In your trousers close to your prick or in your jacket on top of your heart?'

'What must I do to show you I'm sincere?'

'Don't you know?'

Richard wondered whether there were some simple clue he had missed in what Gabriel had said but he could think of none. He looked at his pile of clothes on the floor and decided it was no longer a case of whether he would like to wear them but of whether they would fit. His shirt would be too tight and his trousers too short. If he put them on now, he would never breathe with ease or walk with confidence again. This was his last chance to assert himself. He bent down, but instead of picking up his clothes he reached for the duvet.

'Would you mind if I went back to bed for a while?'

'Is that all?' Gabriel asked him pointedly.

'No. I'd like it very much if you'd come too.' Gabriel looked at his mother. Richard sensed something pass between them, the exact nature of which was too subtle for him to make out.

'All right,' he said with a shrug and jumped into bed. Richard slid in more shyly and was learning to adjust to the sharp, raw presence alongside him when he looked up to see the woman gazing down at them.

'Oh, I beg yours, I was miles away! Don't mind me: don't mind anyone. Enjoy yourselves while you can. That's my philosophy.' Richard felt reassured by a world in which philosophy had been reduced to mottoes. 'If you can't have fun while you're young, what'll you have to look back on when you're my age?'

'Come on, Mum, you're only forty-five.'

'Why, you cheeky monkey!' His mother took a swipe at him. 'I may be thirty-eight . . . thirty-eight, mind, and not a day more, but,' she added with a touch of sadness, 'right now I feel older than God.' For a moment Richard invested the well-worn phrase with truth. As she leant over Gabriel and stroked his cheek, the family likeness resembled that of a Renaissance devotional painting. He had used to attribute such uniformity to a failure in the artist, but he was no longer so sure.

'I'll see you later, then,' she said to Richard as she drifted to the door. 'Stay as long as you like. Or do you have things to do?'

'Yes, several, but I can cancel them. I'm a free agent.'

'That's all right, then.'

For the first time in his life, Richard felt that to be true. He turned to see Gabriel lying languidly on the pillow with a sly grin that made him look less like an angel and more like a Cupid, although the pair no longer seemed to be such opposites. Richard wanted to take him in his arms, to taste his lips and to share his grin, but he remembered in the nick of time that his mother was still in the room.

'Thank you so much for the tea and . . . everything.'

'That's all right, love. Any time. We don't charge.'

At once the room fell silent. Then, with one breath, all three burst out laughing. Richard rested his head on Gabriel's shoulder, nibbled his neck, and lay back content.

The Fig-Leaf

FRIENDS, I have long believed, should be able to tell one another everything. At the same time, they are understandably concerned to spare each other pain. I have never felt the conflict between these impulses more keenly than on the evening that Janet revealed to me that she had been raped.

Janet and I had met at Oxford, sharing what – in a reference to our favourite Greek restaurant – she dubbed our 'moussaka days'. Our friendship was sealed when we acted together in several plays. I later secured my links with the stage by joining a theatrical agency. For a long time, Janet addressed me as 'Mr Ten Per Cent'. She was wrong about the figure (I am, in fact, Mr Fifteen) but right about my having achieved a mere fraction of my potential. After several years and a promotion to junior partner, I had allowed the attractions of a lifestyle to compensate for the lack of a life. Janet too had come to appreciate that the dreams of her youth would not be fulfilled – at least not during her youth (she claimed that the blackest day of her life was when she realised that she had outlived Keats). She had become an English teacher and was making her way through the capital cities of Europe, as if the glamour of the setting made up for the tedium of the job.

We stayed in regular contact, although the heady days of flat-share land (Janet) and bedsit land (me), when we insisted that taking the Tube from Parson's Green to Kilburn was as easy as walking from Somerville to Queen's, had long passed. The initiative for our meetings – as for so many others – was generally mine. With more and more of the names in my address book having partners squeezed in beside them – an affront both to the neatness of my pages and to the loneliness of my life – I compensated by cultivating the unattached. Over time, most of them also defected and I fell back on the instant camaraderie of my profession. In Janet's case, I could blame the emotional distance on the geographical. We saw each other at most twice a year during her duty visits to her mother, and then spent so long catching up that we were unable to move on. Moreover, we had passed the age of heart-spilt correspondence. So I was almost as shocked that she should choose to confide in me as by the confidence itself.

I was at a loss to know how to respond. I had prided myself on my sensitivity to women ever since university, when I was trying to win their trust while most of my friends were trying to worm their way into their beds. Rape, however, reduced me to platitudes. I recalled a discussion in my men's group (a judicious balance of gay and straight with a floating bisexual) at the time of a particularly brutal assault the previous year. The straight men took on the collective guilt of their orientation, while the gay men looked on smugly, saved by a technicality. But, while I have never been a single-issue activist or only marched to further my own cause, I admit that the problem of rape has not come high on my list of priorities. Far from seeming an aberrance, it has always struck me as the essence of heterosexuality: the male–female relationship at its most pure. To my mind, the act of penetration is intrinsically aggressive. The snake in the Garden of Eden lay coiled beneath Adam's fig-leaf.

There are women who would deny me the saving grace of my sexuality, claiming that I am fatally compromised by my gender. Janet's friend Sheila declared that for a man to express solidarity with a rape victim was like the West sending aid to Africa and then charging it huge rates of interest. She was particularly contemptuous of gay men whom she regarded as time-servers, hiding behind women to conceal their own inadequacies and, in the process, weakening feminist resolve. She felt that no man, gay or straight, could truly understand how a woman felt. It was the difference between sympathy and empathy. I accused her of splitting hairs, but then she had always insisted on strict definitions, once refusing a battered transsexual a place in the women's refuge where she worked.

Janet was staying with Sheila during a brief visit from Prague, and we were all three attending the thirtieth birthday party of a university friend (my privileged status as the baby of the group allowed me to approach such occasions with a kind of equanimity). Both Janet and I were horrified by the literal and metaphorical flabbiness of men whom we had not seen for years, but she voiced her disapproval with a vehemence which I attributed – erroneously, as it turned out – to Sheila. In a crude attempt to curry favour and to show that I, at least, had not abandoned the passion of youth, I expressed horror at a savage rape that had occurred in my neighbourhood the previous week, adding, like a Sixties socialist, that it might have been averted by the provision of better street lighting. 'I was raped,' Janet said, 'last summer.' Then, either to calm her nerves or to make a point, she handed me a bowl of olives.

The bowl hovered between us as I tried to make sense of her remark.

'Yes, I thought that would make you sit up,' she said.

I seemed to detect a note of satisfaction in her voice as she registered my unease, but it might well have been my own attempt to hold on to recognisable emotions.

'I'm afraid it's not just something that you read about in the papers.'

'When? You never said anything.'

'It was when I was teaching in Rome last year.'

'But you wrote that you were having the time of your life.'

'Yes, I had been – at least one of them – up till then. And it's not the sort of news that you scribble on a postcard of the Trevi fountain.' Both her voice and her composure were starting to crack. We were in a corner of the room, conveniently away from the crowd. Only the poster of Titian's *Tarquin and Lucretia* on the wall opposite us caused me unease. Janet, however, seemed to be oblivious to anything but the pain of her recollections. 'I was so full of hope,' she said, emitting a sound halfway between a cry and a croak. Several heads turned our way and, to my shame, I found myself miming inebriation. I felt utterly help-less, unable to decide whether to encourage her to talk, which risked reviving harrowing emotions, or to change the subject and appear indifferent. So I relieved her of the bowl and waited for her to take the lead.

'Did I ever mention Filippo?'

'The architect?'

'Yes.'

'Didn't you go out with him for a few months?'

'So I suppose you think it was all my fault. It wasn't really rape: I was giving off conflicting signals. After all, "get away from me" does sound a lot like "come on". Especially in Italian.'

'No, of course not. Please don't make it hard for me.'

'Hard for you!' She sounded incredulous.

'Well, of course it is: trying to imagine – or rather, not to imagine – you being attacked.'

'Yes, I'm sorry.' Her manner changed. 'I shouldn't have brought it up. How selfish of me to ruin your evening!'

'You know I didn't mean that.'

'I've done it again: the life and soul of the party.'

I reflected on all the changes that I had noticed in her during this last visit, which I had attributed to the influence of Prague. 'You know you can always tell me anything, anything you like, if it's a help.'

'Nothing helps. Though nothing hurts that much any more either. I carry my body around like a corpse.' She dismissed my objection. 'Oh yes, a freshly scrubbed, beautifully embalmed corpse, but a corpse all the same.' I plucked up the courage to touch her, albeit only her hand, and felt the chill in her fingers. 'I'd known him for months. We'd slept together for weeks. But he wasn't right for me. Any more than I was for him. Unless his needs were so basic that a woman was no more than a piece of gruyère. But he had always been perfectly charming. I didn't know that many people in Rome and I wanted us to stay friends. So, even though I'd made it quite clear we were no longer lovers, I invited him over for a meal.' Her body began to shudder. 'It was all very light-hearted: two friends who had known each other in a way that went beyond friendship. Then, at around midnight, I suggested it was time for him to go home. His whole manner changed. He accused me of luring him there to effect a reconciliation. He refused to leave and began to paw me.' Her voice quavered, but she seemed to feel an obligation to conclude the story. 'At first I thought – or at least I told myself – that he was just playing the fool. I should have gone easier on the Chianti. But he became more determined. I started to feel frightened. And then it . . . it just happened.' Once again she threw back her head and emitted a death-rattle of a laugh. 'If I'd been knifed, I could show you my scars.'

'I don't know what to say.'

'No. I don't suppose you do. I didn't either. All that expensive education is designed to keep the primitive at bay. And then it appears, suddenly, in your bedroom . . . in your bed. He didn't just put his clothes on and slink out. He lay down beside me as if what we had been through was a particularly boisterous act of love. But, once his lust had died down, so had his strength, and I was able to get rid of him quickly. I shall never forget the winsome smile he gave me at the door, which had no doubt worked on every female custodian of that boys-will-be-boys culture. Well, it didn't work on me. Nor did anything else. I went through a complete transformation: new flat; new clothes; new hairstyle. And it didn't seem like a cliché at the time. I felt a desperate need to ring the changes. It wasn't that I didn't want to look like the woman who had attracted him: I didn't want to be her. That was what I resented most: he hadn't simply violated my body; he'd stolen my whole identity. And I had been stupid enough to let him. I mean I'd liked the guy. Me, who'd always prided herself on her judgement of character.'

'That has nothing to do with it. You can be driving along a motorway and be hit by a drunken driver. Does that mean you should have stuck to B-roads?'

'It isn't the same. Nothing else is remotely the same.' She must have seen my pained expression, since she squeezed my hand. 'I'm sorry. It's just that it's all come flooding back when I thought that I had it under control. It's bad enough my judgement betraying me without my memory doing it as well.'

She stood up and went in search of Sheila and a lift home. I was on the brink of urging her to stay, insisting that it would not be healthy to leave so much unresolved, when I realised my insensitivity. I was not simply drawing her back to the scene of the crime, but rubbing her face in the stains on the carpet. I watched her say goodbye to our hosts and then cornered her for a quick word as she was putting on her coat.

'Did you report it to the police?'

'The Italian police? Are you kidding? He was my friend, remember: a healthy, full-blooded Italian male. And I was a trouble-making, prick-teasing foreigner.' She broke off as she heard Sheila approach. 'Look, I'm really sorry. I didn't mean to dump all this on you.'

'Don't be silly. I'm . . .' I was about to say *glad*, which was not what I meant at all. 'Honoured that you felt you could.' She understood and kissed me warmly on the cheek.

'I know. But, as you see, life goes on. Look, I'm here for another week. Give me a ring and we'll fix up a date. Perhaps we could go to the theatre?'

'What would gay men do without theatre?' Sheila asked, as she enveloped Janet in an intimacy that I knew now I could never fully share. 'They might have to face up to the truth of their wretched little lives.'

Dismissing Sheila's taunt, I called Janet as soon as I was back in my office and familiar with my schedule. I invited her to a revival of *Annie Get Your Gun* in which I had two clients, both dancers (like them, I had yet to escape from the chorus). I had chosen a musical in case our spirits needed a lift, although the production turned out to be so leaden that we'd have done better at *The Dance of Death*. In the interval, we dashed to the bar for a much-needed drink. As we waited to be served by a barman who seemed to have picked up the conductor's tempi, I became conscious of a man staring intently in our direction. While I was loath to say anything that might remind Janet of her ordeal, I decided that it would be worse if she turned round and caught him. 'I'm sure it's perfectly harmless,' I said, 'but you ought to know there's a man staring at you.'

'Don't be silly,' she replied. 'He's been staring at you from the moment we walked in.'

I was astounded and turned to face him, to be rewarded by a broad smile. I was angry, less at his brazenness than at my own transparency. I had always prided myself on being enigmatic. In my one foray into the Lonely Hearts columns, I had described myself as straight-acting, to the alternate amusement and disgust of various partisan friends. Here I was, to all appearances, enjoying a night out with my girlfriend, and he was ogling me as if I were on the dance floor of a gay club. I toyed with the thought of asking him what he wanted (although 'What's your problem, mate?' would have seemed as unnatural in my mouth as some of the red skins had on stage), but I was diverted by the barman's finally taking our order. 'Now you know how it feels,' Janet said, which struck me as excessive, although I was grateful for any antidote to Sheila's separatism.

We returned to the auditorium to find my 'admirer' (Janet)/ my 'stalker' (me) blocking our path. I brushed past brusquely. He maintained his smile and took his seat which, I was sorry to see, offered a near-perfect view of mine. During several of the less gripping moments, I cast a surreptitious glance his way and, each time, found myself catching his gaze. To avoid giving him further encouragement, I fixed my attention on the stage, not even wavering during the interminable choruses of *There's no business like show business* (a statement which, on this showing, was unlikely to hold true for either of my clients). I kept my resolve through all the curtain calls, but my hopes of a speedy escape were thwarted by Janet's visit to the loo. I was waiting outside the door, subject to the ultimate exclusion, when the man sauntered up to me.

'Did you enjoy that?' he asked.

'Yes, on the whole,' I said, my unease at his approach accentuated by the setting.

'What do you mean "on the whole"?

'Well,' I replied, determined not to mince words, 'some of the staging would have disgraced a village hall. Some of the principals would have been more at home at the end of a pier. Some of the choral singing was as patchy as their "Indian" skin. Shall I go on?'

'I thought it was great.'

'I'm happy for you. Though I'm surprised you were able to judge.'

'Why's that?'

'Every time I looked up, you were looking at us.'

'Maybe that's what was great.'

I was amazed. People only came out with lines like that in films. I began to wonder if this might be a set-up: a gay *Candid Camera*. The thought made me break into a smile, which he quite misinterpreted.

'Would you like to come for a drink? We could go to Laverne's. Discuss the show and anything else you might care to.' I was appalled by his presumption, which would have offended someone far less reserved than me.

'That's very kind. But I'm here with my girlfriend.'

'She's not your girlfriend.'

'How do you know?'

'I know.'

In spite of myself, I found his honesty infectious. 'No, she's not my girlfriend.'

'Then you'll come?'

'I can't just dump her. I have to take her home, especially after . . . she's been through rather a lot lately.'

'Boyfriend trouble?'

'Isn't that a tautology?' His lack of response was a sign that I would have to rely on my wits rather than my wit.

'Put her in a cab. I expect she'll be glad of an early night.' He sounded increasingly reasonable.

'Well, I'll see. I'll have to ask her. If you don't mind waiting in the foyer . . .'

'I don't mind waiting for you anywhere.'

Although I resented the spring in his step as he walked off, I knew that my consulting Janet was a mere formality. She emerged, moments later, in full Sheila-mode, complaining about the queue and pointing to the lack of women's lavatories in West End theatres as a flagrant case of sexual discrimination.

'Victorian architects probably believed that women peed in pellets like camels,' I said, but she was not to be appeased. At any other time, I would have joined her in a discussion of male prejudice but, for now, I simply wanted to tell her about my date. I confessed that I found the man attractive. She declared that to be obvious. I began to worry. It seemed that everyone could see through me but myself. Nevertheless I refused to be put off. Having moaned for so long about unattainable men, I could not afford too many scruples now that one had landed in my lap.

'But you don't know anything about him. These days you have to take extra care.'

'Don't worry,' I said, 'I'm the Marie Stopes of safe sex.'

'I don't just mean what you do, but who you do it with.'

'Believe me, I'm not as green as I look. I can tell when someone's on the level.'

'I thought I could too. And remember what happened.'

'He was straight.'

'He was a man. Still, I suppose you're old enough to take care of yourself.'

'If I don't meet somebody soon, age will be academic. But thanks for the warning. Now what about you? You never liked taking the Tube at night, even before.'

'I'll get a taxi. It's no big deal.'

'I could always go with you and then come back,' I said without enthusiasm.

'Now what would you do if I took you up on that?'

'Go. No question.'

'Yes, I know. You're one of the few people who restore my faith in human nature, at least the forty-nine per cent of it that's male. But, believe me, I'll be fine.' As if in proof, she flagged down a passing taxi, squeezing my hand as she climbed in. 'Have fun. You deserve it.'

'I intend to. I'll call you in the morning.'

'Not too early. Day of rest.' Her voice trailed away as the taxi pulled out. I was about to re-enter the theatre when I felt a hand on my shoulder. I swivelled round. The man had been standing behind me the whole time. He must have been listening to our conversation. I began to have second thoughts about going anywhere with him, but his reassuring smile put paid to them. With no further words, he hailed a cab.

'To Laverne's,' he said to me as it drew up.

'To Laverne's,' I repeated, having no idea either who or what it was.

'Frith Street,' he informed the driver as we moved off.

'I'm Duncan,' I said, in a belated introduction.

'Hello, Duncan,' he said, patting my thigh. I waited for him to elaborate.

'So what's your name?' I asked.

'Me? Oh just call me The Man.' I now felt certain that he had seen too many B-movies. Just call him The Man! That was all very well, but how would it work in practice? 'Same again, The Man?' 'How's life treating you, The Man?' 'Would you like to go to bed with me, The Man?'

'I can't call you that,' I said, torn between arousal and embarrassment.

'Suit yourself,' he said.

'What does your mother call you?'

'She's dead.'

'Oh, I'm sorry. Your father?'

'He's dead, too.'

'Oh Lord! Sisters? Brothers? Cousins? Uncles? Aunts?'

'All dead.'

'Where did you grow up? Atlantis?'

'Newcastle-under-Lyme.'

'So you have nobody in the world?'

'I didn't say that.'

'No. My mistake.' For some reason I felt satisfied, even though I had discovered next to nothing about him, not even his name. His readiness to sit in silence offered a challenge to one who regarded every conversational gap as an affront. I was aware, however, that I set too much store by words, and forced myself to follow his lead. A brief contretemps over paying the fare was resolved in his favour. He insisted that the entire evening would be his treat. While professing to take offence, I savoured the rare thrill of relinquishing control.

We were ushered into the club by a bouncer who appeared to be on loan from the Natural History Museum. As we walked into the crowded bar, I could make out a pianist playing show-tunes and felt grateful to the man (I had banished my qualms by shifting him metaphorically into lower case) for maintaining the theme of the evening. When I examined the clientele, however, my gratitude waned. It was composed largely of overweight businessmen in shiny suits, desperate to throw off the shackles of suburbia, accompanied by effeminate young men who aped the more outrageous women on their TV screens. Their whoops and screeches made it impossible to say anything of import, even if one could make oneself heard. I consoled myself with the champagne that the man had ordered. Now that I was sitting at his table, he all but ignored me, preferring to swap a few words with the various acquaintances who drifted past. I was not unduly concerned, enjoying my drink and the Cole Porter medley. I was, however, unnerved by the hard-boiled air of some of his associates. I had thought him so discriminating . . . but that was simply because he had chosen me.

He struck up a heated exchange with a fey young man who left, flashing me a look of compassion. I turned away, refusing to be pitied by anyone with peroxide hair. The man finally directed his attention to me. I thought it only fair to set out my ground-rules: condoms for everything, including oral sex. He seemed so startled that I wondered if I had, after all, misjudged his intentions and he had invited me for a discussion of classic Broadway musicals. His subsequent smile dispelled my anxieties. He took my hand, stroked my cheek and tweaked my ear, the latter somewhat painfully, but I said nothing for fear of destroying the mood.

'Are you all set to go home, then?' he asked.

'Oh yes, please,' I replied, hoping that I did not seem over-eager. 'I don't want to sound corny, but your place or mine?'

'Mine, I think,' he said.

'Mine may be nearer.'

'But I'm sure mine's bigger,' he said with a laugh. And it might have been the champagne, but I found my tolerance of innuendo greatly increased. We took another cab to Belsize Park and I was once again assailed by doubts, as much about my performance as his intentions. Going home with a stranger was so far outside my regular behaviour that I could not but be apprehensive. His coyness about his name made it the ultimate in anonymous sex. On the other hand, I could think of nowhere less threatening to have met than at the theatre. And, as I looked at the muscular figure sitting next to me, I knew that his grip extended way beyond the hand squeezing my knee.

We entered his house, which was as lavish as his extravagance with the champagne had led me to expect. The only thing that seemed out of keeping with the surroundings was him. I asked about his job and he told me that he worked in an office. Given that no one beneath the rank of managing director could afford to live in such a fashionable area, I assumed that this meant *work* as in *for himself*. He explained that the house belonged to his lover, before adding that I had no cause for concern since he was currently on a six-month secondment to a bank in Hong Kong. Neither the interval nor the distance removed my misgivings. As a single man, I had an enormous respect for the sanctity of couples. I would never forgive myself if I were the cause, however oblique, of one breaking up. He paid no attention to my scruples, citing his open relationship and insisting that, even as he spoke, Robert, his lover, would be sampling some local attraction – or at least he would if they weren't eight hours ahead.

Whether it was the effect of the drink or the hour or my libido, I allowed myself to be convinced. He led me upstairs but, before entering the bedroom, I snatched a moment to myself on the pretext of visiting the loo. On coming out, I found that all the lights in the house had been switched off. I had an uneasy suspicion that, given my earlier reticence, he supposed me to be someone who could only make love in the dark. I edged my way to the room, worried more about damaging his ornaments than injuring myself. I found him standing naked by the window. He walked over and pressed me to him. I was exhilarated by his touch and scrambled out of my clothes. He drew me on to the bed and we began to embrace. He immediately took the initiative, pinning my arms above my head and covering my face with kisses, before sweeping his tongue across the roof of my mouth. He thrilled all of my senses in turn, as he lapped my lips, whispered in my ear, pinched my nipples and licked me from neck to groin, leaving a thin trail of saliva glistening on my chest.

He grabbed a bottle of amyl nitrate and held it first under his and then under my nose. Ignoring my protests that I suffered from asthma, he pressed it to each of my nostrils in turn. A burning haze and jagged sharpness passed over me. My heart raced. I began to cough.

'No more,' I spluttered.

'Don't be such a wimp,' he mocked, and took an extended sniff from the bottle. I tried to wriggle out from under him but was pinned down by his knees. Then, without ceremony, he wrenched my legs in the air and thrust two fingers inside me. 'Nice and tight. Just how I like it.'

'Don't!' I screamed, as shocked by the intrusion as by the pain.

'I'm going to fuck you longer and harder and deeper than you've ever been fucked in your life.'

Things were moving both too fast and in the wrong direction. I made another attempt to break free but was locked in a brutal embrace. The man's strength, which had once excited me, now filled me with fear. I needed to keep all my senses alert but, like a poster boy for over-indulgence, I appeared to have lost at least half of them.

'Why are you doing this? I told you how things stood at Laverne's.'

'Oh, don't worry. I'm the condom king. I'm not going to risk catching anything.' He took out a packet of Durex and tore it open with his teeth.

'I don't just mean the virus. I'm not into penetration. To me, it's not an act of love but an assertion of power.'

'Maybe power turns me on.' He laughed and sniffed some more amyl.

'Surely the thing about being gay is that we can discard traditional roles? We can make love in different – more reciprocal – ways.'

'So you're kinky are you?'

'No, not at all! You've completely misunderstood. Look, I think I should go home. This is obviously not working for either of us. No hard feelings?' He responded by placing my hand on his rigid penis. 'Wouldn't you rather get some sleep?' I suggested.

'Just shut the fuck up!' he said and slapped me across the face. The pain I now felt was devoid of anything sexual. 'See what you've made me do. Why must you spoil everything?' His disappointment goaded him, and he gripped my neck in his armpit like a snake. I prayed for the strength that was supposed to surge up *in extremis*, but my muscles appeared to have atrophied. I tried to dissociate myself from what was happening by imagining myself back in my flat, listening to the original cast album of *Candide*, but a sting in my wrist brought me sharply to my senses. I looked up. He was tying me to the bedposts. I laughed out loud: half in disbelief, half in embarrassment that we should be acting out such a cheap scenario. But he mistook my confusion for scorn and slapped my face still harder. This time I tasted blood.

'Don't you fucking laugh at me, bitch!' he yelled. For a few moments the insult filled me with hope. *Bitch* had to be a joke. But the glint in his eye soon set me straight. The man was an obvious psychopath, with an imagination steeped in porn films, who was preparing to murder me. I had the clear vision of a drowning man – except that the water I was drowning in was spit.

My mind at first refused to accept the evidence. This was no schoolboy poised on a parapet targeting unsuspecting strangers, but a grown man aiming gobbets of spit at my face and then rubbing them in with his palm. I could not conceive of any possible pleasure he might derive from the act. There was no giving, no touching, no sharing; it was an expression of pure contempt. Then, without a word – even of derision – he wrenched my legs in the air and again plunged his fingers inside me. I yelled out, twisting and turning and tearing at my bonds. But the emptiness of the house mocked any hope of rescue, just as the tightness of the knots resisted all my attempts to break free.

'I know what you really want is to be fist-fucked,' he said. 'A tight little arse like that.'

I willed myself to pass out: to put an end to the torment by denying him the thrill of my humiliation; but I remained agonisingly alert. Excruciating pangs shot up my spine as I forced his fist out of me, heaving like a woman in labour. A momentary relief was followed by a hard smack on my buttocks.

'Please let me go,' I said. 'I'm truly sorry if I've spoilt your evening. I never realised you were into all this.'

'Everyone is,' he said. 'They just don't like to admit it. They think it isn't nice.' Then he rammed his penis into me like a drill. The pain was as relentless as the man was ruthless. He felt nothing for me. I was just an object into which he could pitch himself. This was not an act of affection but a test of strength. I knew I was crying; I knew I was bleeding; but every pore in my body felt dry. He accompanied his lunges with slaps, as though I were a horse he was breaking in. I was no longer Duncan: I was no longer a person; I was Suffering; I was Rage. He was assaulting me, filling me full of his filth and hate, sullying the core of my being. Finally, in a flurry of wheezes, he came. Then, moments later, he shifted his weight and slid out. He tore off the shrivelled condom in disgust.

My insides felt like a lavatory. I wanted to flush myself away. My eyes filled with tears that smarted like grit. I waited for his breathing to settle before asking him to untie me. I tried to sound as if I had caught myself on a bush. With much bad grace, he unfastened my left wrist, leaving me to unfasten the right. My fingers were stiff but I persevered until I had worked myself free. I suspected that he had fallen asleep, but I moved noise-lessly so as not to provoke him. I struggled into my clothes as though I had changed shape. I could feel myself seeping into my underpants. Groping in the dark, I inched my way down the stairs, no thought in my head but escape. I tugged at the front door, only to discover that it had been locked from inside.

Unable to stave off despair, I curled up on the mat like the animal to which I had been reduced. I lay there helplessly until, gathering all my remaining strength, I forced myself to go back to the room. The man was stretched out on his side, his penis protruding contemptuously. Images of carving-knives and cleavers formed in my mind, but I quickly dismissed them. They debased me almost as much as the assault itself. My one concern was to return to the sanctuary of home. I tapped him on the shoulder. Any hope of a gentle awakening was dashed by the depth of his sleep. He sprang up, confused as much by my presence as by my clothes. I explained the problem. He asked why I could not wait until morning. I replied, with an assumed jauntiness, that I could never sleep in a bed in which I'd had sex. Cursing me for my selfishness, he dragged himself up and grabbed the key.

Even as he fumbled with the lock, I suspected that he might change his mind and try to detain me. But his power had dwindled with his passion, and I was satisfied that I would prove to be the stronger. He had scarcely turned the key when I seized the door and bolted down the steps. I was convinced that, in spite of his being stark naked, he would follow me. My fears accompanied me down the road which, although deserted, echoed with voices and footsteps and sobs. Now that the imme-diate danger was past, I could allow myself other emotions. I hated the man but I blamed myself. I was nearly thirty years old, yet I had abandoned my principles as readily as a child lured into a stranger's car by a bar of chocolate. I scratched my face on an overhanging branch and was reassured to find that I could still feel simple pain. I was forced to walk the entire way to Kilburn, since every cab-driver in north-west London appeared to have conspired to lengthen my ordeal. The journey cleared my head, although nothing could cleanse my body. On reaching home, I stepped straight into the shower and let the water penetrate each pore of my skin. I ripped up my underwear and, even though it was not my sheets that had been stained, put fresh linen on the bed. I rocked myself to sleep.

I told the Agency that I had the flu and, for days, I refused to leave the flat. I was certain that I would bump into the man on every street corner. I convinced myself that he had indeed followed me home and was lurking outside in the shadows. Friends phoned, and it was as much as I could do to remain civil. I was in no mood for idle chatter, and yet there was no way that I could talk about the attack: I had suffered enough without exposing myself to scepticism and prurience. Many people refused to accept that a man could ever be raped. Others felt that it was what all gay men secretly desired. Their belief was not wholly unfounded. I recalled one – admittedly frivolous – discussion in my men's group, in which rape was cited as compensation for being in prison. Meanwhile Sheila and her sisters held it to be the ultimate heresy: an attempt by men to deny the uniqueness of women's suffering, and to turn themselves from perpetrators into victims.

There was one person whom I felt sure would sympathise – or rather empathise (I had discovered how much difference a prefix could make) – yet it was precisely because of her own ordeal that I was loath to burden Janet with mine. I delayed any disclosure until after her return to Prague. Then, one Sunday afternoon, tormented as much by the apparent restoration of normality as by the sewer flowing underneath, I opened my heart to her on the phone. The irony was that she felt as guilty as I had on hearing her revelations, except that her reasons were more specific. She declared that she had distrusted the man from the start but, since I had been so clearly smitten, she had put the suspicions from her mind.

'We're neither of us very reliable judges of character,' I remarked bitterly.

'Oh, I don't know. We must get it right sometimes,' she said. And, although she was more than six hundred miles away, I felt as if she were sitting next to me on the couch. Since then we have grown even closer, with a friendship that is neither defined by memory nor compromised by passion: a friendship that is as strong and as supple, as extensive and as intimate, as love. Now, if anyone ever questions my relationship with Janet, suggesting that our commitment to each other prevents us from finding a partner or that we are using one another to escape from our sexuality, my response is always the same: 'Yes, it does. Yes, we are. Isn't it great?'

The Marriage of Convenience

JUSTIN AND LOUISE were married in style but, although they made their vows in St James's Piccadilly and their speeches in the Café Royal, they reserved any personal declaration of love for the honeymoon. Then, on the back of a carefully selected postcard – four miniature snapshots with 'Greetings from Ibiza' blazed across them – they sent the same message to all their friends: 'Having a blissful time. We are very much in love. Thinking of you whenever we can spare a moment. Kisses, Justin and Louise.'

The honeymoon was a present from Justin's parents. Justin had initially turned down their offer, citing pressure of work on his spring collection. But they insisted that he owed it to himself, not to mention Louise. And, while she would never have admitted to it, he knew that she felt the same. He allowed himself to be won over, although not as far as his parents would have liked. His extensive phobias ruled out anywhere more exotic than Turkey, besides which, as he pointed out, the southern hemisphere held no allure for Louise. A host of wildly salacious travellers' tales had inspired him to visit Ibiza, and the honeymoon gave him the perfect excuse. Having found a hotel that was mixed enough to satisfy his parents (who were, after all, making the reservations) and lax enough to suit him, he looked forward to a stimulating break. So he was appalled when his father handed him his tickets in the Café Royal lobby and told him with a rugby-club grin that he had managed to book the honeymoon suite.

Justin decided to wait before breaking that piece of news to Louise. In any event he was soon caught up in a flurry of farewells, his hopes of a discreet getaway thwarted as two hundred wedding guests spilt out into Regent Street. He longed for his more ebullient friends to tone down their catcalls but was forced to admit that the matching lime-green going-away outfits he had designed for the occasion must bear some of the blame. He trusted that his stuffier relations (in particular his wealthy Uncle Desmond) would attribute the unrestrained kissing to his profession. He followed his new wife into the car, which was covered in so much foam that it looked as though it were about to be shaved. When he shared the thought with Louise, she smiled for the first time that afternoon. As they drove off to the clanking of a tin-can accompaniment, they turned to bestow a final wave on the sentimental family, cynical friends and bemused tourists gathered in their wake.

Halfway down Piccadilly, the driver stopped to detach the train and clear the window of foam, a task that was eased by a sudden cloudburst. 'At least the rain held off until now,' Louise said and then felt absurdly conventional, as she did once again in the departure lounge at Heathrow when she advised Justin against ordering another drink. 'Who's counting?' he asked, before adding, 'You're not married to me, you know!' Louise could not tell to what extent the remark was studied, but it had the effect of calming her nerves. The challenge of what lay ahead overwhelmed her. They had been best friends for years but it was a taxis-at-midnight friendship, whereas, now, thanks to his father's intervention, they faced two weeks of each other twenty-four hours a day. Under the circumstances, it was little wonder that he wanted another drink and, what was more, she would join him.

The flight was rough and Justin threw up discreetly into a paper bag. She restrained herself from informing him that he was anal even when he vomited. He promptly fell asleep and she took the opportunity to examine the man who had provided her with the new name on her passport, who had provided her with the new passport itself. She recalled all the years in which London had seemed as magical to her as the Emerald City. Now she was not only living there but she had married the Wizard. For, despite Justin's calculated air of insouciance, she knew that he was not merely wise but loyal and generous and sensitive to women. And, although she was not supposed to value such things, he was also extremely good-looking, with ash blond hair, limpid green eyes and cheek-bones far more delicate than her own. Above all, he was healthy. She had lost far too many friends over the past few years to contemplate the loss of one who was so special.

They landed on time, but the promised private chauffeuring to the hotel turned out to be in a packed coach. They were all set to protest when they bowed to the greater grievance of a group that had lost its luggage. While waiting to leave, Justin took a broad survey of their fellow passengers. They were largely couples, although he was pleased to note the presence of several single men. Louise was amused by his interest. Her affection for him both surprised and perplexed her. She had never before felt so close to any man. After fleeing New Zealand, she had embraced her sexuality as a political imperative: it was not just a question of who she was but of the way that she viewed the world. Yet she sometimes feared that she had acted too emphatically. Love had so many facets that some of them must involve men. She glanced at Justin who was eyeing a young Sri Lankan and felt a painful conflict of emotions. She resolved to rise above it and to enjoy the trip for what it was: a holiday not a honeymoon. It had been years since she had had a free fortnight and she was determined to put it to good use.

'What did you do on your honeymoon, Lou?' she could already hear people ask.

'I read Proust.' Her smile at the prospect was transmuted to Justin, who responded so warmly that she was plunged into further self-doubt. He informed her with relief that, whatever else, there were no children on the coach. Justin affected to loathe children, although she suspected him of being a closet Santa Claus. He had cruelly disappointed his grandmother, who had seen their marriage as the chance to add a 'great' to her name, by informing her that they were both far too absorbed in their careers to consider starting a family. In some unforeseen way, which she could attribute only to the stresses of the day, Louise felt some of that disappointment herself.

They arrived at the hotel and were shown straight to their suite. Justin's parents had done them proud. The sitting room was filled with flowers, the sight of which brought tears to their eyes: Louise attributing hers to her allergies and Justin his to exhaustion. They moved into the bedroom and stared at the large, beautifully appointed but undeniably solitary bed.

'I'm so sorry,' Justin said, 'I'll ring down and ask them to change it.'

'Not at eleven o'clock at night, you won't,' Louise said, adopting an air of pragmatism. 'Even at this hotel, it might seem rather odd. We are supposed to be on our honeymoon.'

'True.'

'Still, we have slept together before.'

'We have?'

'Although it obviously didn't make much of an impression on you.' She was unable to suppress a note of irritation from her voice. She was terrified that she might betray herself. Although the notion that she might have anything to betray simply increased her irritation.

'So when did the dastardly deed occur?'

'After Juliet and Tammy's Alternative Valentine's Day party.'

'Oh God, that. When Fiona took your bag and you said I was the only man you'd feel safe with.'

'Did I really? Yes, I did.'

'Though I think even Bill Clinton could legitimately have called it sleeping. As far as I remember you were on the bed and I was on the couch.'

'Yes, I don't know why I brought it up. I'm not thinking straight.'

Justin raised his eyebrow but had the grace to refrain from the obvious pun, which would have left her more flustered than ever. She felt as though she were betraying the convictions of a lifetime – or at least of an adult-time. Her childhood convictions had been very different. Then she suddenly smiled. What was attractive about Justin was his delicacy . . . his consideration; in other words, his feminine qualities. He was very different from the average man. Her smile faded. In the ways that were attracting her right then, he was exactly the same.

'It's all right. You needn't look so horrified. I don't intend to claim my conjugal rights.'

'No, of course not.' She choked back a gasp, which turned into a giggle. She was lucky that he had been making a joke.

'So you don't need to roll out the barbed wire. Just you stick to your side and I'll stick to mine. We can pretend we're Clark Gable and Claudette Colbert.'

'You should know that Hollywood references are lost on me.'

'Do dykes have no culture outside country music?'

'I'm shattered, Justin. Can we save the repartee for the morning? I'm desperate to get some sleep.'

'Whatever. Do you want to use the bathroom first? I promise I won't peep.'

'Right.' Pausing only to grab a sponge-bag and pyjamas from her case, she hurried out.

Justin flung himself on the bed and wondered if it were mere tiredness that was making him feel different. He attached no sacramental significance to marriage. St James's had been purely to please his mother (the vicar holding sexual equality in higher esteem than canon law). There was nevertheless no doubt that he had undergone a significant change. He observed himself as though he were a character in a play: *Here you may see Justin the married man.* Several of his friends had accused him of acting cynically. He was poised on the brink of an international career, and in US boardrooms a wife was a distinct advantage – even for a dress designer. In response, he had pointed them to his record. He had never dodged a fight or ducked an issue. Louise's plight, however, was more pressing than his own scruples. Her visa was about to run out and she faced a flight back to Auckland and a family whom she detested with a venom that never ceased to amaze him: so much so that, as far as he knew, she had not even told them of the wedding. A husband had been her only hope, and he was the obvious candidate. They had warmed to each other from the start, braving the frostiness of her hardline friends. She, on the other hand, rejected separatism. She believed that the way forward lay in coming together as brothers and sisters . . . or, in their case, he reflected, husbands and wives.

'A penny for them!' Louise said, as she emerged from the bathroom. 'Although, given the way you jumped, I'd be prepared to make it a pound.'

Gazing up at her, Justin felt exposed, even though she was the one in pyjamas. He was struck by the patch of skin below her neck. It was so fresh and flawless. She looked surprisingly girlish in such masculine attire. It clung to every curve in her body. Women's bodies had always held a strong fascination for him, although he had explored it exclusively on his drawing board.

'I'm done,' Louise said. 'It's all yours. But I think there's something wrong with the loo. Don't yank it.'

'I never yank anything. It makes you go blind.'

'Oh, ha ha,' she said, masking her genuine laugh with an ironic one. She leant over and lightly kissed his cheek, which surprised him since she had never shown any physical affection for him before. To his even greater surprise, he liked it. He retreated to the bathroom where, standing at the mirror, he took a long cool look at his body. It was a pleasing Tanning Shop shade of brown (he gave thanks for all the misspent lunch hours), but he worried that she would find him too skinny. Then he remembered that this was not some censorious stranger he had met in a club, but Louise. She would not find him anything at all. He brushed his teeth and worried about the purity of the water. He used the loo and worried about yanking it. Then he put on the unfamiliar pyjamas and returned to the bedroom.

'I thought you'd be neatly tucked up.'

'I didn't know which side you liked to sleep on.'

'I don't really have a preference, although I suppose, ideologically, it should be on the left.'

'Oh dear. Me too.'

'Then we'll take it in turns. You first.'

They climbed into bed with a first-night-at-boarding-school bashfulness. Each was acutely aware of the other's body, not daring to move for fear of an inadvertent – or, worse, inappropriate – touch. Justin prayed that his toothpaste masked any lingering trace of alcohol: Louise that she would not succumb to wind. In spite of their unease, they fell rapidly asleep: Justin dreaming of a grand hotel full of dwarves; Louise of a vast plain inhabited by giraffes. On waking, although both were exercised by the symbolism, they claimed to have remembered nothing. The casual intimacy of the past was compromised by their new relationship. Justin ordered breakfast but, when the trolley arrived, it simply intensified their misgivings for, set among the fruit and the rolls and the coffee, was a bottle of Spanish champagne. When Justin read out the compliments of the management, Louise declared that she felt as if she had stolen a disabled person's parking space.

In spite of their reservations, they ate – and drank – heartily, after which they prepared for a day by the pool. Justin felt roguish and put on his skimpiest pair of trunks, intended to emphasise both the ambiguity of his appeal and the masculinity of his body. Louise put on a fluorescent orange bikini that Justin had designed for her and which she had initially refused to pack. Having relented, she was wearing it now to please him – although a part of her hoped that his pleasure would go beyond professional pride. She even allowed herself to be flattered by the unabashed stares she received from two hirsute Italians in the lift. She longed for Justin to look at her through their eyes, although the truth was that he had eyes only for them.

They made their way outside to find all the sunbeds taken. They appealed to the attendant who procured two from his store, but neither Justin's mime nor Louise's bikini led to similar success with a parasol.

'You have to be down here at seven to bag your places,' a well-toned man bronzing effortlessly nearby told them. 'It's the Germans,' he added to Justin, as Louise went off to dip her toes in the pool.

'You're reading a German paper.'

'No. I just lay it out every morning to make sure no one will talk to me.'

'You started talking to me.'

'Yes. Funny that.'

'I'm not getting up at seven o'clock for anything.'

'You're right. It can be a royal pain if you've been doing the clubs the night before.'

Justin smiled. Once again his instincts had proved to be impeccable. 'I aim to go in for a fair bit of that myself,' he said.

'Who've you brought with you? Your sister?' the man asked.

'Not exactly. She's more like my wife. In fact, we're on our honeymoon. But we're each doing our own thing.'

'That's a new one on me. I've heard of open marriages before but this is my first open honeymoon.'

'It's a long story.'

'It sounds it.'

'What's your name by the way?'

'Mike.'

'Hi Mike, I'm Justin.'

'And I'm Lou. Good to meet you.'

Justin scowled as she dispelled the mood as swiftly as a call of last orders. 'You're dripping on me!'

'You won't melt. Justin, is there no way we can wheedle an umbrella from somewhere? Even covered in oil, I shall burn to a frazzle.'

'You heard what the guy said.'

'I heard but I didn't follow.'

'"No" is pretty universal.'

'Don't worry, Lou,' Mike said. 'You take mine. I've been here for ten days. My body's pretty much inured.'

Justin cast an appraising eye over the evidence.

'No, I couldn't.'

'Why ever not? It'll give me an excuse to sit over there by Justin. Or are you worried about burning too?'

'Not at all. Look at me. I've caught the sun at home.'

Louise flashed him a sceptical look which he steadfastly ignored. She lay back on the recently vacated lounger and gazed at the two men. She felt a pang which she compared to that of a mother grateful that her son had found another little boy to play with and yet sad that each new companion took him further away from her.

'What are you smiling at?' Justin called across.

'You,' she answered pertly.

'Just get on with your Proust. You don't need to bother about me.'

'But I do,' she replied with forced nonchalance. She bitterly upbraided herself. She had complained often enough about men foisting themselves on women, now here she was trying to do the same to him. Justin was her friend: her very own knight in shining armour, but he had made it quite clear that, once the dragon was dead, it was business as usual. She was appalled by her selfishness. She ought to be pleased that he had found a kindred spirit – after all, he was on his honeymoon. She resolutely turned the first page of *Swann's Way*.

Justin watched as Mike folded himself languorously on the lounger beside him.

'I don't want to cause a row,' Mike said.

'I beg your pardon?'

'Between you and your wife.'

'She's not that kind of wife.' Justin was torn between loyalty and lust. As ever, lust triumphed. 'It was a marriage of convenience.'

'How very nineteenth century!'

'When the law's nineteenth century, we don't have much choice. I expect you've grasped the situation.'

'I made an informed guess.'

'Louise is from New Zealand and had come to the end of her visa. She was so desperate she was even considering advertising. We'd known each other a couple of years, ever since she went to work for my accountant. We hit it off so well that I asked her to become my business manager. I'm a designer. So, apart from anything else, it made good commercial sense. But, above all, it appealed to the romantic in me – like Auden marrying Erika Mann to save her from the Nazis. I'm not suggesting that the Kiwis are in the same league, but still . . .'

'Point taken. Though it's ironic. Everyone else I know wants to get out of England.'

'According to Louise, however bad things are for us, they're a hundred times worse down under.'

'Then they have my deepest sympathies.'

'And mine. Which is why I made her the offer. And it thrilled my parents. It's pathetic really. I came out to them when I was at St Martin's and they've known several of my boyfriends. They must think I was going through an adolescent phase till the age of thirty-two. I suppose that's why they went way over the top with the wedding: to convince themselves as much as everyone else. Louise felt a dreadful fraud but I just sat back and enjoyed it. A good deed for which I'm showered with presents: what could be better?'

'But why on earth have you come to Ibiza?'

'A chap must be allowed a little fun on his honeymoon.'

'So I see.'

Justin pretended not to notice as Mike's gaze strayed to his trunks, which had clearly created the requisite stir. They chattered on, bypassing several stages on the regular route to intimacy. They were so engrossed in their conversation that they were taken aback when Louise came to claim Justin for lunch.

'Everyone else has gone in. The pool's deserted.'

'Why don't you grab a table? I'll just finish this story I'm boring Mike with and then I'll be right with you.'

'Fine.' For all her good resolutions, Louise could not help feeling ill-used. She might not expect Justin's full attention but she did merit some consideration. She was determined not to lose face in front of Mike. 'Thanks again for the loan of the umbrella. It saved my life.'

'Glad to be of service, ma'am,' he replied, saluting her in a way that Louise found infantile but Justin found hilarious. 'It's yours for the afternoon. I'm going trolling on the beaches.'

'You are?' Justin felt his trunks become visibly skimpier.

'Would you like to tag along?'

'I don't know,' he lied. 'It all depends on Louise.'

'I'm sure you won't miss him, will you?' Mike asked, exposing her to the full force of his tanned smile. 'You don't have him on a ball and chain.'

'Of course not.' Louise's voice became ice. 'Justin can do whatever he wants. He's a free agent.'

Justin feared that his wants were becoming embarrassingly obvious. He crossed his legs. 'Well, if you're sure you don't mind. And you did say you wanted to make headway with Proust.'

'I've read quite enough for one day, thank you.' Louise refused to let him off lightly. 'About a spoilt boy obsessed with bedtime kisses.'

'Sounds my kind of guy,' Mike said, and Louise saw that she was bested. 'Meet you back here at three-thirty then?'

'Yes sir,' Justin replied. He followed Louise to the dining room, longing – but not daring – to suggest that they invite Mike to join them. Irritated by her disapproval, he determined to merit it. 'Is something bugging you?'

'Sometimes you can be really dense.'

'What?'

'I don't mind if you humiliate me, but I do mind your humiliating yourself.'

'That's awfully big of you, but I'm afraid you've lost me.'

'The way you threw yourself at that man.'

'Don't be absurd. We had a perfectly friendly conversation.'

'The whole hotel was watching.'

'Then I pity them if they have nothing better to do,' he declared grandly.

'It's when they start to pity me that I worry.'

'Don't. Not everyone has your suspicious mind. Look at us: we're a couple of newly-weds. We positively reek of post-coital bliss. Half the people in the hotel know nothing, and the other half couldn't give a damn.'

'I wouldn't be so sure.'

'Besides, there's nothing to stop you hooking up with someone. I've already spotted several foxy sisters.'

'I never knew you were such an expert. Anyway, who says I want a woman?'

'What?' Justin choked on his calamares.

'I mean not just for the sake of it. We don't all share your high-speed seduction techniques.'

'More fool you then.' Justin felt himself being forced into a position of which he did not altogether approve.

'What's more, he's probably riddled with disease.'

'Oh, thanks a bunch!' Justin pushed his plate into the middle of the table.

'I'm sorry.' Louise acknowledged that she had gone too far, not in her concern for him but in her manner of expressing it. 'But you can never be too careful.'

'And you know that I always am. You can at least trust me on that point.'

'I do,' she said, placing her hand on his. 'I promise.' Further conflict was forestalled by the arrival of the sorbets. After lunch, they returned to their room for a siesta. Louise moaned about the heat and yet, the moment that Justin left for his rendezvous with Mike, she rolled across and lay in his warmth.

Justin met Mike by the pool and they took the bus to the coast. They strode rapidly across three bays and Justin noticed that first the women and children and then the clothes disappeared. By the time Mike began to slow down, they were surrounded by a beachful of naked men. In a gesture of jubilation, Justin tore off his trunks. He wondered if his penis might catch the sun and if he dared ask Mike to rub in some oil. He sauntered along the sand beside Mike, who appeared to be in his element, as attuned to the aesthetic as his mother would be in the National Gallery. He longed to know if any of the men had noticed him or if, in the abundance of bodies beautiful, his own had been relegated to the Reserve Collection. His speculation was swiftly resolved as a succession of heads turned his way, but he balked at the nakedness of the glances (so much less innocent than the bodies). Heterosexuals at least maintained a modicum of decorum, if only because women would not allow it any other way.

'Let's check out the action in the dunes,' Mike suggested. Justin agreed, with a pang of nostalgia for his Suffolk summers. He realised that he had not set foot on a sand-dune for twenty-five years. A very different sight awaited him from that of his childhood memories. Behind each mound were men engaging in every permutation of pleasure. It was as though the meagre camouflage had removed any remaining restraint. Justin thought with longing of Louise. Hers was a world immune from all this, a world of feelings rather than sensations, and it was one to which he was eager to return. Yet the suggestion struck at the core of his being. He was a gay man, and both his identity and his heritage had been dearly bought. He turned to share his misgivings with Mike, who had meanwhile jumped into a clump of human foliage with a shout of 'last one in's a sissy'. In the face of the sort of coercion that he had resisted all his life, Justin shook his head, put on his trunks and returned to the bus stop alone.

Mike's taunt echoed in his head through both the lengthy

wait and the bumpy ride. He wondered if it might provide the reason for the frenzied fumbling in the dunes: not the liberation of desire, but the determination not to be thought sissies. He would have liked to test the theory on Louise, but he had no idea how to phrase it. They had discussed everything about their respective sexualities bar the mechanics. And, although he found himself reflecting increasingly fondly on hers, he had no doubt that she would be disgusted by his.

He had no opportunity to raise the subject at dinner, since Louise never once mentioned Mike or the beach or their lunchtime quarrel but launched into a long and, to Justin, inexplicable discourse on the nature of memories and whether they were systematically ordered like books in a library, readily accessible with the correct code, or random and out of reach. Then, leaving him to chew over her remarks, she announced that her nerves were shot from all the excitement of the last few days and she was in desperate need of an early night. Having surprised both himself and her by his offer to escort her upstairs, Justin felt strangely deflated when she turned it down. As he stood to see her out, he found that he too was flagging and decided that, after a quick brandy on the terrace, he would follow her. No sooner had he found a table and evaded the attentions of a persistent guitarist than Mike joined him.

'I'm off into town in an hour or so to nosy round some of the clubs. Want to come?'

'I'd have thought you'd be exhausted after your exertions this afternoon.' Justin tried to sound reproachful but not priggish.

'Not me. I'm a five-times-a-day man, me,' Mike said with a laugh. 'But what happened to you? I looked up and you'd disappeared.'

'It's not really my scene. I prefer a prick I can put a name to. So you'd better count me out. Besides, I told Louise I'd be up shortly.'

'She Who Must Be Obeyed, eh?'

'Not at all. She was feeling off-colour. I think she must have had too much sun.'

'I gave her my parasol. What more can a man do?'

'Nothing. You were very kind. But you're not her husband.'

'Don't tell me she's holding you to the vows?'

'I don't see why you're being so disagreeable. You know the score. Of course I'd like to come along.'

'So what's stopping you?'

'I'll go up and check on Louise. If she's feeling better, I'll come. Just for an hour or so.'

Justin walked through the foyer feeling trapped. The sensible thing would be to go upstairs and stay there. He would far rather snuggle next to Louise than go out clubbing with Mike. But that preference itself disconcerted him. He sensed a change in his body greater than any he had known since adolescence. It was pointless attributing it to the climate since he had felt nothing like it in Cap Ferrat. He crept into the bedroom. To his surprise, Louise was fast asleep. He had supposed her to be beating a tactical retreat, but that was to project his own impulses on to her. He felt more at sea than ever. He had been certain that she would be awake and he would be able to ask her advice (it was strange how much he was coming to rely on it). She would be justly enraged if he disturbed her: he was her husband not her son. And yet he could not escape the world of the office where she was the provident manager and he the impetuous designer who, for all his acclaim, felt that he was turning out sketches much as he had done at school. He decided to take her impassivity as a sign that he should accept Mike's offer, putting an end once and for all to his confusions. So he hurried down to the terrace and declared himself ready to paint the town pink.

They began the evening in a homely bar run by two middle-aged Englishmen who resembled a pair of bookends, except that one had hair on his head and the other on his chin. They downed a beer beneath the benevolent gaze of minor members of the Royal Family, before moving on to the harder stuff, in every sense. Shortly after 2 a.m., Justin made his first ever appearance in a backroom. The pitch blackness illuminated by the odd cigarette put him in mind of a ghost train, except that instead of feathers brushing his face there were hands. Since Mike was determined to be a participant rather than a guide, he was left to stumble about on his own. He was cursed in a variety of impenetrable accents, which challenged his belief that the language of love was as important as the act. He searched for the exit, but there was no break in the darkness and what he thought were walls were men. Hands emerged to maul him, followed by mouths, one of which claimed its prize. He was ashamed, and humiliated that his shame had not communicated itself to every organ of his body. He speculated on the man who was engorging him: was he young or old, thin or fat, good-looking or ugly? He almost added *alive or dead* since, for all he knew, he was in the grip of some spirit of pleasures past with a vampire-like yearning to drain him dry. He felt as though he had been cast into Hell, while from all sides he was greeted by the moaning of men in seventh heaven. But their ecstasy was too easy: sex had to be more than a discharge. By siting it in the back of a bar, they made it as banal as after-hours drinking. He was determined to hold out for more: a more that, despite his best endeavours, was personified by Louise. So, peeling himself from his partner and groping his way around the room, he headed for the door. As he did, he tripped over a man in a sling and slid into a pool of vomit.

He felt as disgusting as he smelt. He tore off his shirt and walked into the street, desperate to expose his body to the air, which was too muggy to offer even a symbolic purge. No taxi would stop for him and he trudged back to the bus. Reaching the hotel, he braved the censorious eyes that followed him through the foyer and went up to his suite. Safely installed in the sitting room, he made out the silhouetted figure of Louise asleep in bed. He longed for her to wake but of her own accord, so he tramped into the bathroom and turned on the shower full blast.

'Justin, is that you?'

'Give me a moment. I'm wet.'

'What time is it?'

'Around three-thirty. I'm not sure.'

'Where on earth have you been . . . Good God, what's happened to your shirt? It smells disgusting.'

Satisfied that he had removed at least the visible dirt, Justin returned to the bedroom. 'Give me that. I'm going to chuck it.' He crumpled the shirt into a ball and pounded it into the bin.

'Tell me what happened!'

'I slipped in something vile in a backroom. I went cruising with Mike.'

'I see.'

'For the first and last time, believe me.'

'The last?' she asked tentatively.

'I don't think gay bars hold much attraction for me any more.'

'You prefer to meet people in different ways?'

'Or maybe different people.'

He sat down beside her on the bed and sank his head into her lap. She smelt warm and doughy. He sensed her hesitating over where to put her hands before slowly starting to stroke his hair. He was suffused with peace. He clasped her more tightly. Her presence was comforting and, at the same time, challenging. He felt both their bodies stir under the unfamiliar touch. He wondered if she were half-asleep and unaware of what he was doing. He wondered if he were half-drunk and unaware of what he was doing. Nevertheless, he did not break off but gently undid her pyjama jacket and caressed her breasts.

She felt his hands on her breasts and, for the first time with a man, she did not feel alone. She undertook her own exploration, fondling his chest and encountering the unexpected springiness of his nipples. She tentatively loosened the towel around his waist and found herself faced with his erection. The organ that had oppressed her so profoundly in the past, that had seemed so arrogant in its demands, so contemptible in its egotism, now seemed so right. She was pleased that it was big. And she brushed it lightly with her fingers.

'I'm sorry,' he said, 'but it's the way I feel.'

'Don't apologise,' she said, 'maybe I feel the same way.'

'You do?' Justin spun between amazement, apprehension and delight. 'Do you mean you'd like . . .?'

'I think so. That is if it's what you have in mind.'

'Absolutely! But I'm afraid of disappointing you. You know what they say about the flesh being weak.' The tinniness of Justin's laugh betrayed his anxiety.

'You needn't worry. And you have nothing to prove. I'm as new to this as you. It'll be my first time in years.'

'It'll be my first time ever.'

'Really?'

'Mad, isn't it? Would anyone design a car without ever having looked beneath a bonnet?'

'Do you have any condoms?'

'Of course. They're extra-strong ones, specially intended for . . .'

'Never mind. I'm sure they'll be perfect.'

'Shall I switch off the light?'

'Not unless you particularly want to.'

'No. I want to see everything.'

'Me too.'

They lay in each other's arms, their conversation stilled to the sound of their breathing. Justin had never imagined that the female body could be so accommodating: not just the perfect vehicle for his clothes but the perfect complement for his desires. He slid his mouth over Louise's stomach and into crevices from which he had previously shrunk. He licked timidly between her legs and found a richness where he had feared blood. Scarred by his own rough partners, he entered her with meticulous tenderness. Even so, he met with such an intense shudder that he hurried to withdraw, only to be checked by an eager hand and an assurance that she was trembling not from pain but from pleasure. So he thrust harder and harder until he thought that they would both burst. Finally, when neither could hold back any longer, they came at the very same moment. Their pleasure was as indivisible as their bodies. There was no incongruence in their love.

They slept through the morning. Justin woke first in a glow of satisfaction, which turned to shyness when he saw where he was resting his hand. He was determined to preserve the mood and, disentangling himself from Louise, issued detailed instructions to the kitchen regarding their lunch. Half an hour later, a waiter wheeled a trolley into the sitting room, and Justin roused Louise by smearing her lips with champagne.

'Champagne – and it's French!' Louise exclaimed, as Justin replaced his fingertips with a glass. 'Are they mind-readers? Or will we be brought a bottle every day?'

'Apparently the people in the room underneath complained about the noise. So the management put two and two together.'

'No, really? Oh you bastard!' She flung a pillow in his face.

'Take care. Remember the *Vogue* photo-shoot.'

'I'm sorry. I'm a little confused.'

'Lucky you. I'm completely baffled.'

'Justin, are we mad?'

'Probably. Does it matter?'

'Not to me. But I thought that it might to you.'

'It's only straight men who resort to the "God was I drunk last night" excuse.'

'And you're not straight?'

'I'm afraid not. But I think I can be for you. Isn't that the ultimate female accolade?'

'In my case, you'd have to become a lesbian.'

'That might be beyond even my capability. Can't we just enjoy what we have and leave labels to the baggage handlers at airports?'

'I can if you can.'

'That's settled then. We're going to stay here for ever and ever – or at any rate for the next twelve days. We won't set foot outside the room but send down for meals and sunbathe on the balcony and talk and sleep and make love until we break the record.'

'I think I achieved a personal best last night.'

'That was just the Commonwealth Games. I've got my sights set on the Olympics.' Louise placed a kiss like a medal on his chest.

They stuck to their plan, keeping to their room for several days, to the satisfaction of the more conventional of their fellow guests and to the bemusement of Mike, who left three messages which Justin chose not to answer. He had not spent so long alone with anyone since he had been quarantined for measles at prep school. When he told Louise, she feigned outrage and asked if he were comparing her to an adolescent boy. 'Pre-pubescent, if you must know,' he replied. 'And, no, I'm not. Certainly not with Brick Henshaw. Or with anyone else for that matter. That's what's so amazing. There are no comparisons. There can be no comparisons. There's simply you.'

Louise, recalling his impatience with his mother's emotionalism and fearful of the one comparison that he might make, choked back her tears. She distracted herself by pushing him down on the bed and sliding her tongue along his stomach. She was amazed at how much she savoured the tanginess of his skin. She had always presumed that sex would present an obstacle to their intimacy. Now she found that it was the reverse. She relished the immediacy of his responses – the flagrancy of his excitement – which she matched with a passion that startled her.

After a week, feeling guilty at having seen so little of the island, they hired a car. They used it once before deciding that they could see all that they wanted from their room. They even bought presents at the wildly overpriced hotel boutique, although Louise drew the line at 'Greetings from Ibiza' T-shirts.

'You may see them as ironic, but you're not the one who has to wear them. I let you get away with the postcards, which might have come from Christchurch in the Fifties. I'm sure people will think we're being camp.'

'No. It's precisely because they're so tacky, they'll know we're sincere. Don't forget I've built a career on subverting bad taste.'

'I still think you'll find we've some explaining to do.'

Louise was right. The only bad taste that concerned their friends was in the message, and they quizzed them about it as soon as they arrived home.

'Why on earth did you send those postcards? All the authorities required was proof of a marriage. They're not going to cross-examine the chambermaids or give Lou an internal examination at Heathrow.'

They could only smile at their friends' disbelief as they assured them that what they had written on the cards was true. They intended to live together as man and wife.

'You must be insane,' an ex-lover of Justin's informed him. 'A leopard can't change his spots.'

'Maybe not. But what if he discovers he's actually a cheetah who's been rolling in the mud?'

Louise, who was listening, laughed. 'Of course there are issues,' she said. 'But there are for any couple. At least we're wise to them. Be happy for us please.'

Few of their friends were inclined to oblige. Those who took the relationship seriously berated them for their defection: those who were more cynical placed bets on how long it would last. Neither Justin nor Louise, however, was deterred by such disapproval. Far from renouncing their honeymoon romance, they found their love for each other deepening as they integrated it into everyday life until, after nearly a year of marriage, Justin rang his grandmother with the news that she would soon be able to add the coveted adjective to her name.

'Of course it does happen,' one of Louise's friends told another. 'My secretary had an arranged marriage and she's potty about her husband.'

'It's not the same,' her companion replied. 'Lou comes from New Zealand not Karachi. It was meant to be a marriage of convenience. Love shouldn't have come into it at all.'

Virtual Love

'DO YOU WANT green beans or courgettes with your veal?' Keith called from the kitchen, as Craig prepared for another evening of domesticity. 'Craig . . .'

'I heard you.'

'Then why not answer me?'

Craig found himself mimicking the querulous rhythm in his head. Keith knew that he took no interest in what he ate, always provided that it was not salad. Keith's brief flirtation with the *Cranks Recipe Book* had placed a greater strain on their relationship than almost anything else over the past six years. He was sure that he only consulted him in order to make him feel guilty, to underline the uneven distribution of their household chores. that Craig's gardening was seasonal and his do-it-yourself sporadic, whereas Keith's cooking and cleaning and shopping took place every day. But then Keith gleaned almost as much pleasure from picturing himself as a drudge as he did from performing the tasks themselves. His face, while polishing the pine, was little short of ecstatic. It would be as cruel to deny him his secular martyrdom as to deny St Catherine her wheel.

'Courgettes,' he shouted. 'I'd prefer courgettes.'

'Oh that's typical. Just when I've opened the beans.'

Craig smiled. Until he moved in with Keith, he had never appreciated the truth behind situation comedy.

'Fine. Then make it beans. It really couldn't matter less.'

'I knew I should have gone for courgettes. I'd have rather. But I was afraid you'd see it as only thinking about myself.'

'No, I wouldn't, Keith. Believe me.' The fact was that he longed for Keith to think more about himself: at work, at home and, not least, in bed. The problem with living with a doormat was that you automatically wiped your feet on it. Keith put him in mind of a doormat with 'Welcome' stamped across it – although, as far as he was concerned, that message had worn a little thin.

Six years ago, three months had struck him as a long-term relationship. He was twenty-seven and as self-confident as the exigencies of the London gay scene would allow. He enjoyed an income that screamed Spend Me and a lifestyle that obliged. He had a job as a tour agent that enabled him to travel the world, sampling all the local customs – not to mention the customers. And yet, in those rare moments that he dared to articulate it (generally, late on a Sunday afternoon), he was aware of a dissatisfaction. While determined to avoid any parody of his parents, he felt the need for somebody to share his life: somebody who could give the *me* meaning. Just when those feelings were becoming harder to ignore, he had met Keith in an off-licence. That in itself was a minor miracle, since Keith was as abstemious as he was shy. On this occasion, he had been buying a bottle of wine to take to a party. He had ended up drinking it in bed with Craig.

In retrospect, it was clear that alcohol had played a still greater part in bringing them together. Craig had long lived by his libido but, while sex came easily to a man of his statistics, he found that it was increasingly difficult to enjoy sober. But the drinks that he took to stiffen his resolve had quite the opposite effect on his body, and left him feeling more wretched than before. Keith dispelled his anxieties. When he was with him, his drinking was purely social. Nor did he have to bolster himself in any other way since Keith, who sold china at Selfridges and whose contact with foreign culture was confined to tapas bars and tango classes, was totally dazzled by his traveller's tales. Although he soon tired of Keith's admiration, Craig experienced a sense of peace in his presence that he did nowhere else. And yet, when he thought of him, as he did suprisingly often, it was with far more than gratitude. So, on their six-month anniversary, taking the initiative as he had always known he must, he invited Keith to share his flat.

Keith moved in a week later, along with his potted plants, his Teasmade and a collection of Capo di Monte figurines, on to which Craig directed the hostility he had previously reserved for his aunts. Although Keith took up remarkably little space, his very self-effacement became oppressive and, after eighteen months, Craig suggested that they sell the flat and buy a house. They took out a joint mortgage on a Fifties semi in Willesden, which was the closest they came to an official recognition of their union. Craig left all the decorating decisions to Keith, both because they mattered so much more to him and because his taste, though predictable, was sound. Keith had never been happier, but his very pleasure stood as a reproach to Craig who, for all the affection (a longer and a safer word than love) that he felt for him, experienced a gnawing edge of discontent. The world was full of available men and yet, when he had broached the subject of an open relationship, or even the occasional threesome, he had caused Keith such palpable pain that he had felt unable to mention it again.

It nevertheless struck him as bitterly unfair that he should pay the price of Keith's insecurities. He might be on the wrong side of thirty, but he still commanded his share of attention. He reflected with relish on the body-builder in Key West only last summer who had asked him where he was studying. Keith, who was conclusive proof that travel did not broaden every mind, accused him of flaunting himself. 'If you've got it, flaunt it,' he had replied, for want of anything more cutting. And therein lay the rub: he had it and Keith did not. Of course, Keith had many admirable qualities, but that elusive *it* was not among them. A less honourable man would have had affairs behind Keith's back, but he had never been unfaithful to him – at least not in England (he had decided very early on in their relationship that abroad did not count). He lived, however, in a constant state of intellectual infidelity, while enough of his Sunday School training remained to leave him uneasy about adulteries *in his heart*.

His fantasy lovers were all that Keith was not: impulsive, rough, and, in every sense, dirty. They had not settled for wolf-cub badges in love-making, but had gone on to become leaders of the pack. He longed to spice up his sex life, but Keith interpreted every suggestion as a criticism of what had gone before. Thinking he had hit on the perfect analogy, he compared it to trying out a new recipe, which Keith wilfully misread as an admission that he wanted 'fresh meat'. He refused to settle for Saga Holiday sex when he could still hold his own at Club 18–30. If only Keith would give him a sign that an orgasm was more than a prelude to a conversation about curtains; if only he would not describe making a pass as 'hitting beneath the belt' or inform him, as he switched off the light, that he was 'in the mood for a nice cuddle'; if only he didn't make romance seem as unappetising as a choice between green beans and courgettes.

'*C'est servi!*' Keith's chirpy tones penetrated his reverie. He had been taking a French evening class for two years. At first Craig pretended that it was an alibi for a weekly assignation with a fetishist. He conjured up ever more bizarre images of Keith, swathed from head to toe in rubber, throwing cream cakes at a bank-manager naked except for a bib, but they swiftly collapsed when he joined 'the other husbands', a phrase that even now filled him with horror, for an open evening at the end of term. Two hours of listening to the group's stilted prattle was torment enough, but it was even worse when, on holiday in Corsica the following summer, Keith had insisted on testing his language skills on every unsuspecting stranger. He had enjoyed himself so much that he proposed returning the next year. Craig, however, refused, citing the hundreds of places they had still to visit. In the event, he made a third booking for Key West.

'*Blanquette de veau.*' Keith lifted it from the oven as tenderly as Pharaoh's daughter picking Moses out of the rushes.

'Looks good,' Craig said, praying that Keith was not about to fetch his Polaroid, as was his wont for his more notable efforts.

'*Bon appetit,*' Keith said. Craig strummed his fingers on the table and Keith warned him that he would scratch the varnish. To demonstrate his indifference, he strummed all the harder and caught his nail in the crack.

The veal was fine, but the beans were overcooked.

'That's your fault,' Keith said.

'It always is.'

'I'd like to see you make dinner for a change.'

'No, you wouldn't. Forget "green beans or courgettes?", it'd be "HP or Heinz?".'

'Just once in my life I'd like a little appreciation. Might I remind you that I've also been out at work all day? Megan had one of her headaches and I was run off my feet.'

'Ah, me pins is killing me,' Craig croaked in his best Dick Van Dyke cockney.

'You're vicious. I think you enjoy it.'

'That makes two of us.'

'What?'

'Don't act the innocent. You deliberately provoke me so that I'll lash out at you. You're a closet masochist. You're longing for me to knock you around.'

'Stop it, Craig!'

'What's wrong? I've told you before. We should feel free to

discuss our fantasies. Is that what would turn you on: a bit of rough-house?'

'Please, not while we're eating.'

'No problem. We'll wait half an hour for our food to digest and then I'll take you upstairs and give you a good belting.'

Keith stood up, drawing himself to his full height. 'Please excuse me. I don't feel hungry any more and, as my company obviously annoys you, I shall go up to bed and read.'

'Don't be such a prat. Sit down. Pass me your glass.'

'I may be stupid, but I can tell when I'm not wanted.'

'Oh no you can't, or you'd never visit any of your friends.'

Keith stared at him warily as he unravelled the insult. 'You bastard,' he said at last, and left the room.

'Look, I'm sorry – ' Craig found himself addressing an absence. Deflecting all the blame on to Keith, he determined to continue the meal. But, despite the very different ingredients, it tasted as stale as the shepherd's pie his mother had served up one morning for breakfast after he'd spurned it the night before. He gulped down two glasses of wine in quick succession and, although the bitter flavour did not disappear, it was diluted. The more he drank, the more convinced he became of his own good faith. He was not the one who had made a crisis out of a courgette.

He finished dinner, only to be gripped by a deeper hunger, but it was not one that could be satisfied by food. He contemplated going upstairs and apologising to Keith, but decided that that would be merely to confirm the pattern of a relationship which was in danger of becoming a permanent apology. He wanted sex, pure sex – or, rather, impure sex: passionate, bestial and sticky. He wanted a tireless, hot-blooded lover: one who excited him – one who incited him; one with whom he would be unable to distinguish between pleasure and pain; not one who was as fragile as a piece of bone china. He cast a reproachful look at the display cabinet, where the spotlights gave the figurines a particularly malevolent glow, and tried to work out which of them Keith most resembled: the crusty pipe-smoker; the emaciated priest; the tight-lipped crone in her bonnet. He felt gratifyingly wicked as he plumped for the last.

He would not allow himself to be laid low by an old maid's scruples. Keith might have rejected him, but there was a legion of virtual lovers waiting at the flick of a switch. Unlike Keith, he subscribed to the new global community whose members existed in a unique space, midway between their own reality and their correspondents' keyboards. Old loyalties had been superseded in a world where it was possible to travel from Kansas to Krakow in the span of a single orgasm. So, having assured himself that Keith was safely out of commission, he switched on his laptop, attached the modem, and typed in the single word: Stud.

Craig had long enjoyed what he playfully described as a 'healthy interest in pornography'; indeed, it was the sun-kissed Californian landscapes of the films he had watched in his teens that had first inspired his interest in travel. For years, he had thrilled to the exploits of the various Rocks and Randys, those all-American boys who had had to wait for the advent of the video camera to live up to their names. He had tried to share his passion with Keith, who had simply carped at the inept editing (the eye that could spot a crumb on a floral carpet was a match for any stunt penis) and blamed the jaundiced skin-tones (the result of third-generation copies) on the faddy West Coast diet. It was after he had interrupted a spectacularly torrid scene in a Jacuzzi with the news that they were out of shampoo, that Craig decided he preferred to watch alone – and at work.

To the fury of Craig's senior colleagues, their boss, having discovered that 90 per cent of internet transactions involved pornography and feeling it his duty to protect his female staff, had put the firm's entire web business in his hands. Craig immediately made contact with the illicit majority via a seemingly legitimate search for Water Sports in the Baltic. A few judicious reports to his boss supplied him with the pretext for hours of surfing, while subscriptions to selected adult sites provided a never-ending range of films. There had been only one close shave, when he had been so engrossed in *A Weekend on the Danube* that he had failed to hear his secretary's knock, but the angle of the screen had shielded him from exposure, and he had managed to convince her that he was engaged on a conference call to Budapest.

For Craig to spend a weekend on the Danube was an anomaly. Although he worried that it was a sign of insularity, he passed the bulk of his leisure time in Hoxton. It was fortuitous that his all-time favourite porn star was an Englishman, Todd Trent, whose name contained some of the monosyllabic ring and alliterative irony of its American counterparts. Physically, Todd was his ideal. Craig could reel off the official statistics (six foot one, a hundred and ninety pounds, blond hair, blue eyes, ten inches uncut) as mechanically as the Lord's Prayer. He was the one Englishman to have made it big in the American porn industry (a fact that had been hammered home in countless journalistic puns) but, having reached the age of thirty-five – an affront to the youth-orientated US market – and lacking the body-hair crucial for more mature appeal, he had retired. He had not, however, turned his back on the cameras. Exploiting the new technology, he had made his home into a permanent film set and broadcast the results over the web.

Whatever hour of day or night Craig entered the site, he found himself enchanted. Although he still shuddered at the memory of the Warhol film of a man asleep to which he had been dragged by an art-student boyfriend, he was happy to gaze for hours at the sleeping Todd. Even when he was awake, most of Todd's activities were mundane – cooking, eating, downing vitamins, listening to music, lifting weights – and yet they held an intense fascination for Craig. It did not hurt that Todd spent much of the time naked – on his diary page (which Craig regarded with the same indulgence as his film dialogue), he railed against the compulsion to wear clothes. Yet, for Craig, the attraction went way beyond prurience. At times, particularly when the camera was out of focus, he quite forgot that Todd was nude. What he valued was the chance to share his idol's most intimate moments. He had never felt so close to any man, always excepting Keith.

Fortunately for his fans – although Craig, who had set up a standing order to the site, preferred to see himself as a sponsor – Todd appeared to have an almost insatiable appetite for sex. He required 'servicing' (his word) at least twice a day, and there was no shortage of men ready to oblige. Craig speculated endlessly on the identity of Todd's partners who, with a rare exception (whom he came to know almost as well as he did the protagonist), constantly changed. He wondered if they were exhibitionists (in which case, they displayed remarkable restraint about playing to the cameras) or if they remained in ignorance that they were being filmed (a prospect that excited him all the more). It was probable, however, given Todd's aggressive marketing of his personal services, that the majority of them were clients: men so devoted that they were prepared to renounce their anonymity for a taste of his flesh.

No matter who he was with, Todd's dominance stood unchallenged. As one who had yet to recover from the discovery that his favourite cockney character actress hailed from aristocratic stock, Craig was reassured to find that the private Todd lived up to his public persona. The star of a barracks scene, as seminal in its way as Eisenstein's sequence on the Odessa steps, turned out to be equally insatiable in his bedroom. That celebrated organ (of which Craig possessed a much prized, although little used, latex copy) remained an object of universal veneration. The one disappointment was that the 'money shot', of which Todd had shown himself such a master, was rarely visible, his partners displaying more concern for their own pleasure than that of his fans.

As he watched Todd pounding into a man whose lack of conventional appeal suggested that he could only be one of his clients, Craig was convinced that it was time that he treated himself to a private encounter. He deserved Todd in person and not just on screen. He was too young to reserve his greatest ecstasies for his own right hand – a hand that was currently working furiously in order to sustain the same rhythm as his hero. But, just as he was daring to hope that this might be one of those rare occasions when they climaxed at the same time, he was interrupted by the doorbell. The shock that ran through him stopped short of his penis, and he struggled to squeeze it into his pants. Dispatching Todd unceremoniously into the ether, he hurried through the hall, only to receive an even greater shock when he opened the front door to find him standing on the step.

'Well, aren't you going to invite a bloke in?' The voice was unmistakable, a blend of seduction and menace.

'What do you mean? Who are you?'

'You're telling me you don't know?'

'How can you be here? I've just been watching you. Not five minutes ago. You were . . . with a friend.' A thought suddenly struck him. 'Was it a film? Is the whole twenty-four-hour thing a con? Do you replay old tapes in the hope that no one will notice?'

'I'm not a Jehovah's Witness, mate. I don't normally answer questions on the doorstep. Are you going to ask me in or not?'

With a deep sense of unease, Craig stepped aside and ushered Todd into the hall. He cast a swift glance across the road, but none of the curtains quivered.

'Whatever you do, no noise! My boyfriend's asleep upstairs. He knows nothing about you.' Craig led Todd into the living room and closed the door. He gazed intently at his laptop, as if he expected Todd to vanish back into it like the genie of the lamp.

'Don't worry. Keith'll hear nothing.'

'How do you know his name's Keith?'

'Me, I know everything.'

'Look, you're making me very nervous. Tell me truthfully, is this one big wind-up?'

'What do you mean? It's what you wanted, isn't it?'

'Yes, but how . . . ? I know.' Craig's face crumpled with relief. 'It's my friends, isn't it? Barnaby and Dennis and maybe Aidan. They clubbed together. Bastards! But why? It's not my birthday.'

Todd was looking around the room. 'Nice pad you've got here. Bit too *Ideal Homo* for my taste, but still . . .' He smiled as he saw the computer and then stooped to pick up two tissues which Craig had dropped on the floor. He held them to his nose. 'That's a relief. I'd have been most cheesed off if you'd finished without me.'

'There's an obvious explanation. I had too much to drink. I must have flicked the wrong command on my keypad.'

'I give the commands round here,' Todd said, his tone noticeably changing. 'What's the matter? Are you afraid you're asleep? Shall I pinch you?' Without any warning, he grabbed Craig's balls, causing him to let out a muffled shriek. 'Satisfied? Why are you so uptight? I'm here just as you wanted. Six foot one, a hundred and ninety pounds, blond hair, blue eyes, ten inches uncut. A real man. Not like Keith. Not one who worries about sweat stains and dry rot and how often he should visit his mother. Not one who makes a production number out of whether to cook green beans or courgettes.'

'What?'

'Todd has only one use for a courgette and, if you're lucky, you may find out.'

'It's Keith, isn't it? He called you. It's some particularly twisted form of revenge. But how did he find out? Did he go through my "Favourites"? He can't even use the Net!'

'If all you're going to do is moan about how I got here, I might as well go.'

'Yes, perhaps you should . . . No, I take that back. I'm so flustered.' For all his apprehension, Craig was loath to pass up the opportunity. 'I know that your time's valuable.'

'No, just expensive.'

'Would you like a drink?'

'That might not be wise.'

'Because it might affect your performance?'

'Among other things.'

'Look, you'll have to give me a clue. What is it you want from me?'

'Do you need to ask? Come over here and be one of Todd's boys.'

'But I'm thirty-three . . . thirty.'

'It's never too late. Besides, I like all sorts.'

'So I've seen. You're a real stud.' Craig grimaced, as the phrase that was so erotic on the screen sounded stilted in his mouth.

'On your knees!'

'What? Just like that? Shouldn't we get to know each other first? A little foreplay?'

'Since when has Todd been into foreplay? Have you learnt

nothing from all the hours you spend at my site? Now take off your clothes!'

'But – '

'No buts. Off!' Craig obeyed, fearful that his body, impressive enough in the local gym, would disappoint Todd who had had his pick of men on two continents. He stood in nothing but his pants, trying to conceal a premature erection. 'The Calvins, too. Don't be shy, boy. There's no use trying to hide it. Todd gives any man a hard-on. It's my sexual chemistry.'

'I thought that had to happen between two people.'

'Well, I have it all on my own.' As if in proof, Todd whipped off his shirt and sniffed euphorically at his armpit. 'Come closer,' he ordered and plunged his tongue down Craig's throat. Craig gagged at the searingly sour breath. He whimpered as Todd bit an earlobe as sharply as if he were piercing it. He longed for a moment of tenderness to offset the pain but, instead, Todd pushed his head on to his sweat-soaked chest and directed him to suck on the nipples. Locked in an acrid stranglehold, Craig reflected with new-found fondness on Keith's deodorised flesh. His desire for dirty sex did not preclude basic hygiene. He gulped for air, but Todd thrust his face back down the thin line of hair from his navel to his groin and on to his penis. Craig was revulsed by the stench. The *uncut* of his fantasy turned out to be rancid. 'Suck it!' Todd charged, impaling him ever deeper until he thought that he would choke. 'Not much of an expert, are you, boy? I'm surprised Keith stands for it.'

'He has no complaints.' Craig tolerated the insult for the sake of the respite. 'Besides, you're so big.'

'You ain't seen nothing yet,' Todd said. Craig felt his sphincter involuntarily contract.

'Don't you want to suck me too?' Craig asked. 'It works both ways.'

'Not with Todd. Your job is to service me. Now lick my arse.'

'No, I'm sorry, but that's something I never do.'

'Lick it! If you have any idea what's good for you.' The 'six foot one, a hundred and ninety pounds' of Craig's litany flashed through his mind and he set to work. It was soon apparent that Todd had not properly cleaned himself for days. Craig prayed that his tormentor would swiftly climax and then, displaying his characteristic contempt for his partners, disappear. His thoughts were interrupted by the command that he feared most. 'Lie back on the sofa and lift your legs in the air.'

Craig recognised that resistance was futile, but there was one risk that he refused to take. 'Did you bring any condoms?'

'Not me. Todd rides bareback.'

'I've got a packet upstairs. It won't take a minute.' Although, given the state of his sex life, they were probably out of date, he presumed that even obsolete condoms afforded some protection.

'How often have you seen me put on a condom?'

'Maybe not in person, but I supposed you did it out of shot. The camera doesn't pick up every detail.'

'Liar! You were thrilled by the prospect of flesh on flesh.'

Craig was as ashamed of his fantasies as he was alarmed by Todd's clairvoyance. Caught at a disadvantage, he allowed himself to be steered on to the sofa. While Todd was manipulating him for ease of access, he wondered whether to scream for Keith. Their combined weights would surely be a match for the hundred and ninety pounds. But he dismissed the thought even as he felt the first wave of pain from Todd's penis. He had willed this on himself and now he must suffer the consequence. He was determined at all costs to protect Keith.

'Go easy,' he pleaded as the agony became unbearable.

'Easy?' Todd laughed. 'What kind of word is that?'

'You're really hurting me.'

'You've enjoyed watching others long enough. Now it's your turn.'

'No more, please! You'll tear me apart!'

Todd pressed his palm over Craig's mouth, brooking no interruption as he reached his climax. Craig felt the reverberations run through him, followed by the immense relief of reclaiming his own rhythm as Todd slid away. He tentatively slipped his fingers between his buttocks to see if the moisture seeping out of him was blood or semen. It was both.

'You're a good fuck, mate. I'll give you that.'

'I'm glad you enjoyed it.' He wondered whether Todd's egotism encompassed irony.

'Now, if you could just show me the way to the khazi. I need to piss. That is unless you . . .'

'No. No, thank you,' Craig said hurriedly. 'First on the right. Please go quietly. My boy- . . . my lover's asleep upstairs.' Craig defiantly substituted the unfamiliar word. After watching Todd walk naked from the room, he lay back on the sofa, careful to avoid the added offence of leaving a stain. He was full of self-loathing, not just for the sex but for the stupidity. It was only now that he had been brutalised that he appreciated what a brute he had been. When he had made love to Keith, he had used to fantasise. Now that he had made love to a fantasy, he thought of Keith. A single taste of his tenderness, his loyalty and concern was worth more than any number of uncut inches. He felt like Dorothy in *The Wizard of Oz* (which, by no coincidence, was Keith's favourite film) discovering that true enchantment was to be found at home.

His one desire was to go upstairs to Keith but, first, he had to dispose of Todd, who was spending an inordinate time in the lavatory. He felt sure that Todd would be as eager to leave as he was to see the back of him but, in case of doubt, he resolved to expedite his departure by gathering up his clothes. Panic gripped him when he discovered that they were nowhere to be seen. The simple explanation, that Todd must have taken them with him, lacked conviction, since he would have sworn on his life – on his soul, had he believed in it – that Todd had left the room empty-handed. A further shock awaited him in the hall, where he found the cloakroom unlocked with no sign of recent occupancy. Moreover, a rapid search of the house not only failed to reveal Todd's presence but confirmed that the front door was locked from the inside.

Craig's mind was at odds with his senses. The rip in his shirt and the blood on his buttocks dispelled any notion that he might have been dreaming. On the other hand, unless Todd had squeezed through a window, he must have vanished into thin air. Craig could see no solution to the mystery, until a stray glance at his laptop suggested a way of obtaining, if not concrete evidence, then at least corroboration. He typed in the now incriminating password and made straight for Todd's home page but, instead of the familiar flame effect, he found a stark message announcing that, due to a fault, 'the page cannot be found'. Frantic with frustration, he tried to enter the site via various links, but always received the same message. Finally admitting defeat, he lay back on the sofa, trying to clarify what had happened and wondering if it were not only old loyalties but old logic that had been superseded in this virtual world.

Longing for the touch of his flesh-and-blood lover yet unwilling to expose him to the least trace of Todd, he wearily climbed the stairs and ran a bath. Just as he was poised to ease himself into the water, Keith stormed into the room.

'What on earth are you doing? It's half-past two!'

'It's a long story. I need to unwind. Go back to sleep. I won't be long.'

'Fat chance, with you stamping around like a herd of elephants!'

'I'm sorry. I'll be as quiet as I can.' He bent over to step into the bath.

'Craig, you're bleeding!'

'It's nothing. Just a scab.'

'A scab? There? Let me look.'

'I meant a scratch. I was itching. You know how you're always ticking me off.'

'With good reason. Be sure to put some disinfectant on it. You don't want it getting infected.'

'There's always good reason when you tick me off, Keith.'

'If you're referring to dinner, I admit it was my fault. I don't know what came over me. I'd had a rough day.'

'It wasn't your fault. It never is – except for the way that you say it is. Though even that's a very minor fault compared to mine.'

'I can't believe . . . What's got into you? Have you been drinking?'

Craig burst out laughing. 'Oh Keith, I love you so much.'

Keith narrowed his eyes and stared at him. 'Come here!'

'You're the boss.' Craig padded across the cramped confines of the bathroom towards Keith. He puckered his lips in expectation of a kiss, only to find Keith smelling his breath.

'You're drunk!' Keith exclaimed in disgust.

'No, no!' Craig protested, but his very vehemence appeared to prove Keith's contention.

'That's all this is. Maudlin sentimentality.'

'No, not maudlin. Whatever else, not maudlin.' Craig felt his eyes water and was unable to decide whether it stemmed from steam from the bath or something brimming inside him. Catching a glimpse of Keith's mole-like penis through his pyjama trousers, he was overwhelmed with longing. It was Keith who was the real man, not Todd who, whatever the nature of his recent manifestation, would always remain a fantasy. Furthermore, it was Keith whom he loved. He looked at the enticingly foaming water and was struck by an idea. 'Would you like to have a bath with me, Keith?'

'What? Now?'

'When better?'

'But it's two-thirty in the morning. Besides, we'd never fit.'

'We'll have to cuddle up close.'

Keith looked perplexed. Craig expected him to refuse – to pour cold water on to the bubbles – but, with that quiet determination for which he loved him, he slowly unbuttoned his pyjama jacket. 'If you like,' he said. 'Why not?'

The Isolation Ward

'FIVE MINUTES, gentlemen, please!'

Lawrence did not lift his eyes from the page. He knew that he must fill it with words. He had to come out on top: Grade One; Grade A; a First. He no longer knew what exam it was; he no longer knew what age he was. He could not spare a moment to check. All that mattered was to write.

'Pens down, gentlemen, please!' Lawrence paid no attention. He was sure that he could squeeze another minute. He scribbled as if his life depended on it. Time was running out and he had so much still to say.

'Mr Rippon,' the invigilator's voice rang out.

'Mr Rippon,' the night nurse's voice rang out. 'Look lively now, Mr Rippon. We'll just take your temperature.' Lawrence woke up from a nightmare that was finite into one that had no end.

The nurse thrust a thermometer into his mouth with an end-of-shift sharpness. Lawrence gasped as the plastic chafed his ulcerated tongue. He willed the mercury to stick at a respectable normality, only to be disappointed when the nurse took her reading. 'We'll have to do better than this now, won't we?' Not for the first time Lawrence wondered whether the ubiquitous plural were a means to withhold genuine sympathy.

'You just sit tight and Sandra will bring you a cup of tea.'

'I'm going nowhere,' Lawrence said. It was only when she failed to respond that he realised he had not opened his lips.

The night nurse left, taking with her his last hope of oblivion. Lawrence braced himself for his returning consciousness, which was now synonymous with pain. He tried to reclaim his body without disturbing its equilibrium. Let sleeping legs lie, he thought, relishing the vestige of humour, until the crack in his chest when he chuckled pulled him swiftly back to sobriety. He shifted his buttocks a fraction and squirmed as if he had sat on an open blade. The spasm tore through his bowels and left him fighting for breath. It hurt, but it did not overwhelm him. Lawrence had acquired a tolerance of pain that amazed him. Ever since school he had supposed himself to be a coward, but that was because of his loathing for the rough-and-tumble of the sports field. He wondered how many scrum halves and prop forwards would be able to endure the punishment being dealt out by his body. Which, in turn, caused him to question whether the strength that he had assigned to acceptance were not a final – futile – attempt to prove himself a Man.

His internal examination complete, he turned his attention to his bed: the few square feet that had become his entire world or, given his lack of any transcendent belief, his universe. His gown and sheets were both sodden: if he were to wring himself through a mangle like a character in a cartoon, he was sure that he would fill buckets. For one dreadful moment he feared that he had made the ultimate return to childhood. He soon realised, however, that it was sweat. No matter how rigorously he followed his drinking regime by day, his efforts were undone at night. He reached for his glass of water as if it were the stone of Sisyphus. The effort of sipping exhausted him, and he fell back on the drenched pillows. He used to be aroused by sweat – far more so than by more intimate secretions. Now it seemed like a cruel parody of sex: the one body fluid that he still produced.

Sandra brought him his tea. Her hospital plural was even more transparent than her predecessor's: the 'How are we doing today then?' thrown out to cover her retreat. She had forgotten to leave him a straw, and he groped on his locker for the half-clogged one from the night before. Enough moisture seeped through it to remind him of how much he disliked the drink. It conjured up a boyhood in which the kettle had seemed to be permanently on the boil. As soon as he had left home he had taken up coffee. He sometimes thought that, of all social distinctions, that between tea- and coffee-drinkers was the most revealing. He had bought his parents a cafetière one Christmas, but they had never used it. 'I like the box,' his mother had said, which must have been why she had left it in it. She did not trust machines. She still did all her washing by hand, as though she were somebody's maid.

He drifted between sleeping and waking. In the past, he had known few more delicious sensations than snatching the last precious seconds in bed before leaping out into the chill morning air (it was strange how his memories were always of winter), an awareness of the impending doom adding piquancy to the pleasure. Lately, when the transition had grown starker, he had braved his landlady's disapproval by neglecting to shave in order to linger in the warmth. 'I hope you're not growing a beard, Mr Rippon,' she had said, 'to my mind, they make a man look shifty.' Lawrence had eaten his bacon and eggs in itchy silence. With Mrs Hodson gazing at the photograph of her husband, lost at sea when barely old enough to grow whiskers, and Lawrence visualising underwear models with designer stubble, landlady and lodger had for a moment been united in their thoughts.

There was nothing to disturb his reverie. He was as secluded as a private patient. His one previous stay in hospital – to have his tonsils removed at the age of eight – had been in a crowded children's ward (he remembered being rebuked for a misdemeanour involving plasticine). Now he had been shunted into a side ward. He wondered whether the reason were medical or moral. He imagined the consternation it would cause if he were placed among decent diseases, next to somebody's husband or brother or, worst of all, son. In London he would have been admitted to a dedicated ward, with artful nude paintings on the wall and dance music on the sound system. But London was where he had been infected: London was what he blamed for his infection and, when the virus had begun to take effect, he had fled. Having no wish to return to Yorkshire, he had settled on the South Coast.

Hastings was a town where tolerance was seasonal, where the raffishness of April to September was followed by the dour respectability of October to March. It was as if, during the latter six months, the town's inhabitants were determined to rid themselves of any taint of the behaviour on which they depended during the former. Lawrence knew that neither Beth who served his lunch in the Norman tea-room, nor the Singhs from whom he bought his daily paper, let alone Mrs Hodson, would have shown him such sympathy had they not supposed his illness to be some sort of breakdown brought about by overwork.

He would not have censured their censure. Lawrence's respect for the prohibitions of his boyhood religion was one of the greatest ironies of a life that was steeped in them. He had shrugged off its consolations as if they were his mother's hand-knit sweaters, but he was unable to divest himself of its 'as ye sow, so shall ye reap' mentality. Nevertheless, his chief regret – even while lying supine in a sump – was not for what he had reaped, but for the modesty of what he had sown. He would have liked to have scattered whole fields with wild oats, instead of one trifling furrow. He had tried to discuss these issues with the chaplain, who had shied away from any mention of morality or metaphysics, deftly switching the conversation to the test match. Lawrence had followed his lead to spare him pain.

Recovering from an overhasty stretch, Lawrence reflected that it was easier to spare others pain than it was to spare himself, which was perhaps the ultimate expression of the chaplain's belief that it was more blessed to give than to receive. His own pain was like a blitzkrieg, shredding his nerves and mangling his thoughts. He cried out for relief, only to be mocked by the arrival of breakfast: an instant whip with enhanced vitamins and diminished taste. Nevertheless, it was the only food that did not aggravate the lesions in his throat. Lawrence waved away the tray, but the nursing assistant – a callow, camp young man, for whom Lawrence's condition provided a more effective deterrent than any number of government pamphlets – urged him to eat, with the warning that the doctors were threatening to feed him through a tube in his chest. Lawrence was outraged less by the prospect of a further invasion than by the flagrant waste of resources. His mind was as jumbled as a child's building blocks; his body was as foetid as a cesspit; he was ungrateful and incurable; and yet, for reasons of professional pride, they insisted on keeping him alive.

An acute cramp made him vomit up the instant whip. Two nurses came to his assistance, dispensing playgroup rebukes which, against the odds, Lawrence found comforting: his feebleness seemed to be validated when he was treated like a child. They raised his headrest and placed him on the bedpan. The pain far exceeded the humiliation. Ever since the day when he had woken to find that his sheets had been pulled down and his gown pulled up while a party of African doctors examined the lesions on his penis, modesty had been as alien to him as sunbathing. He was able to observe his body with the same objectivity as the beetle colonies he had studied at the museum, and present his bedpan to the nurses with as much indifference as a child who had yet to learn shame.

He rolled back and they began to wash him. Their sponges grazed his flesh. He lay like a puppet in their hands and dreamt of a Petrushka-like awakening. After giving him a clean gown, they changed the sheets, raising and lowering each side of the bed in turn. He felt like a cartoon character trapped on a factory conveyor belt (he wondered whether his increasing recollection of cartoons were the last stirring of his intellectual life or another sign of his return to childhood). He savoured the one sensual pleasure left to him: drinking in the freshly laundered smell of sheets that would soon – far too soon – smell of him. One of the nurses brought him his pills, the painkillers which – in yet another irony – were agony to swallow, before injecting the antiretrovirals which, in the absence of any serviceable vein, were pumped through a line in his chest.

As she left, the nurse switched on the radio, filling the room with a shopping-mall medley. Lacking the energy to think, let alone read, Lawrence was glad of the distraction. He closed his eyes and prepared to glide between layers of consciousness, only to be roused moments later by Welcome, wheeling in her trolley. Welcome, a large West Indian with a smile that lived up to her name, was the one non-medical member of staff to venture into his ward. She sold a selection of confectionery and toiletries throughout the hospital. Lawrence had never bought anything from her, and he doubted now that he ever would, but she still did not neglect him. She always had some new piece of information to impart. This morning it was that her daughter, Mercy, had been chosen to play Mary in her school's nativity play.

'A black Mary: that's a turn-up for the books. But what I want to know is: what colour is the Baby Jesus doll?'

Lawrence found it hard to speak and hoped that his smile was communicating itself to Welcome, whom he would have hated to offend. He seemed to recall that he had taken part in a nativity play. He was supposed to have been one of the Three Kings, but his mother had refused to make him a crown – not from any republican sympathies, but in strict adherence to the Bible's insistence on Wise Men. So he had been downgraded to a servant at the inn.

'How are you feeling today?' Welcome asked. Lawrence felt immeasurably grateful for the *you*.

'Not too hot, I'm afraid. It's as though they've replaced my blood with acid which is eating away at my veins. Sometimes it's so hard to draw breath, I might be climbing the Himalayas.'

'So I don't suppose you'll be wanting anything off my trolley?'

'Not today, Welcome, thanks. Though I may well do tomorrow. Don't forget to drop by.'

'I won't,' she replied. 'Thank Heavens all my customers aren't as tight as you or I'd be out of a job.' Lawrence smiled, although it was a familiar complaint. He closed his eyes since it was generally the cue for her to leave but, today, she had something else on her mind. 'It's a terrible affliction. Why, Lord? I ask myself. Why?' Welcome had a son who performed on the club circuit in London. He impersonated Tina Turner, Shirley Bassey and Diana Ross. She had presumed that Lawrence had seen his act, in the same way that his students in Ghana had presumed that he knew the Queen. Although she declined to put it into words, it was clear that Welcome lived in constant fear of a time when her hospital visits would no longer be professional.

'You say he's a sensible boy?' Lawrence asked in an attempt to reassure her.

'Weren't you?'

'Oh, but I was sensible in all the wrong ways.' He thought back to a family row in which he had dismissed common sense with all the hubris of his scholarship-boy mind. He was paying for it now.

'Anyway,' Welcome said, sniffing, 'the Lord gives and the Lord takes away. It's all in His hands.'

Lawrence would happily have dispensed with the homily. He had never been convinced by any of the attempts to reconcile a loving God with human suffering. He had more respect for the ancient Greek method of distinguishing God and Fate. But Christians had a mania for unity: 'One church, one faith, one Lord'. Nevertheless, if anyone could convert him to a religious standpoint, it was Welcome. She blew him a kiss – which was the closest that he ever came now to the real thing – and pushed her trolley out of the room. He decided that, in future, he would call her Mother Courage. After which he fell asleep.

He was woken by his doctor, who had come to listen to his chest. He lay back impassively. While the doctor probed and prodded, Lawrence felt as if he were wired up like a laboratory animal – although even a rat would inspire people to protest about its treatment. He resigned himself to the pain by imagining the doctor targeted by a group of anti-vivisectionists, who smeared blood on his front door and placed a bomb beneath his car. He broke off in shame. The doctor had the sandy complexion of an overgrown public schoolboy. Lawrence had decided that he had been an athlete in his youth and had married his childhood sweetheart, to whom he made love by both the book and the calendar. Even so, the affront that Lawrence caused was to his practice rather than his morality. In spite of having been a model patient who had never missed a single pill, he had developed resistance to the drugs. His one remaining hope was to enrol in a medical trial in London. Since Lawrence, however, avoided London in a way that, under different circumstances, he would have described as 'like the plague', the doctor was reduced to providing palliative care.

The doctor and Lawrence were locked in a battle of wills – the only battle for which Lawrence still had the strength – over morphine: the one wanting to prescribe it and the other determined to refuse it, ever since two drug-crazed weeks in which he had lain awake half the night conducting frenzied conversations with people whom he knew not to be there. The doctor dismissed his objections. 'What's the point of keeping your mind clear if it's blinded by pain?' Lawrence chose to regard the question, like so many of those put to him in hospital, as rhetorical. The doctor retired, leaving Lawrence to doze through lunch – which was breakfast with a different flavour – and the news. He was startled to hear the word 'nuclear' among the items. He had once been a passionate supporter of CND but, although he found it hard to admit (even to himself), he now viewed the atomic threat as more of a comfort. He was dying, and there was a part of him that wanted the rest of the world to accompany him: less like a pharaoh interred with his possessions than an emperor entombed with his wives.

A student nurse came to spruce him up for visiting hour, which Lawrence likened to feeding time at the zoo. She approached him so warily that Lawrence suspected that she did, indeed, regard him as an animal. 'I shan't bite or spit at you,' he said. 'You're perfectly safe.'

'I'm sorry. It's just . . . it's just . . .'

'Don't worry. I understand.' There was nothing he understood better than being struck dumb.

'I daren't tell my boyfriend I'm nursing you. He'd never come near me again. He thinks nurses today should be paid danger money.'

'Unless you have an unusually intimate bedside manner,' Lawrence said, 'you've no need to worry.'

'Yes, of course. I know that,' she snapped, seeming to forget that she had been the one to bring up the subject. 'Anyway, worse things happen at sea,' she said as she marched off.

Visiting hour was as empty a phrase to Lawrence as bedtime. Friends came high on the list of things that he had left behind when he moved. Lovers having proved unfaithful and confidants disloyal, he had resolved to spend the rest of his life alone. Meanwhile, Mrs Hodson's strict 'no guests in rooms' rule had removed the last trace of a temptation which, by himself, he might have been too weak to resist. His solitude had been shattered by the arrival of two fellow refugees from London, a couple whom he had met in a support group and who had mistaken shared symptoms for genuine sympathy. After a chance encounter in a cinema, he had been unable to escape their Englishman-abroad intimacy. They had made several visits to the hospital, gazing at him as at their own mortality. They quizzed him so intently on his health that he felt like a canary sent down a mine. He hoped that they would not return this afternoon and decided that, if they did, he would feign sleep.

The only other person who might come – and the only one whom he hoped would – was both more and less than a friend: he was a *buddy*. Like Mike and Peter, Derek had entered his life through the virus, although he himself was not infected. He was a volunteer with a charity that provided practical and emotional support. Lawrence had contacted it when it became clear that Mrs Hodson was no longer satisfied that museum life alone was responsible for his pallor, or that sea air would be sufficient to cure his cough. Nevertheless, as soon as Derek arrived, Lawrence did his utmost to drive him away, insisting that his commitment was an attempt to conceal a deep psychological need. Derek refused to be deterred, which convinced Lawrence less of his good faith than of his good training but, little by little, he allowed Derek into his life, until he came to hold what was left of it together. Sometimes he would muse that, if only he had met Derek sooner, he might have loved him: he might never have fallen ill. At which point he would quickly break off, since talk of 'if only's' offended him almost as much as talk of cures.

Then, in a coincidence neat enough to make him believe in telepathy, Lawrence looked up to see Derek sitting by his bed. 'I'm sorry,' he said. 'Have you been waiting long?'

'Not here. Though I waited more than forty minutes for a bus. Believe me, when my textbooks become international best-sellers, I'm not going to buy a Mercedes or a Porsche but a fleet of buses which I shall present to the town of Hastings.'

Lawrence laughed, but his laugh turned into a spasm of pain. Derek watched anxiously. 'You'll have me in stitches,' Lawrence wheezed.

'I went round to your room. Nothing's gone missing.'

'Nothing's worth taking.'

'I don't know. I had my eye on your weights. I never knew you trained.'

'I did for years in London. When I moved down here, I joined the YMCA. I even put up with the daily bromides on the black-board: you know "It only takes two muscles to smile but ten to frown" – which struck me as perverse given that they wanted us to exercise as extensively as possible. But, when I found my first lesion, I thought I'd better quit before there were complaints.' The effort of so long a speech left Lawrence gasping for breath. He lay back on the pillow and closed his eyes. He opened them to find Derek peering over him, holding out a glass of water. He humoured him by sucking on the straw.

'I've sorted through most of your books. You're quite sure you want me to sell them?'

'Any that are worth it. The rest I'd just chuck away.'

'I thought I was well-read, but compared to you . . . Have you really read all of them?'

'Pretty much. Once upon a time, I was reckoned to have quite a mind. And quite a body too. Though I don't suppose you want to hear about that.'

'No?'

'Not when it's in such a rush to decompose that it can't even wait for me to die.'

'I also found some photographs. In your quiet way, you were a bit of a hunk.'

'I sometimes wish I'd been one of those men who neglect their bodies, but I made mine the centre of my life. Now look where it's got me.' He gazed down at the coat-hanger frame that formed barely a ripple in the sheets, and a tear appeared in his eye.

'Now, now,' Derek said. 'Enough of that.'

'Quite right. Please don't ask for sympathy as a refusal often offends . . . Did I ever tell you about the type of beetle that was my special field – my daily companion for almost twenty years? The necrophore. The name gives it away. They bury dead animals – mice, voles – laying their eggs in the corpses so as to breed more beetles to bury more dead animals. Forget worker ants, I can't think of any insect that offers a better metaphor for human life.'

'I don't come here to be depressed, thank you very much! I can get enough of that at school.'

'You're so good for me, Derek. You're the only person who still makes demands on me.'

'I'm afraid I've one or two more to make. A couple of them final. I've sifted through your bills and written out several cheques. Do you think you can sign them?'

'Of course.' Lawrence edged himself up the bed, determined not to let Derek see the effort that it cost him. He winced at the Somme-like disparity between exertion and result. 'I'm sorry, but you'll have to help me.'

'No problem,' Derek replied prematurely. He grappled Lawrence into position and guided his hand. Lawrence's writing was so faint that at first he supposed the ink had run out. He asked Derek for another pen. Then he realised that what had run out was his strength. He reflected starkly that he could not ask for another life. Derek placed the cheques in their respective envelopes while Lawrence sank down on the pillows. He felt as though the steel claws of a mechanical digger were tearing through his flesh. Derek said that he would leave him to rest and return tomorrow.

'Don't feel that you have to,' Lawrence said.

'I don't.' Derek squeezed his fingertips with a tenderness that Lawrence relished, despite the bone-crushing pain. He watched as Derek left to spend the evening with his lover, a Buddhist architect, whom Lawrence to avert a three-way disappointment had refused to meet. He lapsed into a stupor until he was roused by a nurse with the news that he had some very special visitors. Two figures stood by his bed, but he was unable to make them out. He presumed that his vision was failing and then realised that it was clouded with tears.

'Mam . . .?' It might be because he was lying in bed, but he felt a child again. 'Mam, is that you?'

'Yes, lad,' she replied. 'It's me.'

'And Jack.'

'Yes, it's me too, kid.' And, for the first time since his arrival in hospital, Lawrence was convulsed with sobs.

'There, there, lad.' His mother leant forward to comfort him but Jack held her back. 'Why, Jack? Whatever is it?'

Lawrence saw himself through his brother's eyes, zipped up in a body-bag, carted off by masked men in protective clothing, and mused wryly that it was they who were more likely to pose a threat to him.

'You can touch him,' the nurse said, choosing her words with care, 'but watch out: he's very poorly.' Lawrence was amazed at her unwonted tact. He began to speculate on her own background, when his mother clasped his hand to her bosom. It was the first thing in weeks that had felt soft.

'Why don't you pull up those chairs?' the nurse said to Jack. 'I'll leave you in peace. If you need anything, just ring the bell.'

'Thank you, staff nurse,' Jack said, his precision betraying his unease. His voice sounded so deep that Lawrence wondered whether, consciously or not, he were seeking to distance himself from his disreputable brother. He felt disorientated by the intrusion and anxious as to how much the two of them knew.

'You're nothing but skin and bone, lad. What do you weigh?'

'About six stone, I think.'

'Six! But that's no more than a bairn!'

Lawrence wished that he had thought to soften the blow. Meals were the centre of his mother's life and her one means of expressing affection. He realised what his skinniness must represent to her. At least if he had died of obesity, he would have died of love.

'I wasn't expecting you,' he panted. 'How did you know?'

'Your landlady,' his mother said. 'That Mrs Hickson – '

'Hodson, Mam,' Jack said.

'Mrs Hodson, aye. She wrote such a lovely letter. Why didn't you tell us, lad?'

'Tell you what?' Pressed like a corsage to his mother's breast, Lawrence's arm had gone dead. He decided to regard it as a dummy run.

'About the cancer,' Jack said with studied emphasis.

'Oh, that.' Lawrence registered his new diagnosis: cancer, a disease that had been virtually rehabilitated by his own.

'What are you thinking of, Jack? I've already told you: I won't have that word spoken.'

Lawrence thought of a word – or, rather, an acronym – that she would find even more distasteful.

'Lawrence, lad, did you never mean to tell us?'

Lawrence covered his embarrassment with a cough. The one consolation of his godless death was that he could dispense with conventional pieties: no grieving family or sanctimonious priest. The hospital was obliged to respect his wishes, while Derek wholeheartedly approved of them. Lawrence had not thought to include Mrs Hodson in the equation. He presumed that she had stumbled upon his address book while rummaging through a drawer. It was not her prying that surprised him so much as her restraint. Curbing her innate *Schadenfreude,* she had been content to report his admission to hospital and leave them to draw their own conclusions. That Jack had drawn the correct one had been clear from the start. His mother, however, clung to the belief that illness was the expression of a moral universe. As he gazed at his brother's desperate face, he realised that, for all his helplessness, he still had power. One word from him could either bind his family together or tear it apart.

'Why didn't you tell us? What were you trying to prove?'

'I didn't want to worry you.'

'Worry us?' Her disbelief removed his advantage. He knew then that he would have to maintain the fiction, even though it was the story of his life.

'The last time I came home. Two Christmases ago . . .'

'The time you rowed with your dad.'

'Yes.'

'It's beyond me. Two grown men falling out over politics.'

'You're right: when there are so many more important things to fall out about.' He realised that his father had told her nothing. 'How is Dad?'

'He's grand. Fit as a flea.' Then, as if afraid that extolling his father's good health might seem callous, she added, 'Of course he's in a right state about things at the plant. He's fifty-five.'

'I know.'

'Not much call for a fifty-five-year-old welder in this day and age.'

'No, I don't suppose there is. Is he here?' He strained to see if there were a third figure assuming his familiar place in the shadows, but it was wasted effort.

'He couldn't take the time off work. Not right now. It's too risky.'

'He'll come soon,' Jack interjected, giving Lawrence a shock reminder of his presence.

'I'll look forward to that.'

'Are you hurting?' his mother asked, in a voice redolent of witch-hazel and iodine.

'Oh yes. Can't get away from that.' He heard his tone harden. 'It feels like some mad scientist's conducting experiments inside my skin: letting off constant explosions, each one more caustic than the last.'

'Can't they give you something for it?'

'They can and they do. But I don't want to spend what's left of my life spaced out. The pain reminds me I exist. It's the only sensation I have left.'

'Nay, lad, you mustn't say that. It's not true.'

Lawrence longed to shatter her defences. The pain was hurtling through his veins at wall-of-death velocity. It was as much as he could do to stop himself screaming. He wanted to share it with them both like a family inheritance, rather than claiming it all for himself.

'About my funeral . . .' he said, and felt his mother's bosom heave.

'Have you no consideration?' Jack hissed, putting his arm around her shoulders.

'I'm the one that's dying,' Lawrence said, the rawness of his throat reducing the scale of his protest. 'I was going to leave a letter but, now that you're here, there's no need.'

'You'll pull through,' his mother sobbed. 'All it takes is a little faith.'

'That's just it, Mam,' Lawrence said. 'I don't have any. I don't want any kind of religious service. I want to be cremated and I don't want a plaque. Nothing. I want it to be as though I'd never been. You can scatter my ashes anywhere you choose. I'm not fussy. Why not try the allotment? Dad'll be pleased. He'll have found a use for me at last.'

His mother was now openly crying. He himself was delirious with pain, but he could not stem the invective. It was as if he had to push himself to the limit before he could pass out. Jack raised his hand and, with a nod to their childhood, Lawrence thought that he was about to hit him, but he merely reached for the bell. His mother stood up. 'I'm sorry, lad,' she said. 'I'm so sorry.' She edged out of the room. Jack followed with the promise to come straight back: Lawrence did not know whether to feel grateful or alarmed. He closed his eyes and fought for breath. The demented violinist was scraping another cacophony on his guts. He coughed up blood. He felt no panic since it had happened before, but the rusty smell made him vomit. He fumbled for the bell, but a nurse was already in the room. For a moment he wondered whether he were the victim of an elaborate conspiracy in which his own body played a part, then he remembered that Jack had already called her. She wiped him and helped him to wash away the metallic taste.

The nurse left and his brother returned. Lawrence was quite discomposed. A few moments had been enough to erase the visit from his mind. He watched with curiosity as Jack, looking Sunday-suit solemn, sat by his side and took hold of his hand. Jack's clasp coupled pleasure and pain even more sharply than Derek's. Although they had touched so often as children, both by accident and design, they had fought shy of each other for years.

'I'm sorry, Lal.'

'Are you?' So little made sense to him any more. 'What for?' Jack made a gesture, at once expansive and equivocal. Lawrence immediately understood. 'You know, don't you?'

'I knew as soon as we got the letter. I think I even knew before: when we hadn't heard from you in so long.'

'You made it quite clear that I wasn't wanted in Skipton, you and Dad.'

'We wanted you, kid. It's just . . . why did you have to go and tell him?'

'I didn't have to; I chose to. It would have been far easier to tell Mam. That's the usual way. But, while she'd have stuck by me, she'd never have understood why it mattered. Dad should have understood. So should you.'

'You must tell me something, Lal. You must.'

'What is it? What's wrong?' He had never seen Jack so disconcerted.

'Is it my fault?'

'What? This?' Even for a pillar of the local chapel, that was taking the "brother's keeper" line too far.

'When we were lads . . . I was two years older . . . You know what I mean.'

'Oh, Jack.' Lawrence would have smiled if his lips had not been so lacerated. It seemed that self-reproach was a family trait. 'Believe me, it has nothing to do with you.'

'I can't get it out of my mind. Maybe if I'd kept my – '

'Jack, listen, that had nothing to do with anything. For you, it was just a lark. Mucking around. Playing with each other's cockstands. For me, it went a lot deeper. And I'm very grateful for those times, and for every one of the memories.'

'Don't think of them, Lal, please.'

'I can't help it. They're all I have left.'

'I've always admired you, Lal, so much.'

'Strange. For me, it's the other way round.'

'You were so bright. So full of sparkle. Like Guy Fawkes' Night all the year round. Other kids could look after themselves with their fists, but you had the words. I thought one day you'd be Prime Minister.'

'No, Jack, I don't hate enough.'

'You should never have moved to London. You'd have been all right if you'd stayed up north.'

'It's not like something they put in the water to soften it.'

'You should have taken that job in Durham.'

'Don't you see? I had to get away. I wanted to be myself.'

Jack said nothing but his eyes brimmed with feeling. Lawrence looked away.

'And were you?'

'For a while. It was a golden age when we stood together nipple to nipple. Before God decided to wipe us out.'

'Don't talk like that, Lal.'

Jack's piety goaded Lawrence and he resolved to ask him how he squared the Bible with his conscience and his conscience with the world. Then he began to cough and everything deferred to the struggle for breath. He beckoned Jack closer, determined to articulate more than suffering.

'I learnt to dance. Did I ever tell you?'

'No, kid, tell me now.' Jack stroked a dank strand of hair away from his eyes. He seemed to have forgotten about not wanting to touch him or, if he remembered, then he no longer cared.

'I used to be such a clodhopper. Two left feet: that was me. Then I started going to discos and discovered that dancing was the most natural thing in the world if you were attracted to your partner.'

'And were you?'

'Was I what?' Lawrence knew the answer but needed to hear the word.

'Attracted?'

'Oh yes. All the time. At once too much and not enough.' In fits and starts and rasps and spasms, Lawrence told Jack a little of his life in London and in Hastings. He spoke about Derek, who was young and strong and self-assured and who had managed to make a life for himself after the Fall. He expressed his conviction that, if there were to be any hope for the world – if there were to be any hope for *his* world – then it lay with men like Derek. 'My generation, Jack, we're dead wood. We should be chopped down to make room for the rest.' As if to emphasise his point, he was convulsed by a frenzy of hacking, leaving Jack's exhortations to fall flat.

'There are so many ghosts, Jack. So many of us lingering on, before our deaths and after our time.'

'No, Lal. You've so much to live for. We're taking you home.'

'This is my home now, Jack: this splendid isolation. And I'm so alone.'

Jack watched in horror as blood began to seep from Lawrence's mouth. He rushed into the corridor calling for help. Two nurses followed him to the room, accompanied by his mother, who had been huddled in the nurses' station, clutching a cup of tea. Jack tried to dissuade her from entering, but she brushed him aside as though he were still in short trousers. She froze at the sight of her son, lying motionless on the pillows, speckled with his own blood. The nurses set about sponging him clean. One attached a drip to his arm, while the other injected him with morphine. She promised that he would feel no further pain. Lawrence's lips moved mutely. As soon as they were given leave, Jack and his mother drew close to the bed. The nurses fell back, while remaining within easy reach.

'Get Dad to come,' Lawrence whispered.

'Yes, I promise. I'll ring him right away. Does it hurt, kid?'

Lawrence shook his head barely perceptibly. 'I'm so tired. I feel Stonehenge . . . on top of me.'

'We're with you, Lal. We'll lift it off.'

Jack leant over the bed and cradled his brother, confident that his touch could no longer hurt him. His mother clasped Lawrence's hand and placed it first to her lips and then to her breast. All at once she understood everything: everything he had hidden from her; everything she had hidden from herself. None of it changed what she felt for him, but it was too late to let him know. She was crying, but her tears seemed to reach beyond her heart to a place buried deep within her womb. Jack rocked his brother gently in his arms. 'You sleep now, Lal, sleep peacefully. Sleep till you regain all your strength.'

The nurses crept away, leaving mother and son on either side of the damp, deserted body. And Lawrence was no longer alone.

Visiting Hour

IF IT HADN'T happened in Cambridge, no one would have been interested. I'd have been one more petty crime report, a couple of columns in the local paper, 'Clothing Store Fraud . . . Policeman's Son Jailed', squashed up against the car boot sales and the tap dancing demonstration at the WI. It was the setting that gave it significance. I was no longer just a criminal but a symbol. You could almost say a parable: the poor man at the rich man's gate; the shop assistant seduced by a world of privilege and glamour. The *Daily Telegraph* called me a victim of my own pretensions. Cheek! I'm nobody's victim. I'm a free and independent spirit. Still, I kept a copy for my scrapbook. I'm not ashamed. My future triumphs will taste all the sweeter when I look back on what I had to overcome.

I mustn't waste time on recriminations. It's not often that I have the cell to myself. Jenkins isn't one of those illiterates who see writing as a personal insult, but he always seems to choose the moment when I pick up a pen to ask questions. And he takes offence if you don't answer. A lot. He's all right on the whole, I suppose. Though he does have his funny habits, like the way he won't shower. He thinks the screws have put some drug in the water. And he washes his feet in the slop-pail. He says it toughens the skin. I made the mistake of asking why it mattered: he wasn't Mowgli. He'd no idea who that was and he made like he was going to clock me. But I wriggled out of it in the nick of time when I said he was a character in a Disney cartoon (I knew better than to say it was a book).

I never thought I'd be grateful for the quiet. Whenever we played loud music at home, our dad would tell this story about jukeboxes where you could put on a disc of five minutes silence. If there was one in here and I had the money, I'd put it on twenty-four hours a day. There's a non-stop racket: screws shouting; dogs barking; keys scraping in locks; some con freaking out in his cell. But in Visiting Hour it dies down. It's a sign of respect – even from blokes that have no visitors. Jenkins's mum has come down from Sunderland. His wife ran off, but his mum takes the bus every month even though she's got one leg shorter than the other. My mum wouldn't come, nor my dad. Not that I'd want them to. They sent me a letter telling me I'd brought disgrace on them and they disowned me. Don't they know there are nonces in here and rapists and murderers and all sorts? Their folks still visit them. All that 'he may have done wrong but he's still my John or Jack or Joe'. And here's me, serving a muppet sentence for a muppet crime, and they've disowned me! Sorry, but it's too late. They never owned me in the first place. I disowned them when I was ten.

They're very religious. They go to church every Sunday, sometimes twice. It used to kill me at Christmas that we had to wait for our presents till after the service. Other kids woke up and dived straight into their stockings, but we had to thank God first. The worst time of all was Remembrance Sunday when my dad wore all his medals. I thought Jesus was supposed to be a man of peace. Hypocrites! Where's all their Christian charity now? Have they never heard of the Prodigal Son? I go to chapel here, mainly for a change of scene. It's like the hospital: for a moment you can forget where you are. The hymns we sing are the same as on the out, even if the voices sound more like ones you'd hear on the terraces. And on Sundays the screws bring their wives. In the choir, I can stare straight at them without anyone telling me to turn round. I never thought I'd miss women so much. Maybe I should have let my sister come. She wrote to me and offered, which was decent of her, especially seeing as we'd never been that close. But I put her off. I can only have so many visits and I'm saving them for my friends.

I never thought I'd say it but I'm glad that I used to share a bedroom with my brothers. It's made me better able to handle being cooped up with Jenkins. I told him one night that we were like a couple of battery hens. He looked as if he was about to deck me. It seems that where he comes from hen is another word for woman. I've come to learn that Jenkins is a man you should only ever tell what something is, not what it's like. All in all it's not too bad in here. Not that I'd recommend it, but you can see how some blokes get attached to the place. Life's better for them here than it is on the out. They have a roof over their heads, three square meals every day, hot and cold running water. And it's not only the old lags. I was talking to this young lad at association. He was explaining how he broke into a school just so as he'd get sent back inside. The judge called him a habitual criminal, said he had a personality defect. For a moment I was afraid that I might be looking at myself. Then I realised that I have friends.

How I wish that one of them would send me a letter – or even a postcard, it doesn't have to be long. I'm sure they can have no idea what it's like being locked up in here. Robin once said that boarding school was like prison so I expect they think it's just cold food and homesickness and games. There again, they may be saving up all their energy for one giant celebration when I'm freed. I'll be the hero of the hour. There'll be a fleet of Rolls Royces to greet me at the gates. They'll compete with each other for the honour of driving me. We'll drink champagne and eat caviar as we head back into town. Then they'll carry me shoulder-high through the Market Square and straight to a slap-up meal. Newspapers will offer me six-figure sums for my story:

'My life inside, by Cambridge martyr'. But I'll turn down the *News of the World* and the *People* and sell it for far less to *The Times* or the *Independent* because I know they'll treat me with respect. I'll be another Nelson Mandela or Oscar Wilde.

I work in the prison library. I enjoy being among books. We're having a stock check at the moment, which can be tricky since, when you ask some blokes for an overdue title, they take it personally. My own taste is for novels. I'm in the middle of *Vanity Fair*. I prefer long novels, except when there are too many characters, which is as bad as life. The most popular categories here are thrillers and horror stories, although history has its fans, especially among the lifers. We have a large shelf of do-it-yourself, with a long waiting-list for *Small Boat Building*. But my interests aren't solely intellectual. I'm learning to make a rug. It hasn't gone entirely according to plan. The border's supposed to be diamonds, but it's come out as squares – not quite square squares. Jenkins started taking the mickey. So I asked him 'Where would Picasso have been if he'd stuck to the rules?' Then I had to explain Picasso in a way he'd understand. 'He was the painter who put women's tits in all the wrong places.' 'That's sick!' he said and turned back to his gallery of pin-ups.

Jenkins doesn't have any hobbies except draughts. We'd play all day long if I let him. He cheats which, I suppose, should come as no great surprise, but I thought there was some code of honour among thieves. Still, I know better than to challenge him. It's not that I'm scared, but tempers are easily frayed and I don't want any bad blood (or any blood at all, for that matter). After all, we're friends, in so far as men inside ever can be, which is nothing like my real friends on the out. I just wish that one of them would get in touch. I'm afraid that the screws could be confiscating their letters. They won't ever have come across a con who knows such distinguished people. They won't be used to the elegant writing. They won't understand the erudite words (they won't understand 'erudite' for a start). They're bound to feel threatened by envelopes that don't have SWALK scrawled on the back or contain some peroxide blonde's pubic hairs.

I date my life from the day I met my friends. The first seventeen years were just a prelude, like BC before it became AD. It's hard to explain how it feels to live in Cambridge and not go to the university. It's like being a Jew at Christmas: a real Jew, one with sideburns, not one of the rich ones who celebrate everything. The whole place is directed towards something you're not part of. I used to dream that one day I'd be a student there myself. Then I could look down on all the townspeople in my turn. I'd cut my old schoolfriends in the street – not snobbishly, but because my mind was on higher things. The trouble is I only got four GCSEs. It's not that I'm thick, but I don't have the right sort of cleverness, I'm not good at cramming for exams. I'm more imaginative. I wanted to stay on to do drama and art A levels. To listen to my father, I might just as well have asked for a two-year supply of Ecstasy and condoms. He'll be sorry. Most celebrities buy their parents grand houses with swimming pools when they make their fortunes. Not me. Like Jenkins says of his 'trick cyclist', I wouldn't piss on them if they were on fire.

I feel sorry for my future biographer, having to find something interesting to say about my parents. My mum has been a bedmaker at St John's for over twenty-five years. When I asked her why she never practised at home, she whacked me across the face. At the end of each term the students give her bottles of sherry, which she doesn't drink. She says that it's useful for stock. Stock! She could open an off-licence. She's too tight to hand it on to me or even my older brothers. She claims that her father was an alcoholic and she wouldn't want to see any of us going the same way. Some chance! Until he retired last summer, my dad was a policeman. I know we can't all be the children of dukes and film stars, but why must I be the one at the other extreme? He even came to school in his uniform. The only kid who had it worse was George Hargreaves and his father was an undertaker. He was regularly beaten up. At least no one tried that with me. Though they did call me Plod.

The happiest day of my parents' lives was when they went to tea at Buckingham Palace (although they were only allowed in the garden, not the house). I suppose it had to do with my dad and the building society siege. My big regret was that he hadn't been killed in action. Then, instead of feeling like an orphan, I'd have actually been one – or, at least half a one. Kids at school would have looked at me like they did at the boys who'd had sex. But no, he just got a flesh wound and an invitation from the Queen. Though it turned out that she didn't say one word to them. She just walked past like she was inspecting the guard. I told them that they should have sold their tickets to touts. I saw on this programme that there was a black market of American tourists who paid five hundred quid each. My dad said that I didn't deserve to be an Englishman. I suspect he may be secretly attracted to the National Front.

If I thought there was the slightest danger of me growing up like them, or like my two brothers with their screaming wives and kids, or like my Auntie Maureen whose party piece is taking out her teeth and clicking them like castanets, then I'd slit my throat on the spot. But there's a line (I bet it's by Shakespeare) about the fairest flowers growing on the foulest dung-heap and that gives me hope. Besides, everything is useful to an actor, even parents who won't let him act. We need something to rub against: Mr Bateman, my old English teacher, calls it 'the pearl of discontent'. He wears badges instead of a tie so you can't take everything he says seriously, but he told us about some Olympic skater from when he was young. He wanted to be a ballet dancer but his dad wouldn't let him, so he took up skating and danced on the ice. 'There's a moral in that,' Mr Bateman said, looking straight at me.

I started acting at school. I won the cup twice but, when I took it home, my dad refused to put it in the cabinet alongside my brother's cross-country bowl (and that was only for under-fifteens!). I wanted to go to drama school, but I was too young to apply. And, although in my fantasies, my father the duke told me to take a couple of years and see the world, in reality my father the cop told me to 'get off your fat arse and find a job'. He was hoping that I'd follow him into the police cadets. He went on about how much things had improved since his day. It was all thanks to Maggie, whom he worships only slightly less than the Queen. He explained that the pay was good, what with all the overtime, and there were plenty of perks. I told him that the only way he'd ever catch me wearing a uniform was in a TV series about police brutality. It was worth the clipped ear to see the look on his face. He wouldn't give way on the job front, so I combed through the local paper and found a vacancy in a clothes shop – and not any old clothes shop but Austin Road (all dinner dances and double garages). They took me on the next day. In spite of myself, I felt excited. I'd be earning my first wage. And, in our family, money's what counts.

While I knew that it could never be more than a stop-gap, I have to admit I enjoyed working in the shop. My colleagues were a friendly bunch, although one of them was just like Mr Humphries off the TV (I took care not to let him swing his tape measure in my direction!). They were all beautifully spoken. You can't sell a five-hundred-pound suit with a voice like a market-trader. It was an elocution lesson in itself to hear their vowels. I soon discovered that I have a knack with clothes. I like handling quality material: I like seeing well-dressed men. Shakespeare said that the apparel proclaims the man, so I'm in good company. I know how to make the best of people. I'm not the sort – like some I could mention – who hear 'bonus' the moment the doorbell rings. They'd do anything for a sale: put a customer in a size 42 because size 44 is on order and then praise the snug fit; insist that rust is his colour since we've run out of beige. No, I respected my customers. I gave them what they wanted – that is, what they would have wanted if they'd had better taste.

One thing I hated was the patter: trying to flog a bloke a shirt or a tie or a sweater to go with the very expensive jacket he'd just bought. If the manager was watching, I had no choice. He called it integrated selling: I called it pushing our luck. The only thing I hated more was when the customers brought their wives. They'd feel duty-bound to criticise every purchase. They'd complain about the clothes, when what they were really complaining about was their husbands. It wasn't the jackets they wanted in a different cut, but the men.

Then came the fateful day: if I were Napoleon, I'd call it my brush with destiny. It was a Thursday afternoon and I was alone in the shop when a student walked in. I could tell he was a student, although not from his clothes, which were country cords instead of the usual denim. It was more a question of attitude: the sense that he would have tipped me if he'd had any cash. I'd left him to look through the shirts when I saw him, bold as daylight, slipping one into his bag. I didn't know what to do. Of course I'd been trained. There was a procedure. But he looked so honest. I was sure that he must have made a genuine mistake, or else that he was on medication. He moved towards the belts, which only confirmed my view: if he were a regular thief, he'd already have been halfway down the road. I went through the standard 'Excuse me, sir' routine, and asked if I could inspect his bag. He came over all huffy and tried to leg it, but I was quicker and snapped the lock on the door. 'I really must insist, sir, or else I shall have to call the police.'

He started to throw his weight around and warned me he intended to make a serious complaint to the manager: if I wasn't very careful, I'd find myself out on my ear. But the more he blustered, the more I kept my cool (I have to admit I was quite proud of myself). Then, as if he'd grown bored with keeping up a front, he tossed his bag on to the counter. 'There you are,' he said. 'Why not strip-search me too while you're about it?' I ignored his tone and opened the bag. Sure enough, there was the shirt. I was expecting him to break down; to beg me to say nothing; to tell me that the scandal would destroy his parents, not to mention his career. But not a bit of it. 'What are you planning to do, then?' he challenged me. 'Turn me in?' I replied that I hadn't decided. I resented the way that he made me feel as if I was the one in the wrong, like some sort of sneak or bully. He seemed to sense my confusion. 'Look,' he said, 'can't we just forget all about it? What will be served by making a fuss? Just a lot of hassle for everybody. I obviously suffered a blackout. Temporary amnesia. You read about it all the time. Old ladies who walk out of Harrods with half the china department in their bags.'

'You're not an old lady,' I said.

'No, I'm the Honourable Pitt Stephenson. My father will retain one of the best barristers in the country. It'll be your word against mine. We'll wipe the floor with you.' He didn't say any more. He didn't need to. I pictured myself sweating in the witness box as I was grilled on my precise angle of vision (I never guessed that, eighteen months later, he'd be the one in the witness box and I'd be in the dock). 'Let's be grown-up about this.' He took out his wallet. 'I'm sure I can make it worth your while.' I was flabbergasted. He was offering me a bribe. I asked him why he hadn't paid for the shirt in the first place. 'I'm overdrawn. You wouldn't believe how tight my father is. He won't even settle my buttery bill.' He then explained that the shirt wasn't for him personally but for one of his friends' twenty-first birthday, which put things in a very different light. I assured him that I'd say no more about what'd happened, at which point all his cockiness vanished and he burst into tears.

He offered to pay for the shirt but the machine refused his card, which only made him more upset. So I told him to take it anyway. No one would be any the wiser: the stock-checking system was criminally slack. 'You're a star,' he said, and I remembered where I'd seen him before. He'd played the lead in a student production of *Cyrano de Bergerac*. He was wonderful. And to think that I'd almost ruined his life!

I told him that I hadn't recognised him without his nose. He said that he felt like a tart who was caught with her clothes on. I apologised. He said there was no need. Then, although it seemed like me who was stealing from him, I told him that I also wanted to be an actor. He suggested I audition for one of the university plays. I was amazed. I thought there'd be strict rules. He said that they'd be prepared to bend them for sexy, fresh-faced boys like me. I wasn't put out by his talk. I knew that in the theatre they always paid compliments in capital letters. They called their enemies 'darling' when even my nan only calls me 'dear'. I said that it might sound an awful cheek but I wondered if we might meet for a drink one evening: I was usually finished by six. He offered to go one better. We could have dinner that very night, provided I was free. I replied that the only date I had was with my mum's fish pie and he told me to meet him at seven o'clock in his rooms in Clare.

I asked the porter for the Honourable Pitt Stephenson. He pretended to look unimpressed. I'd been to St John's with my mum (she dropped the 'Saint' as though she was an atheist) but this was the first time I'd visited a college as a guest. Pitt offered me a glass of sherry, which I drank with particular pleasure. A bell rang for dinner, which they call hall. I had to wear a gown which made me feel a bit of an impostor. I wondered if we'd meet his friends and if I'd understand a single word they said. I had quite a scare when one of the masters said grace and I thought that the whole meal was going to be in Latin. But, as soon as the food came, everyone seemed quite normal. Mostly they talked about money. It wasn't like *University Challenge* at all. At the end, I told Pitt how much I'd enjoyed it. 'Don't be absurd,' he snapped. 'It was the Slough of Despond. No one I know would be seen dead in hall. I only go because I won't have to pay the bill till next June. Now let's slip next door to meet some of my chums.'

Next door turned out to be Trinity Hall. We walked through the first courtyard. 'You don't need the yard. Plain court will do,' said Pitt, who was already taking my education in hand. We went up to the rooms of his friend John Wilkes. 'He's distantly related to *the* John Wilkes,' Pitt said, and I nodded as if the name was as familiar to me as my own. Pitt knocked and a voice called out, 'Enter so long as you're pretty.' I felt like a twelve-year-old sneaking into an 18 film. I was bowled over by the decoration. Every inch was covered in cloth, with great swathes of silk and satin hanging down from the ceiling like the canopy of a stately home bed. There wasn't a stick of furniture, just dozens of different-sized cushions in various shades of red. The light bulbs were also red, which must have made it impossible to study and now made it difficult to tell exactly how many people were there. The room gave off that powdery, purply, candle-shop smell that my dad used to say was 'like a tart's boudoir', and that gave me the biggest thrill of all.

'Well, you certainly meet requirements,' said John, whom I soon discovered spoke as if every line were out of a play. 'Where *did* you pick him up, Pitt?'

'He works in Austin Reed.'

'A shop girl! It's so J. B. Priestley,' said a man whom I later identified as Tarquin (if only I'd been called Tarquin: I'd be a quite different person from Mark).

'His father's a policeman,' Pitt added, much to my horror. I may not have told him it was confidential but you'd have thought he would have guessed.

'Well, he's not exactly my father,' I said. 'He's my stepfather. My real father's dead.' I hoped that the substitution would both remove some of the stigma and give me added prestige.

'God, I wish my father were dead,' Pitt said.

'Then you could pay back the money you owe me,' Tarquin said.

'Though I suppose my ma might marry again.'

'But not a policeman?'

'Somehow I doubt it. Though it might have fringe benefits.'

'Such as taking you down to the cells and letting you watch the interrogations?' John said.

'And perhaps even lend a hand?' Tarquin said.

'Bastards! You must keep away from them, Mark, or they'll corrupt you completely.' I didn't know whether to say 'yes' and risk offending them or 'no' and risk offending Pitt, so I gave a slight laugh and wished that it didn't sound quite so much like the ring of a till.

To my amazement, Pitt told them about the shirt. If it'd been me, I'd have kept it to myself, but he seemed to think that the excitement of his escape outweighed any embarrassment. Not that his account was complete. There was no mention of his bursting into tears or attempting to bribe me. All in all, I felt that he might have done better to have waited until I'd left, but the others seemed delighted both by the story and my response.

'So you're Pitt's guardian angel,' John said.

'You're not just a pretty face,' Tarquin said and kissed me
smack on the lips. I felt sick, which I knew showed my lack of
sophistication. So I made a special effort not to squirm when he
put his arm on my shoulder and invited me to sit beside him.

'Remember, Tarquin,' Pitt said, 'finders keepers.'

'*Droit de seigneur*, old fruit,' Tarquin replied, which made
me wish I had a family motto.

I perched on the cushions, which hurt my back, but I'd have
lain on a bed of nails to be in their company. John handed me
the pipe they were sharing. I'd never taken drugs although,
according to my dad, they were on offer at every primary school
in Cambridge. I didn't want to seem unfriendly so I took a quick
puff and hoped that it wasn't heroin. By swilling the smoke
around in my mouth, I managed not to cough. It was quite
pleasant but I didn't get high. On the contrary, I just wanted to
curl up on the cushions. And that's how I spent the best evening
of my life. John played an old German record. He said it was
'Marlene'. I know better now, of course, but then, I'm ashamed
to admit, I'd never heard of her. To be honest, I didn't think she
sang that well, but Tarquin explained how there was more to a
singer than a voice. I had another puff and gazed up at the cloth.
When I looked down, I found Tarquin rubbing my thigh –
though, since I appeared to have lost all sensation in my legs
and to be seeing double, I couldn't be sure. I was considering the
best way to remove his hand when I caught sight of the time.

'I have to go,' I said, the words fluttering out like butterflies.
'My mum and dad will kill me.' Tarquin refused to hear of it and
pinned me down like we were wrestling, but the others dragged
him off and Pitt pulled me to my feet. He said that I was his
responsibility, which made me feel good. He seemed quite angry
with Tarquin, which wasn't fair since he was only fooling. I've
no idea how I managed to walk: my whole body felt as if it'd

been filleted. But Pitt dragged me to the Market Square and deposited me in a cab. Before he left, he made me promise to visit them again soon: I'd been a hit. And I felt like I had when I won the cup.

I did go back, more often than I could ever have hoped. Tarquin turned out to be Cambridge's top director. He was the one who'd cast Pitt as Cyrano de Bergerac. Now he was planning *Coriolanus*. I asked if he might have a part for me. 'Only a small one,' I said modestly. Though, to tell the truth, I didn't expect it to be quite as small as it was. At school I played leads, whereas for Tarquin, over the next year, I played walk-ons: a plebeian in *Coriolanus*; a servant in *She Stoops to Conquer*; a soldier in *St Joan*. When my sister asked why I was always a peasant, I assured her there was nothing sinister behind it. My job meant that I could only rehearse in the evenings, whereas the main roles – the nobility and gentry – had the afternoons free as well. I felt honoured simply to be acting alongside them. They were all so dedicated. And I didn't mind if they teased me a little. Pitt explained how there was always a scapegoat in every production. It helped to unite the rest of the cast.

There were some who said that my friends should be in here with me – even instead of me – but I certainly wasn't one of them. They'd never last a day. Their accents alone would see to that. And they'd never manage to get up so early. Pitt pretended not to know what a morning was. No, it was much better that I took the rap. Me, I'm a survivor. I can take care of myself. There's a bloke here who was put away by my dad. So far he's been friendly enough. 'I don't bear you any grudge,' he said. Then he laughed. But you never know with laughing in here, whether it's for what they've said, what they've done or what they're going to do. So I keep well clear. I make sure not to get on the wrong side of anyone. Though I worry about Jenkins. I don't think he's quite all there. His wife ran off with another man so he burnt down a church. Why? The man was a security guard not a vicar . . . He sits for hours staring at his pin-ups, groping himself with no thought for me. And, though I wish he was more private, I do like seeing the pictures. I find myself looking at them more and more. It's strange how a picture can make you feel real.

For two years I had a girlfriend, Janice. Everyone liked her, even my mum and dad. They kept inviting her to tea and it was all I could do to get her to refuse. 'What's wrong?' she asked. 'Are you ashamed of me?' In the end I had to admit that it was the other way round. 'That's silly,' she said. 'Besides, if they're going to be my parents-in-law, I want to get to know them. I wouldn't like there to be any ill feeling.' I was shocked. Who'd said anything about marriage? That was the last thing on my mind. Too many actors marry young, before they've become famous and had a chance to meet other famous people. I didn't want children and divorce and bad publicity. Still, if she wanted to dream, I wasn't going to stop her. And she did let me sleep with her. By the swimming pool on Jesus Green. It was great except for the way that she giggled when she got excited. It put me right off my stroke. She's got a new boyfriend now but she still writes to me. She signs off 'Yours faithfully, Janice', so as not to raise my hopes.

While it's true that, on balance, I much prefer women to men, I'm one hundred per cent bisexual. We all are. It stands to reason: we're not machines programmed to function a single way. Until I met Pitt and Tarquin, I'd never kissed a boy at all, not even in puberty when it's expected. That just goes to show how uptight I was. Tarquin explained to me how many great men had been homosexual: Plato and Sophocles (or was it Socrates?); David and Jonathan; Alexander the Great; Michelangelo; and hundreds of others. We watched *The Agony and the Ecstasy* on TV last Christmas and Michelangelo's lover was played by Diane Cilento. I wanted to blurt out the truth, but what would have been the point? All my mum did was coo over the ceiling as though she was on a coach tour. 'We're getting a far better view than if we went to Rome.'

Any normal parents would have been happy that their son was mixing in such high-class circles. Not mine. My dad even threatened to stop me acting, but I told him that, if I was old enough to join the army, then I was old enough to play a soldier in *St Joan*. That stumped him. He insisted that the students could never be my friends. He drew a line between *us* and *them* as rigid as something from the Bible. I'm sorry to disappoint him, but they were the best friends I ever had. The year that I spent with them was the happiest of my life. I used to count the minutes each afternoon until I could escape from the shop and join them for rehearsals. The only black spots were the holidays (it's not like school; their holidays last longer than the terms). The worst was Easter, when Pitt invited a crowd of them to the country for a party. I only found out when Tarquin and John both begged me to bring them something to wear. At first I felt hurt not to receive an invitation. Then I realised that he was being extra-sensitive. He didn't want to remind me that I couldn't get the time off work.

There was one place where we parted company. Although I laughed it off when they groped me and tickled me and grabbed my tights in the dressing room, I didn't really want to go to bed with any of them. I kept having to come up with fresh excuses. I was afraid they'd lose patience, but Pitt said that he was glad to see I wasn't a pushover and Tarquin that he liked a boy who played hard to get. I could tell they didn't hold it against me when they gave me a nickname: Polly. Pitt said it was because I was always cheerful, like *Pollyanna* – which is a film with Hayley Mills. Though somebody else claimed it came from 'Pretty Polly', because I repeated what everyone said. Which was spiteful. Why do I have to remember stuff like that? I spend too much time on my own. That's why it's even more important that my friends come. I wish I knew what was keeping them. If they're not here soon, it'll just be hello and goodbye. I hope they realise that they can't roll up half an hour late as though it was a lecture. In prison, you have to be on time.

Pitt used to make jokes about sex in prison – or something halfway between jokes and dreams. To hear him talk, you'd think it was full of men like him and John and Tarquin, only fitter. Well, I'm here to tell him it's not. The day after I arrived, three men raped me in the laundry. The pain was horrendous – it felt like they were using corkscrews. They treated me with contempt: I didn't count; everything was about them. When they were through, they left me like a pile of dirty sheets. Within minutes, everyone in the prison knew. And though, apart from a nonce, there's nothing cons hate more than a rapist, they seemed to think what'd happened to me was fair game. They whistled at me like I was a tart and made crude gestures with their cutlery. Jenkins was the one who saw me right. He told me the thing to do was to get myself a bloke, someone all the others respected. And I got Clegg. He's the hardest man here. He's in the *Guinness Book of Records* for having done the biggest number of press-ups in one go. The Governor and all the screws went to watch him. At the end, they gave him a bottle of Guinness to celebrate. But, instead of drinking it, he poured it over his head.

I used to think that all students were rich, but a lot of them are quite poor, especially the posh ones. They don't get any grants so they have to take out loans or else grovel to their parents. And there are so many claims on their parents' cash. Pitt explained that his father is still paying duties on his grandfather who died ten years ago. It might seem right that people with the most money should pay the most taxes but it takes no account of all their responsibilities. Pitt showed me a picture of his house. It was as large as a college. His parents were forced to sell pictures that'd been part of the family for hundreds of years. The only antiques in our house are my mum's nan's sideboard and a George V Jubilee mug. It's all very well to say everybody's equal but, if two blokes have to have their legs amputated and one's a violinist and the other's a football player, it's not hard to see who's the worse off.

I was eager to spare my friends any fresh humiliation. One evening a group of us went to Shades, a restaurant I'd never been to before – and, when I saw the prices, I knew why. At the end of the meal, Robin took out his chequebook, but the manager stormed up and, in full view of the other customers, refused to accept any more of their cheques. I couldn't believe it. Didn't he realise that Pitt was an Honourable and Tarquin was the nephew of a bishop? We agreed to have a whip-round, but I was the only one with any cash and that barely covered my own share. John said he'd nip back to Trinity Hall since he thought one of his cards was still good, but I saved him the trouble by placing my own on the plate. I felt a lot less generous the next morning when I realised that the bill had come to more than my weekly wage, but they'd all been so grateful that it seemed only polite to repeat the offer the next time we went out. Until they came to expect it. The judge was quite wrong when he accused me of trying to buy their friendship. Why should I have needed to buy what I already had?

I soon found myself short of money, so I supplemented my wages from the till. I worked out a system of ringing up receipts followed by refunds. In my own defence, I should say that I've never taken a penny from an individual. I've always been the sort of bloke who hands in change when it's left on a seat. But Austin Reed was different: a chain store with branches all over the country. I didn't think they'd miss a few hundred – or, as it turned out, a few thousand – pounds, and I knew that it would make all the difference to my friends. Given the people involved – future actors and writers and teachers (and lawyers!) – it seemed almost a sort of sponsorship. I felt like a modern Robin Hood. I also began to take clothes that I knew would suit them. It helped that we were short-staffed and that the manager liked me, sometimes even leaving me to lock up on my own. I suppose that was why he considered it such a betrayal of trust. But betrayal works both ways. When he started to find discrepancies, he should have called me in, giving me a chance to explain and pay back the money, instead of using the security cameras to trap his own staff.

I was arrested and taken to my dad's station. I knew a lot of the officers, which made it seem even more like they were pulling my leg. They treated me well enough: nobody tried to beat me up or anything. They left that to my dad when he got me home. Four months later I was sent for trial at Peterborough Crown Court. My dad wanted me to say that I'd been lured into it: I was naive and insecure and impressionable and my friends had been using me, since they must have known that I didn't have access to that sort of cash. I replied that just showed what a narrow life he'd led. He'd never met anyone like them. They didn't think about where money came from: they took it for granted. In any case I may have made myself out to be higher-up than I was: more like a trainee manager than an assistant. They would have supposed I had a salary to match. As for the clothes, I'd told them they were samples. And, whatever my dad may have thought, his colleagues must have found me convincing for they pressed charges against me alone.

I was so relieved. Even if my friends had been found innocent, the experience would have scarred them for life. As it was, they were left without a stain on their characters – except for a question-mark over their judgement (although they assured me that their feelings towards me hadn't changed). The first chance I had to escape – my dad had imposed a twenty-four hour curfew – I went to see Pitt. He said that he spoke for them all when he thanked me from the bottom of his heart for keeping their names out of it. He was sure I'd understand why they had to steer clear of me until after the trial. The police investigation had been an ordeal and they were liable to be called as witnesses. It was all so sordid, although Tarquin had succeeded in rising above it: he was already planning an adaptation of *Crime and Punishment*. I said that I hoped there'd be a part in it for me. He smiled and said, 'Of course, darling. Depending on availability,' which I know he didn't mean to sound cruel.

The last time I saw either Pitt or Tarquin was in court. They were called by the prosecution, so I realised that they had no choice about what they said. As soon as I heard words like 'misfit' and 'fantasist', I could tell they were reading from a script. I longed for them to give me a sign – a single smile – to show they were still on my side, but they kept their eyes fixed firmly in front. I've written to them both three times, explaining about visiting orders and enclosing the necessary chits. I didn't expect a reply. I know how much they loathe writing letters and, on the other hand, how much they love giving surprises. So they're sure to blow in out of the blue, just when they think I've given up on them. But I haven't given up on them any more than they've given up on me. I know that some time very soon (not this week: I can hear all too clearly that time has run out), they'll stroll into the visiting room and turn it into the tea-room at the Ritz. I'm looking forward to seeing them so much. But if for some reason they're not able to get away, if they're busy with exams or matinees or they think that the sight of me locked up in here will depress them, I'll understand. I've only fifteen months left to serve – less with remission. If they prefer to wait till I'm out, I'll understand.

Hélène du Coudray ANOTHER COUNTRY
£7.99   ISBN 1 904559 04 2

A prize-winning novel, first published in 1928, about a passionate affair between a British ship's officer and a Russian emigrée governess which promises to end in disaster.

Lewis DeSoto A BLADE OF GRASS
£8.99   ISBN 1 904559 07 7

A lyrical and profound novel set in South Africa during the era of apartheid, in which the recently widowed Märit struggles to run her farm with the help of her black maid, Tembi.

Maggie Hamand, ed. UNCUT DIAMONDS
£7.99   ISBN 1 904559 03 4

Unusual and sometimes challenging, these vibrant, original stories showcase the huge diversity of new writing talent coming out of contemporary London.

Sara Maitland ON BECOMING A FAIRY GODMOTHER
£7.99   ISBN 1 904559 00 X

Fifteen new 'fairy stories' by an acclaimed master of the genre breathe new life into old legends and bring the magic of myth back into modern women's lives.

Anne Redmon IN DENIAL
£7.99   ISBN 1 904559 01 8

A chilling novel about the relationship between Harriet, a prison visitor, and Gerry, a serial offender, which explores challenging themes with subtlety and intelligence.

Henrietta Seredy LEAVING IMPRINTS
£7.99   ISBN 1 904559 02 6

Beautifully written and startlingly original, this unusual and memorable novel explores a destructive, passionate relationship between two damaged people.

Norman Thomas THE THOUSAND-PETALLED DAISY
£7.99   ISBN 1 904559 05 0

Love, jealousy and violence play a part in this coming-of-age novel set in India, written with a distinctive, off-beat humour and a delicate but intensely felt spirituality.

Adam Zameenzad PIGEON-INDIA?ARIA
£8.99   ISBN 1 904559 06 9

A highly original novel about a group of street children in America whose zest for life carries them through the most extreme adversity and suffering.